The Mayhew Junction Historical Society

The Mayhew Junction
Historical Society

Cassie Dandridge Selleck

Published by Obstinate Daughters Press
Lady Lake, Florida 32158
The text of this book is set in Times New Roman.

Book design and cover photography by C. D. Selleck

For my three beautiful Obstinate Daughters

Patti Walker
Katie Emily
and Emily Selleck

Also by Cassie Dandridge Selleck

The Pecan Man

The Truth About Grace (A sequel to *The Pecan Man*)

The Beanie Bradsher Series
(in order)

What Matters in Mayhew

The Mayhew Junction Historical Society

Table of Contents

1 - A Little Bitty Problem 1

2 - La Pâtisserie...9

3 - The Mayhew Junction Historical Society....................15

4 - Poop or Get Off the Pot 18

5 - Front Porch Tales 24

Corinne Barr 31

6 - Home is Where the Car Goes 33

7 - A Reckoning 40

8 - The Proposition 49

Randy Kerner...54

9 - Spring Awakening 55

10 - Historical Significance 61

11 - The Third Box..67

12 - Bad Brain 73

13 - Strategies...80

Gabriella Warren 85

14 - The Final Decision 86

15 - Make Fletcher County Great Again..........................88

16 - The Trouble with LouWanda 92

LouWanda Matthews Crump 100

17 - History Lessons 102

18 - Who's the Daddy?..105

19 - Lunch Date..111

20 - At the Archives 114

21 - LouWanda Meets the Mouse 120

22 - Road Trip 124

23 - Nothing to Crow About 130

24 - Stormy Weather 132

25 - It's Getting Hot in Here 137

26 - Special Delivery 140

27 - Be Careful What You Ask For 142

Sissy Coleman 148

28 - Twin Troubles 150

29 - Heading for a Fall 158

30 - What Wicked Wind Blows? 161

31 - If I Knew You Were Coming, ... 165

I'd Have Baked a Cake 165

32 - Royal Letdown 169

33 - What History Teaches 171

34 - Founders Day Fiasco 178

35 - Batter Up 182

36 - It All Comes Down to This 187

T-Ray Atwater 194

37 - The Aftermath 197

38 - A Time to Heal 201

39 - The Stars of the Show 204

40 - A Bump on the Head 209

41 - All's Well That Ends Well 212

1 - A Little Bitty Problem

Sweet Lee Atwater parked her mini-van in front of Mayhew Elementary School, pulled her quilted floral designer handbag from the back seat and sat for a minute. It was a bit more than two months since she'd gotten the surprise of her life, and she still wasn't used to her newfound fortune—literally, a fortune. Sweet's thoroughly reliable husband Bubba John had gone behind her back for years, playing the lottery with money they could ill-afford to lose. Fortunately for them both, their numbers hit before she discovered his duplicity, and now they were millionaires.

And what did that mean, actually? They still lived in the small town of Mayhew Junction, population roughly ten thousand if you counted everyone in the entire county, who all shared Mayhew's one zip code. Their kids still went to the same small schools, and they still didn't have the first fast food restaurant or even a Walmart for crying out loud. It had taken Sweet a half an hour to talk herself into paying a hundred dollars for the gorgeous Vera Bradley handbag in her lap. She loved it, and she *still* felt guilty for owning it. What they had now was more money than they needed, and fewer worries than before, but that didn't stop Sweet Lee Atwater from worrying.

Besides, money would not help with the problem Sweet currently faced. Her middle child Bitty had always been a little different. She had habits that were endearing when she was a toddler but were apparently disruptive now that she was in a public school setting. Sweet was a few minutes early for a meeting with Bitty's teacher and the guidance counselor. They were going to discuss interventions that might be necessary to make everyone's experience more—what was the word—tolerable? Sweet sighed. Bitty was a bright light in her life, always cheerful, smart as a whip, and incredibly kind-hearted. It was disheartening to watch that little light waver as her daughter grew more and more frustrated with school.

No use sitting here fretting. Time to face the music. Sweet slid from her car, locked the doors and made her way to the entrance of the school office. Signing in at the front desk, she scarcely had time to give her name to the receptionist when the guidance counselor came around the corner, right arm outstretched and Pandora bracelet crackling heavily.

"Mrs. Atwater, so glad you could make it."

Sweet gave the offered hand one firm shake that rattled the bracelet again and wrinkled her nose into a smiling grimace. "Please, call me Sweet. Mrs. Atwater is so formal."

Libby Daniels laughed. "I completely agree," she said in a soft country lilt, "but we have standards here that make it a requirement. Even though it makes me feel old and crotchety, I'm Mrs. Daniels and you're Mrs. Atwater and we're both stuck with it."

Sweet decided right then and there she liked Libby Daniels very much. Though she had never met her personally, she knew the family Libby married into before moving to Fletcher County and they were good people.

"Come on back," Libby said. "Mrs. McMinn is waiting in the conference room."

Sweet knew Delia McMinn well. They had gone to school together many moons ago and Delia's cousin Gabe was a bit of a celebrity in town. Sweet was happy when Bitty was assigned to her third grade classroom. She had not looked forward to this conference, but she relaxed a bit as they settled in to discuss what might be done to help Bitty cope with the structure of the classroom. She had a feeling she was going to need all the help she could get.

***

Delia McMinn started their conference by asking if Mr. Atwater was on his way. She'd known Sweet Lee Atwater since they were children themselves and was pretty sure she knew what the answer would be, but she asked anyway.

Sweet scooted forward in her chair and sat up a tiny bit straighter.

"He's, uh… He's working today." Sweet turned her head toward Libby as she spoke, even though Delia had asked the question.

"No problem," Delia said. "I just didn't want to start without him."

2

"Well, you know Bubba John." Sweet lifted one shoulder toward her ear and surrendered to the truth. "He'd rather nail his foot to the floor than attend a meeting of any kind."

Delia laughed. "I do know Bub…Mr. Atwater. I'll be honest, though, I was sure hoping he would be here. I've seen him with Bitty; he's patient and good-natured. His input would be helpful."

Sweet grinned. "I'll tell him you said so."

Libby cleared her throat and opened the file lying face down on the table in front of her. "So, let's talk about Elizabeth, shall we? You call her Bitty?"

"All my kids have nicknames except the baby. I'm not sure why I thought that was such a good idea." Sweet grabbed a mint from her purse and rattled it open.

"It suits her," Libby said. "She is a tiny thing, isn't she? And precious. We all adore her, Mrs. Atwater. I hope you know that. And we are going to figure out how to help her. I understand she's struggling a bit. Can you talk a little about what you've observed? And tell us your own concerns as well, before we make any suggestions. We want to hear in your words what you think is going on."

Sweet popped the mint into her mouth before speaking, then gave a nervous cough. "Gosh, I don't know if I can put it into words really. She's never been much of a problem for me before, I mean, she's a little different, if that's what you're getting at, but it's really just quirky things, nothing bad…" Sweet trailed off, and wrung her hands in her lap.

Delia reached over and stilled Sweet's hands with one of her own. "We know it's nothing bad. Really. We need to hear how she is at home, and that will help us figure out how to help her at school. Sometimes it's an environmental thing, sometimes not. At any rate, Miss Bailey will be taking all of this down for our reports." Delia nodded toward a small woman in a powder pink suit sitting at the end of the table. They'd been introduced when Sweet arrived, but she melted into the background so efficiently, Sweet had forgotten she was even there.

"So, Mrs. Atwater," Delia continued, "could you tell us why you think we are here today? I promise you, we'll all be chiming in soon."

"Well, I've seen a huge change in Bitty this year and I'm concerned. Every single morning has become torture for us all. She says she hates school and doesn't want to go. I keep asking her why she hates it, but all she says is "It's boring." I ask her if anyone is bothering her, and she says, "Yes, they're bothering me. I don't want to go to school." But when I ask *who* is bothering her and what they're doing, she doesn't have an answer."

Delia chuckled a little and nodded her head. "Sounds like Bitty to me," she said and adjusted the hem of her skirt. "Let's go back a bit further and talk about the things you call "quirky," so we'll have it on the record. What behaviors have you noticed and when did they begin?"

"Gosh, where do I even start? Bitty's always been a little odd. She's my third child, but the next two came pretty quickly, so I may not have even noticed some of the earliest behaviors, if I'm being honest. Or at least I didn't make note of them. She likes to count things at lot, and line them up in order of size or color or whatever strikes her fancy. She's a great organizer, by the way, and keeps her room WAY neater than any of the other kids, which is probably the thing I find the absolute oddest. What kid cleans their room without being asked? But the weird thing is…it's just HER things she keeps neat. She doesn't need the whole room clean. She just wants her stuff left where she put it and she does not take it well if anything is moved. And see, that's what bugs me, because normally Bitty is a sweet, easygoing, cuddly little girl who wants to please *everyone*. Am I talking too fast?" Sweet took a deep breath and looked down the table at Miss Bailey, who looked up and smiled.

"Not at all," she said, still typing.

"Okay, good. Sometimes I get going and I don't know where to stop."

"Let me ask you this, Mrs. Atwater," Libby Daniels pulled a yellow sheet of paper from the file and ran one finger down the center before continuing. "Bitty's test scores show her at well above average in almost every category, as high as the 98th percentile in many of them, so clearly she is bright. Her verbal scores, however, seem out of line with that assessment. So, my question is, how much does she talk at home? Does she engage in active conversation with her siblings? Does she come home and tell you about her day, or do you think she is more of an observer than a participant?"

"Gosh, that's a good question. It's funny, actually. We have a family story about Bitty that we tell all the time. She didn't speak much at all until she was two years old. She'd say *Mama* if she wanted me to pick her up, *baba* if she wanted a bottle, and *binky* if she wanted her pacifier, but she'd just go climb up in her high chair if she was hungry or head for the bathroom if she needed to go. She was potty-trained at eighteen months, not because I did anything special, but because she saw us use the bathroom and decided that was how it worked. So, at her second birthday party, a family friend commented on the fact that she wasn't talking yet. I remember feeling a little defensive, or maybe guilty, I don't know. So anyway, I just shrugged it off. But my friend picks up a book and starts pointing at pictures and saying the words to Bitty. Now, I read books to my kids every night—always have—so I was thinking, oh my gosh, does she think I'm an idiot? And then, suddenly, Bitty was repeating the words back to her. Then a few minutes later, she was naming whatever was pointed out. So, my friend gives me this smug *I told you so* look and I'm shaking my head like *whatever.* And of course, then I look at Bitty and she looks so proud of herself and I feel like the worst mother in the world, so I do what I always do when that happens. I go straight to sarcasm. I look at my sweet little girl, and I say…mind you I'm laughing the whole time…I say, 'Okay, Miss Smarty-pants, how about you say the Lord's Prayer for us.' That's our bedtime routine—I read a book, then we say the Lord's Prayer together. But Bitty hadn't been saying it and I just figured, she'll do it when she starts talking. Well, don't you know that child looks at me and says, 'Our Father, which art in heaven…' and the whole table erupts! I will never live that down. My kid could talk, and I didn't know it." Sweet reached into her purse and pulled out a rumpled tissue. She twisted the edge a bit and dabbed at her eyes. "So, yeah, I guess you could say I noticed, but I thought it was just her version of normal. Does that make sense?"

"Absolutely!" Delia said. "And it may confirm some things I've noticed as well. Bitty is perfectly happy to sit back and watch. She stays in her own little world and is often reluctant to come out of it, especially if she's interested in what she's doing. Getting her to speak in class is a little like threading a needle. You have to be steady and patient and focused on the task. Don't get me wrong— she can speak, and she has a remarkable vocabulary, but she processes things a little more slowly. And she's easily distracted if there is noise in the room, or if her task is difficult or unpleasant for her. And that's where I think she struggles the most right now. We are introducing new concepts every day and some of them are more difficult to grasp. Especially the common core things we're required to teach."

Libby Daniels straightened her spine in one swift moment, and she shot a sideways glance at her colleague.

"I'm sorry, Mrs. Daniels," Delia said. "I know we disagree on this, but I have to be honest. I'm just saying, Bitty gets frustrated a lot these days. And what we are trying to identify here is *why* she gets frustrated."

"No, no," Libby shook her head and held up one hand. "I'm not saying you're wrong. However, I think it's important not to jump to conclusions here. So, let me add my observations and then we'll look at our options going forward."

Sweet frowned. "What do you mean options?"

Libby twisted at one earring and her bracelets rattled and pinged. She pulled her chin down and tightened her neck muscles forming a second chin of pure skin because nothing about Libby Daniels was heavy, except her jewelry. "I mean *options*. Like, where we'll go from here. We need to discuss creating an IEP, which may or may not include further testing and observation."

"IEP?"

"Yes, the Individualized Educational Plan is basically a program we develop based on the needs of the child. It holds us accountable for providing specialized instruction and related services for any student based on their specific disability."

"I don't understand. Bitty isn't disabled." Sweet felt an overwhelming urge to bolt from the room. Her hands clenched the arms of her chair, though she wasn't sure if they were holding her in place or preparing to catapult her from her seat.

"I'm so sorry, Mrs. Atwater. I think I have gotten off on the wrong foot here. Disability in this case is used very broadly. The IEP is a requirement for us and is meant to identify and provide specialized intervention and education for any special needs a child might have. Identifying needs is really what we are after first, and that will require some testing. It could be something as simple as an attention deficit disorder--I'm not making predictions, just giving an example—and even that falls under the legal definition of a disability, which entitles a child to special planning. And that's the key word in IEP: a plan. There are some things we can do on our own. For instance, I'd like to get our Speech Pathologist to evaluate her if she thinks it's warranted. These things can seem a little arbitrary, but I can assure you they're not."

Sweet was confused. "I don't understand. She talks fine, just not a lot. She doesn't lisp or stutter or anything like that…"

"Of course not," Ms. Daniels interrupted. "But there are other things we look at—things like cognitive-communication and social language, or her receptive language, how she listens and comprehends. All these things can be impacted by attention deficits, or really any number of things. A speech pathologist can identify anything that might impact a student's learning experience and give us tools to get them on track. But let's not get ahead of ourselves. For now, let me see what we have available that might help and we'll sit down again soon and see where we are."

"Is that it?" Sweet asked. "I thought we were going to come up with something today."

Delia laughed. "Believe it or not, Mrs. Atwater, this was pretty productive as far as these things go. You have to remember, this is pretty new for you. And while Bitty is certainly a little bit of a challenge, we have seen things like this before. Right now, what you need to know is that we are on your side. And more importantly, on her side. I look at that little face some days and I want to squeeze her to pieces. She is the most precious thing. But by golly, when she doesn't want to do something, it might not get done. And sometimes that's okay. But, as you well know, sometimes it's not. She has to get up and come to school every day. So, we are going to help you and you're going to help us, and we'll figure this out together. Okay?"

The women talked for a few more minutes and then wrapped it up. Sweet left in a bit of a daze. The twins had been so easy, but of course, they'd always had each other. It was hard not to feel like a failure, and harder still when she loved her children with a ferocity that often overwhelmed her. She could only imagine what it was like for her babies. The worst part was, here she was feeling sorry for herself because she'd never be able to have another child, and she couldn't take care of the ones she already had. She was a blessed woman, and she knew it. She had a loving husband, five beautiful children, a house built with love and more money than she ever deserved. But money couldn't fix everything, now could it?

2 - La Pâtisserie

"Will?" Beanie Bradsher called out from the kitchen of The Château, where she had lived since moving out of her flood-ravaged house on the Suwannee River, minus a stint out at the Atwater house while Sweet recovered from surgery. It had been one of the most dramatic Christmases Beanie ever experienced and she still wasn't sure she was quite recovered herself.

"You need me?" Will Thaxton appeared at the doorway with a bundle of firewood in his arms. "Thought I'd stock up in the living room. Looks like we have a cold front coming through, though it always makes me laugh saying that. You haven't seen a cold front until you've seen one in Minnesota."

"Oh, shoot, I needed an extry hand here, but you ain't got one. Can you put that load down and come help me a minute?"

"Sure, I'll be right back," Will said and disappeared down the hallway.

Beanie could afford to get her own place. The part she played in Bubba John's duplicity with his wife had netted her a share of his lottery winnings, which were drawing interest in her account at the bank. She'd bought lotto tickets for him using extra cash provided during Avon transactions. Sweet Lee had been none-the-wiser until Bubba John was forced to confess that they were now millionaires.

Beanie's portion, a mere fraction, gave her a nest egg she could use to build a house on land she'd inherited from her grandparents, but she was comfortable here with the widower Thaxton, and he was happy to have her help, so she stayed. Besides, they were well on their way to opening a bakery—by accident mostly—but plans were taking shape and they were already filling orders for three months in advance. Will had once taken a cake decorating course with his late wife Marie and was surprisingly good at it. Beanie, on the other hand, never had a day's formal training, but made a name for herself with the baked goods she distributed to her Avon customers over the holidays.

Will was in the process of installing glass cabinets in the unused front room of the Château. Salvaged years ago from an old jewelry shop once housed in the small building on the same property, the cabinets were perfect to hold pastries and cookies and other baked goods. The Château, built in 1883, was originally the county courthouse, but had not been used as such since the current courthouse was built in 1907. It had been remodeled as a bed and breakfast over the years, and there were still several rooms left unused in the enormous wooden structure. Will needed to increase his income to stay afloat, and there wasn't a bakery to be found in the entire county, so La Pâtisserie it would be.

"At your service, Mamselle."

Will had taken to using French terminology lately, which vaguely annoyed Beanie, though she couldn't quite put her finger on why. "Sorry it took so long. I washed up first."

"That's okay, I actually need help with this cooling rack here. It's all whoppy-jawed and I cain't have my moon-pies slidin' down into a heap."

"Beanie, we've talked about this. We are making macarons," Will said, rolling the "r" dramatically and giving the last vowel a nasal sound like he'd learned in high school. "They are not moon-pies. There's a difference."

"Look like moon-pies to me," Beanie said, rolling her eyes. "If they's macaroni, where's the cheese?"

Will laughed so hard he could barely hold the baking rack steady while she adjusted the height of the legs.

"Oh, stop," Beanie complained, smiling in spite of herself. "It ain't that funny."

But it was, which was why Will had found himself smitten with Beanie Bradsher months ago. She was only half-serious about the moon-pies. She knew the difference, but she wasn't one for pretense. She also knew how to milk a good joke.

They laughed a lot in this kitchen, and that carried as far as the living room, but no further. Their relationship was like the rack they were fixing, a little off-kilter. Love on Will's side, great friendship on Beanie's, and it looked a lot to Will like "never the twain shall meet." That did not stop him, however, from hoping.

Beanie straightened her body and eyed Will from beneath the brim of her red Stetson hat. "What are you thinkin' about now? I was askin' you to pull this thing out and you was just ignorin' me to death."

Will scrunched his shoulders up and winced. "Lost in thought again, I guess."

"We ain't never gonna get the Patsy open, if you don't pay attention."

He should have known better than to choose a name like La Pâtisserie, but it went with the French theme. When would he ever learn?

"The Patsy?" Will chuckled. "Really?"

"Are you gonna help me or not?"

Beanie knelt again, her crinolines swishing as she pushed them out of the way so her knees rested on solid pine floors and not the tulle she used to make the outfits she wore every day. Will knew for a fact she didn't own a single pair of pants, not even jeans. It took a little getting used to when he first met her, but he couldn't imagine her dressed any other way now.

"I think that'll do her." Beanie stood and tested the cooling rack by nudging it with one finger. It had taken nearly fifteen minutes of lifting and adjusting, but the metal unit was solid and steady now. Beanie dusted off her hands. "Looks like they's a storm comin'. You got gas for that generator?"

Will handed her the towel he'd had slung over his shoulder all morning. "Got some this morning before Williams closed. You see the Weather Channel this morning, too?"

"Naw, I can just tell," Beanie said. "The elements is all a'fluster. Even the birdies are hunkerin' down in the back yard. They's usually clamorin' for feed whenever I get out there, but they was quiet as church mice this mornin'. I think it's gonna be a doozy."

"That's what the weatherman said. Well, not in exactly those words, of course, but…" Will opened the refrigerator, grabbed a container of half-and-half and shook it. "I've got a list going for the grocery store. Don't want to get too much in case we lose power, but we'll need a few things to get by. This is one of them." He set the container back in the refrigerator and closed the door. "The colder it is, the more coffee they drink. Supposed to drop down into the thirties by tomorrow morning."

"I'm guessin' cold, but not that cold," Beanie said. "Hey, could'ja put heavy cream on that list, too? I was just thinkin' about my granny's cream puffs. I wanna try 'em out tonight. I don't reckon anyone'll be put out too bad about the weather if we feed 'em good."

"Ah…choux à la crème!" Will kissed the tips of his fingers and gestured grandly. "Magnifique!"

Beanie snorted and threw the hand towel at Will's head. "Shoo yourself. I got work to do."

Will laughed all the way out the door. Beanie shook her head. "He ain't right," she said to the empty room, but the smile didn't leave her face for a good long while.

***

Beanie was right about the storm. It *was* a doozy. Friday morning found Will outside cleaning up debris in the courtyard and climbing the huge live oak to settle a squirrel's nest into a space at the top of the tree's massive trunk. Will had no idea how the two tiny, still-sightless babies had stayed in the nest when the limb fell but stay they did. It was Beanie's idea to put them back in the tree so the stray dogs in town didn't find them and take them for an easy lunch. Will had his misgivings. He was forever chasing squirrels out of the bird feeders, and now here he was saving two of them to grow up and antagonize him further.

"All God's creatures gotta eat," Beanie said when Will complained. "And what would you do with all them acorns if they wadn't scarfing 'em up for ya?"

"This is true." Will decided he would not tell her how he and his childhood friends used to wander the back woods of Minnesota using squirrels for target practice. When they graduated from BB guns to real rifles around age twelve, they started shooting rabbits, too. Sometimes they'd take their loot to Old Man Michurski, who lived alone in what passed for a cabin about a hundred yards from their swimming hole. All God's creatures gotta eat, indeed.

Will finished up his chores, took his outside shoes off at the back door and tried to sneak upstairs to take a shower. A guest caught him at the bottom of the stairs and asked about a refund for the night since the storm had knocked out power for several hours. After explaining the refund policy that excluded acts of nature, Will tiptoed upstairs and prayed no one would hear him. Beanie was waiting at the top of the stairs holding two lint rollers.

"I'll do the outside and you can do the other when you get your clothes off." Beanie shoved one of the rollers into Will's hand.

12

"The other what?" Will was confused.

"What ain't clothes!" Beanie began to swipe at Will's shoulders with the roller, lifting first one then the other arm to roll the armpits.

Will looked down at his clothes, wondering what prompted the sudden invasion. "Am I that dirty?"

"It ain't dirt I'm after, Will, it's chiggers and ticks. Look, there's one now." Beanie thrust the roller at him and pointed at a tiny red speck, no bigger than a pencil point.

"One what?"

"A chigger, for crying out loud. A red bug. Don't you know nothin'? They'll tear you up good. They like to crawl into the bends of your knees, and they bury under your skin. They's all up in the Spanish moss you was wrasslin' today. You ain't never itched a'tall till you've had a chigger bite. Ticks is just as bad."

Beanie ripped off a section of the lint roller and started back in, leaving no stretch of fabric untouched until all that was left was Will's crotch.

"I'll let you tend to your nether regions yourself," she said, waving the roller in a circular motion toward his zipper.

"Uh, thanks, I think." Will said. "Now, am I to understand I'm supposed to use this roller on my skin as well?"

"Absolutely," Beanie nodded. "Especially in the cracks and crevices, and up your legs. They crawl from the ground up and them ticks can be as small as the chigger. If you wait till you can see 'em with your nekkid eye, you'll already be bit and that's a whole nother problem."

"Isn't that going to hurt?" he asked. "My legs are kind of hairy."

"Roll DOWN your legs," she said, as if talking to a child. "Down with the hair, not up against it. Do you want me to do it?"

"No!" Will said, a little more forcefully than he intended.

Will slid into his room and shut the door. He caught a glimpse of himself as he entered the bathroom, his eyes wide and his lips pulled down. Deer in the headlights if he'd ever seen it, and he had. Many times.

"I left some blue dish detergent on the counter for ya, just in case ya got into some poison ivy."

Beanie's voice rang clear through his bedroom door. As old as The Château was, some of the doors had gaps between door and frame wide enough to pass a pencil through.

"I'm good," Will called back.

"I'd use it if I was you," Beanie hollered. "Cuts the oil from the plant. Kills the chiggers, too."

It took Will a minute to process what she meant by "ull," which is the way he heard it. By then he was in the shower lathering himself with half a bottle of body wash. He had no intentions of rolling himself with sticky tape, though he did give himself a once-over with dish soap. Still, the thought of chiggers and ticks left him feeling twitchy for days.

3 - The Mayhew Junction Historical Society

LouWanda Crump pushed a stack of coupon inserts, catalogs and general junk mail to the outside corner of her desk, swept the crumbs from this morning's convenience store muffin into her hand and emptied them into an overflowing garbage pail salvaged from the demolition of the old colored school ten years earlier. Matter of fact, the desk itself had been part of that deal. She was given whatever she would haul away herself and, since it was only a few blocks from her store on Main Street, she took whatever wasn't nailed down and a few things that were.

Since she'd taken over the fundraising for the Mayhew Junction Historical Society, she'd learned a whole lot more about the history of that school, including the name of the teacher who sat at the desk the last ten years of its existence. Corinne Barr was a force to be reckoned with, LouWanda had quickly discovered. LouWanda reckoned she didn't want to deal with her at all, but it looked like she was going to have to anyway. It was either that or give up her post, which she was not going to do.

Corinne was due to arrive at the store any minute now, which is why LouWanda was tidying up. A little dust never hurt anyone, LouWanda figured, but she'd had enough people talking about her lately without adding Corinne Barr to the crowd. Mouthy as a fishmonger's wife, she thought as she lifted her sweating jumbo cup of sweet tea purchased this morning with her muffin. It left a round pool of water high enough to jiggle when a logging truck roared by outside. Grabbing a handful of used napkins discarded by the telephone, she smeared the water ring across the surface of the desk and called her job done. Moments later a cowbell wired to the front doorknob announced the arrival of LouWanda's guest.

"Correeeen," LouWanda hollered as she sat quickly down in her chair. She had no intention of giving the woman the satisfaction of being greeted at the door. "I'm back here."

LouWanda stood when Corinne's dark round face peered tentatively around the corner into what LouWanda optimistically called an office.

"You found me," LouWanda said and pointed to two dusty chairs in front of her. "Take your pick."

Corinne swiped at the seat of the nearest chair with a gloved hand, then winced and sat down.

LouWanda, nearly six feet in her tennis shoes, towered over the small elderly woman, yet still felt entirely intimidated and she did not like it one bit. She'd always felt nauseous around schoolteachers.

"What can I help you with today?" LouWanda sat then and stared across the desk.

Barr pulled her gloves off one finger at a time and weighed her words before she uttered them.

"Well," she said, her drawl slower and more pronounced with age and the effects of a mild stroke suffered four years prior. "First of all, you can call me Coh-RIN, not Coh-reen. It's not a big thing, but it's an important thing, wouldn't you say?"

"Very important," LouWanda agreed. Best to get off on the right foot here. "I'm a stickler for Christian names myself. I dislike the use of nicknames. If my mama had wanted me called Lou, she wouldn'ta tacked Wanda on there without a space."

Corinne nodded. "I know that's right," she said and wheezed out a short laugh. "It's a funny thing about names. They can tell you a lot. Especially when you're doing genealogy and the like."

"Speaking of which," LouWanda seized on the opportunity to get this thing over with. "I know you have some information you'd like to go into the book I'm writin' about the history of Mayhew Junction, so if you'll just tell me what it is, I'll get right on it. I'm near 'bout finished now."

"Well then," Corinne removed her wide-brimmed hat and set it on the dusty chair beside her. "I'm glad I caught you when I did."

"Why's that?" LouWanda crossed her arms on the desk and leaned forward.

"I thought maybe…" Corinne paused, and concentrated on the very slow process of removing a stack of files from her oversized Coach handbag. Once out, she set the bag on the floor beside her and looked for a spot on the desk to place the files. Finding none, she looked up at LouWanda, who simply stared at her, unmoved. "I thought perhaps you'd be interested in some information I've accumulated over the years. Most of it, in the beginning anyway, was family stories handed down, but then I got into that Ancestry thing and made a few more connections. Fascinating stuff, and I've only scratched the surface."

LouWanda dug at the fold in her beehive hairdo, near the crown where her bobby pins faced straight down. "I don't know nothin' about no Ancestry-dot-com thingie. I got my information from family Bibles and courthouse records and such. Besides, what's all that got to do with anything? I'm writin' about the hist'ry of the town."

"With all due respect, LouWanda, this *is* the history of the town."

"Well, you know what I mean. This is a fundraiser for the Historical Society museum. I'm lookin' at all the industry that made this town what it was back in the day, not who married and died and had babies and such. I'm doubtin' you have anything in that file I'd ack-chally be interested in."

Corinne stared at LouWanda for a moment before speaking. "I'm well aware of the Society's fundraising efforts, as I have contributed several times myself. So has Suvi Jones and the Reverend Milo over to the Bethel Fellowship. I think if you check back through your records, you'll see these have been substantial contributions to this very worthy cause. I realize you only recently took over for Miss Marie, so I have to assume you didn't know. However," Corinne picked up her hat, placed it carefully on her head, and stood, "now you do. So, I can take this up with the committee at your next meeting, or I can make a few phone calls today, but I am not inclined to let this drop, LouWanda. And as far as what you will or will not be interested in…well, let's just say I think you might be surprised at what all I've found. I'll see myself out."

LouWanda waited until she heard the cowbell rattle and clang. "Well, of all the goll-darned nerve of that… that… woman! Who does she think she is anyway? If she thinks she's gonna tell me— "

Corinne Barr's face appeared around the corner of LouWanda's office door. "You might want to keep your voice down a bit. You've got a customer out there. You have a blessed day, okay?"

Corinne was gone before LouWanda let out the breath she was holding. The cowbell clanged twice in succession, which meant the customer was gone, too. Dang it all to H-E-double hockey sticks, what was she going to do now?

4 - Poop or Get Off the Pot

Suvi Jones angled his pickup truck between two large oak trees straddling the back parking lot entrance to the Mayhew Café. He usually parked in front, but he was running uncharacteristically late this morning and all the parking spaces were filled. He'd taken a break from his routine last fall when all hell had broken loose from the news that he was dating a white woman. To be fair, he'd gotten it from both sides, as he had expected he would. He didn't know which was worse, the disapproving looks from the ladies at church, or the ignorant remarks from the café regulars. He did know which was worse, though—it was the fact that Beanie Bradsher hadn't waited for him to sort things out. She dumped him at Christmas, of all things. She hung up on him when he tried to call and invite her to dinner. Okay, so it was two days after Christmas, and he hadn't called for over a month, but he did *try* to explain.

It was all a big misunderstanding if you asked him, but nobody did. First, there was the thing with the red velvet cake Beanie shoved in his face at the Trunk-or-Treat. The town's alternative to a Halloween festival was hosted every year by several churches and was one of the most well-attended functions in the county. He'd never been so humiliated in all his life. What was a man supposed to do, wear the cake and eat it, too?

Second, his relationship with Beanie was an enigma at best, and he knew he was mostly to blame. She had been willing to go public from the very beginning, but it was complicated. In his world, from his perspective, you had to carefully weigh the decisions you made. At any point, it could be life or death or, if he was completely honest, misery or happiness. And at the point where Beanie launched her frustrations in the form of a cake, he had to admit he was miserable. So, he took a break. A long break, now that he thought about it. The longer he took, the harder it was to call her. What would he even say?

It was the Christmas holiday that made him realize how much he missed her, plus all the aunts nattering on about Gabriella Warren. He and Gabe, as she preferred to be called, were just friends. Golfing buddies. That was all. It was bad enough how the town blew things out of proportion. That café round table was just about more than he could take, but he finally decided he wasn't going to punish his cousin Edwina for the sins of her customers. Business was slow enough.

Still, it took him an entire month to gather up enough nerve to show his face in the café again. A man can only take so much mortification before his pride gets the best of him.

Suvi felt a car slide into the space beside his truck. He checked his watch and realized he'd been sitting here with his door wide open for at least ten minutes, thinking of nothing but Beatrice Bradsher. So, he reminded himself about spilt milk and shook the image from his troubled mind.

Suvi ducked his head and unfolded his impossibly large athlete's body from the cab of his truck. He looked up in time to see Randy Kerner walking toward him across the parking lot.

"Mornin', Suve!"

Suvi acknowledged the man with a brief lift of his chin. "Commissioner."

"Missed you at breakfast this mornin'. You runnin' late?"

"I am." Suvi opened the door of the café, then stepped back to allow an elderly couple to hobble out. He felt a hand grasp his bicep and turned.

"Hey, I've got something I'd like to talk to you about, if you have a little time in the next week or so." Suvi glanced down at the offending hand and Randy released his grip on Suvi's arm.

Suvi raised his eyebrows in lieu of a response.

"Nothing terribly important," Randy said. "But it may take a few minutes and I'd just as soon not talk in there."

"Well, you got my attention with that one."

Randy laughed louder than he intended, then caught himself and cleared his throat.

"Do you mind stopping by my office? Maybe on a Monday when the Big Pig is closed?"

"Don't mind at all. You have a good day." Suvi slid through the door he was still holding and released it behind him, leaving Randy Kerner staring at the mass of flyers pasted on the glass.

Sissy noticed Suvi first and made a beeline for the coffee pot. Used to be she could put a cup of coffee on the table at 6:30 and it would still be piping hot when Suvi came in, but he'd become a little erratic lately.

"Hey, Suve," Sissy slid a steaming cup in front of him and flipped her pad open. "Whatcha havin'?"

"Over easy with bacon. No, make that ham instead. Wait…maybe an omelet today."

Sissy didn't know what to make of this abrupt change in a man so formerly steadfast and predictable. "Ham and cheese?" she suggested.

"That'll work. And no toast today. Just pancakes."

Sissy scratched out the order and hustled over to hang the scrap of paper on a clothespin in front of the pass-through window to the kitchen. She used to write *SUVI* across the top with the egg and meat listed. The cook knew as well as anyone else that Suvi wanted dry toast, pancakes, and grits with his order. That's the way he'd had it every single day for years on end. Now all of a sudden, he was coming in late and changing his mind about everything. *Next thing you know, he'll be wanting creamer for his coffee. What in the world has gotten into that man?*

Ten minutes later, Gabe Warren came in and Sissy thought she had her answer, but she was wrong. Gabe, a former LPGA golfer, and a distant cousin of several people in Mayhew Junction's black community, had no romantic interest in Suvi Jones, nor he in her. They golfed together often and commiserated on occasion. They had a lot in common, including the fact that Mayhew Junction was not an easy place to live when you had traveled the world and knew how different it was elsewhere. Still, there was something comforting about being near family, and they had that in common as well.

Gabe stopped at the round table and chatted with the few regulars who were still in attendance. Gabe owned and operated the only real estate office in the county, and she made a point to network everywhere she went. All the social media and technology in the world could not replace word-of-mouth advertising in a place like Mayhew Junction. Gabe was certain of that.

She finished up and made her way to Suvi's table, sliding into the seat in front of him. Suvi acknowledged her with a nod over the top of his newspaper. He had never been much for conversation in the morning.

"What are you doing in here so late?" Gabe asked, waving at Sissy to get her attention.

"Be right there," Sissy called, and went to get Gabe's coffee.

"Up late last night. Couldn't sleep." Suvi folded his paper and tucked it under one leg.

"Still mulling over the offer from your alma mater?"

Suvi sighed. "It ought to be a no-brainer, you know? But I cannot seem to figure out if it's the right thing to do. Maybe the right thing at the wrong time."

"What would make it the right time?" Gabe smiled up at Sissy when she deposited a full to the brim cup of hot coffee without spilling a drop. "Thanks, Sis."

"You eatin' this mornin'?" Sissy slid two plates in front of Suvi and set a squirt bottle of syrup to his right.

"Nah, just catchin' up with Suvi for a minute."

"Gotcha." Sissy was already four steps away, but added over her shoulder, "Holler if you change your mind."

"So," Gabe turned her attention back to Suvi and repeated her question. "What *would* make it the right time?"

"I was hoping you'd forgotten you asked," Suvi grumbled as he shot a healthy dose of syrup over the stack of pancakes still steaming from the kitchen.

"Not a chance." Gabe grabbed a sugar packet from the center of the table. "Come on, Suvi, what the hell? You have the opportunity of a lifetime here. So, what if it's not a head coach position?"

Suvi stopped in mid-squirt. "Really? You think this is about the position?"

"Isn't it?"

"Absolutely not. What kind of idiot would expect to go from coaching a high school team to coaching college ball? I'm happy to go in as a recruiter. Hell, I'm happy to be a Florida Gator again. I just don't know about all the travel. Been there, done that. And Lord knows I'm not getting any younger."

Gabe rolled her eyes.

"What was that for?" Suvi asked.

"Friends don't let friends tell *bald-faced* lies." Gabe stirred half the packet of sugar into her coffee and watched brown rivulets run down the outside of her cup.

"Why was that a lie?"

"Thanks for the confirmation. If it wasn't, you'd have issued a blanket denial."

"You are immensely annoying," Suvi did his best to suppress a grin, but failed. He sliced the pancakes into large square stacks, then crammed a wad of them into his mouth, shaking his head in defeat.

"That's what you like about me," Gabe said. "Cut me off a hunk of that, wouldja?"

"Get your own," Suvi said, but stabbed a block of pancake pieces with his fork and held it out for her to grab.

Gabe held the fork in one fist and plucked off one square of pancake at a time with her fingers—four total if anyone was counting—then handed the fork back to Suvi.

"Okay," she said, still chewing the last bite, "then what gives? Are you afraid to leave Mayhew Junction? I could list your house for rent so you won't lose money. Shoot, I'd be happy to live there myself."

"Well, that's an idea, but it's paid for anyway, so it's not like it's a problem to leave it a while."

"Can't be the restaurant. You aren't making any money on that."

"Tell the whole café, why don'tcha?" Suvi glanced around to see if anyone noticed.

"*What* is your *problem,* Suvi? Anyone else would be jumping at this offer. Can I just remind you, it is the *University of Florida,*" Gabe hissed the last three words out, enunciating the syllables as if Suvi were dense.

Suvi sighed and dropped his fork across his still untouched omelet.

"If I tell you, could you please keep your reaction *somewhat* muted?"

Gabe covered her mouth with one hand and nodded.

Suvi scowled. "Oh, *that's* subtle. Put your hand down or I'm not telling you." When she complied, he continued. "It's just that I've been thinking a lot about Beanie lately. I don't think I gave that a real chance, and I don't know what to do about it. If I leave, it may be over forever, and I guess that's bothering me. That sounds stupid, doesn't it?"

Gabe pinched her lips together and took a deep breath. "No, Suve," she said after a pause. "It doesn't sound stupid at all. I know exactly what you mean."

22

Neither of them said anything else for a good long while. Suvi finished his pancakes, ate half of his omelet, and pushed the plate away. Gabe drained her coffee and left three dollars on the table to cover the drink and a tip.

"What's our tee time tomorrow?" Gabe stood to leave.

"Seven-twenty. Wanna ride together?"

"Nah, I got some stuff to do later. Gonna head up toward Valdosta."

Suvi nodded and Gabe turned toward the door, hesitated, then turned back.

"Suvi, you really oughta go talk to her. I think that's the only way you'll know if there's anything still there. If there's not, and you miss this chance to work for a team you *love*, you'll kick yourself even harder ten years down the road. Trust me on this one." She paused a moment, waiting for Suvi to look up. When he did, she said, "Seriously, Suvi... go."

5 - Front Porch Tales

Beanie was sitting on the Château's front porch when Suvi pulled into the parking space in front of the courthouse across the street. She froze for a moment, the pea pod she was shelling poised over the colander in her lap. She started to rise, then sat back down when the colander tilted and almost scattered a full bowl of peas. It was a reasonably warm day for early March, but Beanie suddenly felt cold. She set the peas on the floor beside her and crossed her arms over her chest, rubbing her upper arms to ward off the chill.

She wondered what he was doing at the courthouse. Probably getting his tags renewed, she thought. Or maybe he finally decided on a new house. The new lady—what was her name? Gabby? No, Gabe. That was it—the real estate lady who stayed at The Chateau when Beanie was still helping the Atwater family. The one people were saying was Suvi's new girlfriend. He sure didn't waste any time. The town hardly got used to the fact that Beanie and Suvi were dating when it all went to pot. Well Gabe could have him.

Suvi sat in his truck for a few minutes, trying to get his nerve up. Maybe this was a bad idea. Maybe he should go into the courthouse and pretend he had business there. Then he heard Gabe's voice in his head. What she *would* say anyway: *Maybe you should grow a pair and go talk to her.*

Fine, he thought. Fine. He looked over at her and smiled, just as he realized she wasn't looking at him. He dropped his head then, shaking it back and forth in disgust at his own foolishness, which is when Beanie chose to look at *him*. So, when he raised his head, he saw the same tight-lipped, indignant glare that preceded a face-full of frosting—something he ever wanted to see again, he was certain. The frosting or the glare. Best to get this over with. He wrinkled his nose and winced, raising his hand to wave at her. She nodded in acknowledgment, then returned the colander to her lap and tried to look busy.

Suvi pulled a handkerchief out of his pocket—thank God it was clean. He took the white square by one corner and dangled it out his open window, waving it back and forth until she looked up again. He waited until he saw her face relax into a smile. Then he got out of his truck and crossed the street in six long strides, stopping short at the stoop.

"Don't be mad at me," Suvi said.

"Is that an apology?" Beanie squinted at him beneath the brim of her Stetson hat.

"Well, no, but I'm headed that way. May I sit with you for a minute?"

"Lord, Suvi, the whole town'll be talkin'. I've barely got 'em to stop askin' me how you're doing? Word travels fast when the news is juicy, but it's kind'ly slow when it ain't."

"Let 'em talk," Suvi said.

"Ha! That's what I tried to tell you, but you wadn't havin' none of it."

"I didn't come here to argue, Beatrice."

"What'd you come for then?" Beanie ripped the string off a pea pod and scraped a row of purple hulls into the colander.

"I came to apologize."

"I ain't heard no apology yet," Beanie said.

Suvi closed his eyes and shook his head. Then he took a deep breath.

"Beatrice Bradsher, from the bottom of my heart, I apologize." Suvi said. "I'm sorry I hurt you. I'm sorry I didn't call. I'm sorry I wasn't willing to claim you as my girlfriend. As it turns out, it was a whole lot easier than I imagined, and I'm sorry I didn't have the…intestinal fortitude…to face the music while it was playing."

"Well," Beanie dropped both hands into the bowl of peas, "If that don't beat all."

"I really am sorry," Suvi said. "I mean it."

"I'm sorry, too, Suvi. Sorry I hit you with a cake, anyway." She didn't want to grin, but the thought of his face dripping with cream cheese frosting and hunks of blood red cake just did her in. She brought the back of one hand up to her mouth until she got her face under control.

Neither of them spoke for a full minute or so until Beanie broke the awkward silence.

"Come on up here and set down then. You want some tea?"

Suvi climbed the cement steps and eased his long frame into the rocking chair next to Beanie. "You got any coffee? I'm tryin' to cut back on my sugar intake."

"I just made a fresh pot. I'll take these peas in and bring you a cup back."

"Need some help?" Suvi offered.

"Naw, Will's in there decoratin' a cake. I don't wanna throw him off'n his game."

"I heard y'all were opening a bakery. How's that going?"

"Oh, it's great, but we'll both be fat as pigs if we don't stop samplin' all the recipes we been testin'. I done gained five pounds myself. Will and I started walkin' in the mornings. We walk clear out to the blue bridge and back. That's three miles one way!"

Suvi didn't know what to do with this information. They sounded like a couple to him and, if that were the case, he was wasting his time here. He said nothing.

"Anyways—I'll be right back."

Beanie found Will bending over the kitchen table, icing a two-tier cake that was a gift for a young couple getting married tomorrow. Beanie thought they should charge for it, but Will said he didn't want to do that until they were officially open. Until then, he'd consider all the freebies as part of their marketing plan. A way to get the word out.

"How's it goin'?"

Will groaned. "Going good, but my back is killing me."

Beanie took two cups out of the cabinet and poured them both full of coffee.

Will looked up from his work. "Oh, thanks, Bean, but I'm all coffee'd out. I just finished a cup."

"Oh, that ain't for you," Beanie said. "It's for Suvi."

Will stood up straight then. "Ow," he said, rubbing at the small of his back. "Suvi's here?"

"Yeah," Beanie grabbed a couple of napkins with one hand, then picked up both cups. "He just stopped by to say hey. Awkward, if ya' ask me."

Awkward, indeed, Will thought to himself, but said aloud, "Oh, okay, well...tell him I said hello."

When Beanie had gone, Will wiped his hands on a kitchen towel. *Tell him I said hello?* How lame was that? He made an effort to get back to his cake but messed up three leaf patterns before deciding he'd be better off waiting until Suvi was gone.

Will hated feeling jealous of anyone. In all the years before Marie's death, he'd never once felt jealous or insecure.

Well, of course not. Marie was his wife. Beanie wasn't even his girlfriend, and likely never would be. All the more reason *not* to be jealous. He rolled his eyes at the empty room and started back on the cake.

On the porch, Suvi and Beanie did their best to start a normal conversation. After a few stops and starts, Beanie threw up her hands in exasperation and got right to the point.

"Why are you here, Suvi?" Beanie leaned forward in her rocking chair and studied his face. "I mean, really...won't your girlfriend ask you the same thing?"

"Girlfriend? What girlfriend?"

"Gabe-what's-her-face. That girlfriend."

Suvi snorted. "Gabe is *not* my girlfriend, Beatrice. Not even close."

"That's not what everybody in town thinks."

"Yeah, well everyone in the town thought *you* were dating Bubba John Atwater, and they got that wrong, too. If I was dating Gabe, I wouldn't be here asking you to go out with me."

"Is that what you're doing?" Beanie felt her face burning and put both palms on her cheeks to cool them.

"I am," Suvi nodded. "Look, I know this is weird, but I don't think I really gave us a chance. Now I have an opportunity to go work for the Gators, and I can't bring myself to say yes unless I know for sure it will never work out for us."

Beanie took a deep breath. "I see," she said. "They offered you a job and you aren't sure you want it?"

"Oh, I want it," Suvi said. "I want it almost as much as I've wanted anything else in my life, but it took me a while to realize why I wasn't jumping at the bit to accept the job. I couldn't imagine not seeing you. And if that isn't love, I guess I don't know what is."

"I see," Beanie said again. And she did see. She stood then and faced Suvi. "Well, I can make this pretty easy for ya', Suve. You should call them up and ask them when you can start."

"Wait," Suvi stood, too. Beanie held one palm up to stop him from going on.

"No, you wait," Beanie said. "Now, I appreciate you coming over here and saying you're sorry and all that. It makes me feel better, it really does. But as far as I'm concerned, it's been over for months now and I'd just as soon not go backwards. It's like a big ol' pot of soup, ya know? You take that first taste and you either like it or ya don't. But you don't leave it settin' there on the stove to spoil."

Suvi scratched at the back of his neck for a moment. "So, I waited too long?"

"I don't reckon that's the onliest reason, but does it matter?"

"I guess it does to me. Is there someone else?" Suvi asked. "Is that why?"

"Don't matter if there is or there isn't," Beanie said. "Wouldn't have nothin' to do with it anyhow."

Suvi hung his head and stared at his fingertips.

"Suvi?" Beanie reached over and placed one hand on his forearm. "Sometimes it's okay to leave things unfinished. If you wanna know the whole truth, I don't think you'll ever be fit to love somebody if you don't take this job and see what happens. It's like they's always somethin' holdin' you back."

"I don't like making mistakes." Suvi said. "What if I regret leaving?

"You're gonna *what if* yourself to death. Listen to me, regret never killed nobody. All regret does is tell you what you did wrong so's you can do it right next time. If you don't go, you won't *ever* know for sure what you want."

Suvi nodded and they were both silent for a few moments.

"I'm going to assume you won't be waiting for me when I get back."

Beanie shook her head. "I been waitin' all my life, Suvi. But not 'cause I meant to."

"I know one thing for sure," he said. "I will miss you, Beatrice Bradsher. I already do."

"I miss you, too." Beanie took a few steps toward Suvi and stretched up on her toes to kiss him on the cheek. Then she adjusted her hat and peered up at him from beneath the brim. "I reckon I'm a little surprised how much I do... miss you, I mean. But it don't change nothin'. Nothin' a'tall. Go on now, Suvi. I gotta get supper done."

Suvi nodded, then strode off the porch without looking back.

Later that evening, after dishes were done and leftovers put away, Will did what he'd told himself a hundred times he would not do.

"So, what's Suvi up to now?" he asked while Beanie was gathering up her newest sewing project. They'd gotten into a routine of watching the weather channel together, then turning to the cooking channel after that. When Beanie looked slightly startled at the question, Will backpedaled fast. "You don't have to answer that."

She scrunched her face and twisted her head. "I don't mind answerin' the question. I was just wonderin' how you meant it. Sounded kind'ly smart-alecky to me, and that ain't really like you."

Will froze, his eyes wandering randomly as he tried to think of something to say that wouldn't get himself into trouble. This was why he had reminded himself over and over, all throughout supper and the aftermath, *keep your big mouth shut.*

"I didn't mean it that way. I was just wondering how he was doing. I haven't seen him around in a while."

"Nope," she said, "and he *won't* be around if he has any sense at all."

Will was not sure at all how to react to that. He wanted to jump out of his recliner and let out a whoop, but he reined the impulse in.

"Why's that?" Will's attempt at nonchalance was feeble, especially since his voice rose nearly an octave.

"Are you catchin' a cold?"

"No, not at all," Will cleared his throat. "Just… you know… allergies."

"Oh," Beanie settled onto the couch and pulled her sewing kit onto her lap. "I could make you some licorice tea if you like. That'll help."

"I'm good," Will said. "Just a tickle."

Beanie focused on threading a needle.

Will switched on the television and punched the numbers for the weather. Jim Cantore was talking about the upcoming hurricane season. When they cut to a break, it was an advertisement for Viagra. Will winced and quickly changed the channel. Anything, dear God, *anything* but that. Why is this happening?

"Thank you," Beanie said without looking up. "I wish they wouldn't have them things on there. Cain't you just imagine some kid lookin' up, sayin', "Daddy, what's erectile dysfunction? Lord, help 'em.""

In his head, Will said *let it go, let it go, let it go, let it go,* but his mouth said, "So, what did Suvi want today? I mean, why'd he stop by? I mean, why'd you say he wouldn't be around if he had any sense? I mean, you never answered that, and you… Never mind. Never mind. I'm sorry."

Beanie dropped her hands into her lap. "Well, if you must know, Suvi came by to tell me he's taking a job in Gainesville."

"You're kidding!"

"You gotta do something about your throat, Will. You sound like you're goin' through puberty again or somethin'."

"Why Gainesville?"

"He got an offer to scout for Florida," Beanie shrugged.

"Wow," Will said. "Wow! That's…that's something. And he's moving?"

"Well, I don't rightly know all that. I'm not even sure he's takin' the job. That's why he stopped by."

"I don't get it." Will turned the sound down on the TV.

"Lord you're nosy, Will. If you must know the whole story, Suvi came by to say he was thinking about taking the job, but first he wanted to know if he still had a chance with me."

"Oh?" Will bit his tongue. Literally bit his tongue and closed his eyes.

"I told him to take the job."

"Oh!"

Beanie pushed her sewing to the side and stood up. "I'm gonna go make you some tea, 'fore you turn into a girl."

Will felt his face go hot as he realized how much fun Beanie was having at his expense. But to tell the truth, he wasn't certain it was embarrassment or joy that made him suddenly feel like his skin was on fire. He fanned himself with the *Country Living* magazine from the table beside him.

Corinne Barr

I was born at home, in a small, sturdy house in Mayhew Junction in 1949. It was not uncommon for black mothers to give birth at home back then. The nearest hospital accepting black patients was sixty miles away. We had several midwives in the Quarters, and my great-grandmother Maribelle Boone, Grandmary to me, was one of them. She was training my auntie when I was born. I can't tell you how many times Auntie Rose said to me, "Missy, I brought you into this world, and it wadn't so's you could be mouthy. You mind your manners, or I'll sho' nuff take you out." My favorite was, "I gave you your first whippin' when you was borned, and if you don't cut it out, I'll give you your last." My auntie aimed to teach me respect, but I learned that from Grandmary, who insisted on good grammar. "If you intend to speak up about things, you had better learn to speak well," she said. "There are plenty of people willing to judge you ignorant because you're black. Best you learn to prove them wrong the moment you open your mouth." I should point out Rose was my aunt by marriage. No child raised by my grandmother ever said "sho' nuff" about anything.

I'm sure that's why I became a teacher myself. I grew up with an overriding sense of duty to the community. My great-grandmother was born in South Carolina in 1882. She married when she was barely seventeen and had her first and only child, my grandfather Frederick, two years later. Her husband Jesse was a brakeman for the railroad, working freight trains up and down the eastern seaboard. He was killed when he slipped and fell between moving cars trying to set one of the brakes. His death benefit was what allowed Grandmary to become a nurse. Fred was just a couple of years old when she enrolled at St. Luke's Hospital and Training School, a nursing college for black students.

When Fred was eighteen, Grandmary moved to Mayhew Junction to be near family, a move she would regret for the rest of her life. She blamed herself for what happened to her son, which is why she felt compelled to stay in Mayhew Junction and take care of his pregnant widow. And stay she did, even after my mother Lula was born and it was clear she was no child of Frederick Boone's. When she told me all this, I asked why she helped raise a grandchild that wasn't really hers. She said, "Hattie was Fred's widow—I knew that much was true. She needed me first, then your momma Lula, then you. How could I have walked away from all that pulling at me? Besides, what would I have gone back to? Fred was all I had left in this world. And in a roundabout way, he gave me a family after all."

I understand the pulling. That's what this genealogy thing is doing to me. Pulling at me, saying tell 'em who you are, Corinne. Tell 'em who you are. This town may not like old wounds broken open, but how are they ever going to heal?

6 - Home is Where the Car Goes

Tate Atwater was the first to notice and speak up.

"Mama, you turnt the wrong way again!"

"It's turned, son, not turnt." Sweet raised her voice enough for him to hear from the back of their minivan.

What had gotten into her lately? This was the third time this month she made a right turn toward her *old* homestead, instead of a left toward the new house Bubba John built as a Christmas surprise. Sweet pulled off the road, checked her sideview mirror and started to make a U-turn only to hear the blaring horn of a car.

Daisy, her two-year-old, covered her ears and wailed from her car seat in the second row.

Sweet slammed her foot on the brake, cursed under her breath, and angled the car back off the road. She put the car into park, swiped the back of her hand across her forehead and peered into the rearview mirror to see all three of her youngest children wide-eyed with mouths open.

"What happened, Mommy?" Bitty spoke when Sweet made eye contact.

"Nothing, honey. I didn't see that car in my blind spot. We're okay, though. Everything's fine."

Daisy held up a half-empty baggy of Cheerios. "Oh dod," she said, looking at the cereal spilled across her lap and onto the floor.

Sweet winced and caught her daughter's eye in the mirror. "Daisy, honey, we don't say 'oh, god' like that."

Daisy frowned at her mother, her head cocked sideways. "Yes, we do," she protested. "And den we say *chit.*"

Tater burst into a fit of giggles in the back and elbowed Bitty, who had resumed quietly counting the beads on her bracelet. "Bitty, did you hear that?" Tate screeched. "Daisy said the S-word!"

Bitty looked horrified. "No way! Daisy said *stupid?*"

"No, not *that* S-word, the *other one!*"

"All, right, that's enough!" Sweet choked back her own laughter and worked her face into some semblance of sternness before turning to face her children. "Now I'm sorry I scared everyone, and I'm very sorry I said a bad word, too, but we are *not* going to curse in this car. Do you hear me?"

"Can we cuss on the bus?" Tate collapsed into raucous laughter at his own wordplay. Daisy, with no idea why, joined her brother, squealing and snorting and clapping wildly. Even Bitty stopped counting long enough to chime in.

"You made a rhyme, Brudder Bear."

Sweet shook her head and closed her eyes and felt herself relax. This was why she loved her kids so much. No matter what was going on, they could always make her laugh. She was going to have to watch that boy, though. If he was this precocious at six, they might have some real problems down the road.

When they all settled down a bit, Sweet checked carefully before turning the car, and headed toward home. After a few minutes, Sweet asked Bitty about her day at school.

"It was bad, Mama," Bitty said, "but I don't wanna talk about it."

"Why not, honey?" Sweet glanced in the rearview mirror and watched Bitty pull at the beads on her bracelet.

"I just don't wanna talk about it."

"Did you have to sit out at P.E. again?" Sweet guided the car down the long dirt road to their remodeled farmhouse.

"No," Bitty said.

"Then what is it, baby? Please tell Mommy why you had a bad day."

"I think I have a bad brain," Bitty said matter-of-factly. "It doesn't cooperate."

Sweet parked the car and turned back toward Bitty.

"You have a very *good* brain, Elizabeth Atwater. Look at Mommy."

Bitty complied.

"There is nothing in the world wrong with your brain. I want you to hear me. Nothing wrong at all, and I don't want you saying that again."

Sweet watched a single tear hesitate at the brim of Bitty's eyelid before sliding down her cheek.

"Then why do I do everything wrong?" Bitty asked. She stared at her mother, waiting for a response and, when there was none, went back to counting beads.

34

Sweet first took a deep breath, and then some time to count her blessings. The house was empty at the moment. The twins were at ball practice, B-Kay playing girls' softball, and T-Ray on the varsity baseball team. Bubba John was still at school. After winning the lottery and completing the remodel of his parents' old farmhouse, her husband decided he thoroughly enjoyed the process. So, he enrolled at the college, something she had never even imagined he'd want to do and was studying to be a licensed contractor. Truth be told, they had enough money to never work again if they managed it right, but even Bubba John, who preferred leisure whenever he could get it, didn't think it wise to do nothing. That was not the kind of role model he wanted to be for his kids.

As for Sweet, she counted every single day a blessing, knowing how close she came to... She couldn't even *think* the word. The idea of her children living without their mother made her nauseous. She wrangled the three little ones inside, sat the older two at the dining room table she'd had since her first Christmas with Bubba John, and plopped Daisy in front of the T.V. for a half hour of Dora the Explorer. She'd learned if she didn't get Bitty and Tate working on their homework right away, there would be mass hysteria the next morning when they grabbed their backpacks and realized it hadn't been done. Routine was the key for her rowdy bunch.

Tate, despite his often-boisterous behavior, always breezed through his homework, needing very little help or encouragement from her. Bitty was another story altogether. Sweet stuck close by in case she was needed. She went to the refrigerator and pulled out a package of chicken breasts and another of thighs, then set them in the sink to thaw in a bath of warm water. Then she started peeling potatoes to boil.

A few minutes later, Tate slammed his folder shut and hollered, "Done! Can I go outside?" She wasn't sure why he shouted when she was only ten steps away.

"Did you do everything?" Sweet grabbed a paper towel to dry her hands and walked toward the table.

"Yep!"

"Yes, ma'am?" Sweet flipped open his folder and looked at the two workbook pages he'd completed. Common Core Math was beyond her, but Tate always seemed to be able to make sense of it. He rarely came home with a paper scored less than 100%.

"Yes, ma'am!" Tate squirmed in his seat. "Can I go?"

Sweet grabbed Tate's pencil and signed the homework log in the folder.

"Folder in the backpack—backpack by the door. Then you can go," Sweet said. "But stay inside the fence and watch for snakes."

"Got it!" Tate leapt from his seat, did as he was told, and flew out the back door at full speed.

"Slow down, son!" Sweet called after him. "You're gonna hurt your…" She halted when she heard what sounded like tumbling buckets, and a shriek from her son. Good Lord, what has he done now? Sweet rushed toward the door.

"I'm okay!" Tate's voice rang out strong, and after a rattle of more buckets or boxes or whatever they were, all was quiet again.

Sweet shook her head and returned to the table. "You doin' okay, Bitty-bug?

No response. Bitty sat hunched over, staring at her paper.

"What's up, baby? Do you need help?"

Bitty's face crumpled and she dropped her head onto her arms and sobbed. "I can't do it. I can't. It's too hard."

An hour later, the work was done and Bitty dragged herself to her room for some "quiet time," as she called it. The chicken was completely thawed, Daisy was asleep in front of the television, and Tate was nowhere to be found.

Mother of the year, Sweet thought, shaking her head in disgust. I'm doing *everything*, but nothing well. Then she poured herself a glass of wine and finished making supper.

***

An hour later, Sweet Lee stirred the pot of Salsa Chicken and replaced the lid. Wiping her hands on a kitchen towel, she looked across the dining room table and into the living room and counted heads. Four children and one husband watching the Turtleman. How they could stand that silliness, she would never know, but she didn't have time to worry about that now.

"Has anyone seen Bitty?"

No response. Not even from Bubba John. Sweet walked into the living room to find him asleep in the recliner, his mouth gaping open. She smacked him on the arm with the back of her hand.

"Hey, wake up," she said. "Have you seen Bitty?"

Bubba John opened one eye and squinted up at her. "I'm sleeping."

"I see that. Supper's ready. I'm trying to find our child."

He raised himself to a sitting position and rubbed his face with both hands. "Where'd you see her last?"

"In your lap, thirty minutes ago."

"Oh, yeah. Give me a minute, hon...I'm a little foggy."

B-Kay stood then. "I'll go check her room. You need some help in there?"

Sweet could always count on her oldest daughter. Not so much her father, or her twin brother for that matter.

"If you'll find your sister, that will be a big help. T-Ray, you and Tater come help me set the table."

"Aw, mom...the Turtleman's about to catch a rack-koon," Tate sputtered.

T-Ray stood, "I'll set the table, Mom. Tate'll just be in the way."

"Thank you, Son. I take it back."

"Take what back?" T-Ray stretched and yawned behind his forearm.

"What I just thought." Sweet poked his exposed belly. "Never mind, thanks for helping."

"I haven't done anything yet."

"Tell me something I don't know, Son." Sweet flung the towel across her shoulder and headed back for the kitchen. "Y'all go get washed up. I'm putting supper on the table in five minutes."

Ten minutes later they were all seated at Sweet Lee's pine table. When they moved into Bubba John's old family home, remodeled and upgraded into a beautiful modern farmhouse beyond Sweet's wildest dreams, the table was one of the few pieces of furniture from their "old life" that came with them. Sweet loved the table for its long clean lines, but it was the sentimental value—what it represented especially—that made even her husband realize nothing could replace it. He didn't even try. He'd given Nonie Crawford, the designer who helped him furnish Sweet's Christmas gift, the dimensions of the table and told her to find new ladder-back chairs similar to the ones they already had.

"Can I light the candles?" Tate asked.

The twins groaned. The little ones still loved the family tradition of lighting a tea candle for each person at the table, but the teens thought it took up too much time. They were hungry.

"Get Daddy to light this for you," Sweet said, handing Tate the long-handled lighter. "Y'all go ahead and start helping your plates."

Tate scrambled out of his chair, and promptly tripped over his own feet, sprawling to the floor and sending the lighter skidding across the polished wood.

"Dude, slow down," T-Ray rolled his eyes and shook his head in disgust.

Unfazed, Tate retrieved the lighter and hurried to his father's side. After a bit of a struggle, Bubba helped Tate hold a lit flame at the tip.

"Can I go first?" Tate asked.

"I'll go first," Bubba John grinned at his wife at the other end of the long table. "I'm thankful for the dinner Mama cooked for us tonight."

Bubba John lit the first candle and looked at T-Ray sitting immediately to his left.

"I'm thankful for no homework tonight." T-Ray said as Tate guided the flame to the next candle. "Ditto," said his twin.

Tate went next. "I'm thankful that rack-koon didn't bite the Turtleman, and also for the frog I found today."

"What frog?" Bubba John and Sweet asked in tandem. "Where is it now?" Sweet added.

"It was dead, Mama. I gave it a' autopsy."

Sweet shuddered. "Did you...never mind. I don't wanna know. Bitty, what are you thankful for, baby?"

"I'm thankful Mr. Dallas wasn't at school today. Can we eat now?"

Bitty picked up her fork and started arranging her green beans into a pattern on her plate. Sweet froze and looked at her husband, who started to speak. She shook her head at him, and he closed his mouth.

38

"Y'all eat before your food gets cold. B-Kay, could you get the sour cream for me? I forgot to put it out." Sweet did her best to look calm, but a cold dread shook her to the bone.

7 - A Reckoning

Corinne Barr pulled her 2015 Cadillac CTS into the parking space in front of the Milestone Baptist Church, about a mile west of downtown Mayhew Junction. She'd arranged the meeting there for several reasons. First of all, it was a neutral location. Not LouWanda Crump's cramped and dusty office, and not her own church where white women scarcely ever tread, least of all LouWanda.

Secondly, it was a contemporary church known for having a moderately diverse congregation, and one whose pastor worked closely with her own pastor on community issues. The information she planned on sharing with LouWanda this morning was going to raise some hackles and Corinne was fairly certain she would need reinforcements of the level-headed kind. And witnesses to boot. So, she called a meeting of the entire board of the Mayhew Junction Historical Society. Even if she didn't gain inclusion into the History of Mayhew Junction book, she would still accomplish the most important task of all—a good old-fashioned history lesson. Considering her background, she figured she was just the one to give it.

Corinne was getting out of her car when LouWanda drove her battered Ford Bronco into the space beside her. She parked about six inches too close, despite the fact that there were numerous empty spaces in the generously configured parking lot. Corinne winced when LouWanda squeezed out of the driver's seat, her door pressing into the side of the Cadillac as she released her ample bulk onto the asphalt. LouWanda slammed her door, licked her finger and rubbed at the spot on Corinne's passenger door.

"Sorry about that," LouWanda said over the top of the car. "It'll buff out, I reckon."

Corinne opened her mouth to respond, then thought better of it and turned toward the church. She recognized Diane Kerner's Suburban by the "Vote Kerner, County Commissioner District 3" placard pasted to its back window. There were four other cars parked in front of the reception hall doors, but she couldn't place who all they belonged to.

"I'm gonna hit the little girl's room first," LouWanda said to her retreating back. "I'll see y'all in there in a minute."

"I'll let the ladies know." Corinne replied, then added under her breath, "Take your time."

She was right. Diane Kerner was already there, making a pot of coffee in the industrial-sized kitchen. Nell Wiggins and JoDeen Avery were throwing a tablecloth over a large round plastic table, and Phyllis Montgomery, who sat on the board of Corinne's church and worked at the County Clerk's office, was bringing coffee cups from the kitchen to put on a table already laden with store-bought cookies. A Tupperware cake carrier sat off to the side, no doubt harboring one of Nell's famous cakes. Didn't matter what kind she brought, it would be decadent, irresistible, and deadly. Corinne could not imagine how anyone could eat those things and not become an instant diabetic. Not that she would be able to resist it. She'd have a sliver. Just a sliver.

Corinne wheeled her briefcase over and placed it beside a chair at the round table. She was glad they'd chosen round over rectangular. That was always such a power struggle, no matter how humble you fancied yourself to be. It would be better if everyone were on equal footing. Well, as equal as could be, anyway.

The greetings were kind and genuine. JoDeen took Corinne's coat and hung it on the rack by the door, then sat down and pulled out the handwork she always had with her. Phyllis hugged her neck and asked about her grandkids. Nell cut everyone a piece of Hummingbird cake and served it with two cookies and a fork. So much for the sliver, Corinne thought as she stared at the three-inch slice of scrumptiousness in front of her. By the time they got down to business, everyone would be in a state of caffeine and sugar bliss, and she wondered how long that would last. She didn't have to wait for an answer.

LouWanda, fresh from the restroom and still drying her hands on a wad of brown paper towels, towered over the table. Her height was made even more impressive by the dark hair piled high on her head in the beehive style she'd worn for years.

"I'm so hungry, I could eat the butt out of a rag doll. Looks like y'all outdone yourselves this time. Wooo-weee, Nell Wiggins, is that your hummingbird cake? I'll take two slices if you don't mind." She yanked the chair from beneath the table and heaved herself into it with a whump.

"Well, hello yourself, LouWanda," JoDeen intoned, looking up from the doily she was crocheting.

LouWanda waved one hand in dismissal, then started in like she'd called the meeting herself.

"Thank y'all for comin' today. I been thinkin' a lot about what we oughta do with the windfall from our fundraisin' efforts, and I thought we should talk about that first." LouWanda had barely gotten the words out before she popped a huge hunk of hummingbird cake into her mouth and crooned appreciatively. "That's some good stuff there, Miss Nell."

"What windfall are you referring to, LouWanda? The book isn't even published yet." Corinne folded her hands and waited for LouWanda to swallow. Unfortunately, she didn't.

"I'm talkin' about the money been donated to puttin' this whole thing together. It ain't gonna cost half what we brought in, and I got some ideas for how we can use what's left over."

Diane Kerner cleared her throat. "Could I interject something here? I mean, I don't want to overstep my bounds, but I *am* the treasurer of the Historical Society, and I'm not sure it is completely accurate to say we'll have that much excess in publishing funds. Not to mention that this is a matter to take before the executive board, not the *Mayhew: Then and Now* committee."

"That don't mean we cain't discuss it, does it?"

"There are protocols, LouWanda," Diane said. "Today's meeting is about the book."

"Oh, phooey on the protocols, Diane. I *am* talkin' about the book. What I want to do will be the perfect send-off for the book at the Founders Day Parade. See, I was thinkin' about how we ain't never had the money to do a proper historical tribute at our courthouse downtown. That thing is a national treasure settin' there on Main Street. I think we ought to have something commemorative out front, like a statue or somethin'. I got just the man we oughta honor, and it ain't because he's my great-great-grandfather, neither. It's 'cause he is none other than Louis B. Matthews, architect and designer of the courthouse itself."

Corinne Barr choked on her coffee. Phyllis Montgomery instinctively reached out and patted Corinne on the back, but never took her eyes-wide gaze off LouWanda's face.

"I'm not sure that's a great idea, Ms. LouWanda," Phyllis said.

Corinne nudged Phyllis with her knee and gave a quick shake of her head.

"Well, why not? Seems the perfect choice to me," LouWanda drew herself up in the chair, dropped her shoulders back and thrust her ample chin forward. "What have you got against him is what I wanna know?"

JoDeen Avery knew a storm when she saw one brewing, so she took matters into her own hands. "I move we table this discussion until the next meeting of the Board of Directors."

"I second that," several women spoke in unison.

"We'll talk about this later, LouWanda," Diane said. "Case closed."

"Well, I never… Fine then, I'll set here and eat this cake. Y'all just go on like I'm not even here, since that's what y'all are dead set on doin' anyhow."

Diane turned toward Corinne and spoke. "I know you have some information to share with us, Mrs. Barr. Please go ahead."

Corinne, sufficiently recovered, patted her lips with a folded napkin, then began, "I had a chance to look at the work that has been done so far on the history of Mayhew project, and I must say it's pretty impressive. It could use a little editing, but I know that can wait until we have all the stories and pictures we want to include in the book compiled and uploaded to a document file—"

"What editing?" LouWanda interrupted.

"Well, you know," Corinne said patiently. "a few word choices, some spelling errors, punctuation, that kind of thing. Nothing big. I can do that myself. Phyllis has volunteered to help me transcribe everything onto Word, so we'll have a file we can upload per the instructions from the publisher. Anyway, that's not really the problem I want to talk a—"

"Why is it a problem at all?" LouWanda demanded.

Nell reached over and covered LouWanda's hand with her own. "LouWanda, honey, I don't think Mrs. Barr is trying to offend you. Let's just let her finish, okay?"

LouWanda huffed and leaned back in her chair.

"I'm sorry, Corinne," Diane Kerner said. "Please continue."

Corinne Barr straightened her spine and hesitated a moment before speaking. She decided to take a conciliatory tack. "I'm afraid Miz Crump and I have gotten off to a bad start, and that is partially my doing. I appreciate you all taking the time to sit down with me and discuss this project. It's as important to me as it is to anyone else, I assure you. I'd like to address a bit of an elephant in the room, so please bear with me as I do my best to tread lightly on the subject. These things are delicate, you know."

Diane and Nell nodded in unison, giving Corinne sympathetic lifts of the chin, which served to calm Corinne's now racing heart. She hadn't expected to be this nervous. Phyllis—the only one present who knew what was coming—patted her leg under the table. Buoyed by the support, Corinne took another sip of her coffee with shaking hands and plowed onward.

"As I was saying, I think Marie and LouWanda have done a fine job of collecting stories and pictures of our little town..." She paused. "But I find the community in which Phyllis and I live has been overlooked in some ways, and I'd like to add some important facts which I believe will round out the book in a more inclusive way."

"Oh, absolutely, Mrs. Barr, I agree," Diane nodded. "Marie and I talked about this before she got sick and she suggested I check with Suvi Jones to find someone who might help us from the—from your community. We were so happy when you volunteered to work with us. We value your input. Really, we do."

LouWanda grumbled something under her breath, which sounded to Corinne like "speak for yourself," and she was sure she heard JoDeen kick LouWanda under the table.

"The problem is," Corinne said, trying not to look at LouWanda Crump, "some of my information may not set well with some people."

"That's putting it lightly," Phyllis said under her breath.

Nell Wiggins winced. "Is it that bad?"

Corinne shrugged. "I guess that depends on how you look at it."

Diane looked at her watch. "Okay, I think we've danced around this enough, y'all. Tell us whatcha' got, Mrs. Barr. We're all adults here. We can take it."

"Do y'all know about naval stores?"

"Like military stores or something?" JoDeen asked.

"Not really," Corinne said. "Naval stores were what they called the turpentine industry. Turpentine was used to waterproof ships, and it was a booming industry collecting sap from the pine trees back in the day, so that's where they got the name."

"Ohhh…" Three of the women joined in that chorus and slumped in their chairs. LouWanda sat up taller and leaned across the table.

"Why we gotta put anything in there about that? We're tryin' to put out somethin' we're proud of. Ain't nobody gonna wanna read anything about that."

"Why not?" Corinne asked. "It's part of our history, though I agree it's not a particularly pleasant part. Still and all, we ought not ignore it. Why, I wouldn't even be here if not for those camps. My own mother was born at Blue Creek."

"Oh, is that where this is goin'?" LouWanda shoved back her chair and stood. "I'm not gonna sit here and listen to my family be defamed more than's already been done."

"LouWanda!" JoDeen looked stricken.

"Don't LouWanda me! I know what she's tryin' to do and I ain't gonna stand for it. I done heard enough about Blue Creek to last a lifetime. I'm sicka bein' made to feel guilty 'bout somethin' I ain't had nothin' to do with. Why she's even bringin' this up, I don't know. Just to get at me, I reckon."

"I promise you I am not trying to 'get at you,' as you say. But it's something that needs to be discussed for a variety of reasons." The more agitated Corinne became, the more difficult it was to speak clearly, so she took a deep breath and slowed her speech even more than usual. "I've been researching my family and others through the Ancestry website. They have a DNA program that is very helpful when trying to compile a family history on people of color. I had always heard stories about my grandparents and wasn't sure what to believe, but I've done my DNA and it confirms one very crucial piece of information."

Corinne stopped to take a sip of cold coffee. "I think you better sit back down, LouWanda."

There was a collective intake of breath as the four women waited for Corinne to speak. LouWanda sagged back into her chair, her eyes already filling with angry tears as she braced herself for whatever Corinne was about to blab to the room.

"My mother, Lula Corinne Boone, was born in 1922, in the encampment known as Blue Creek. Her parents were Frederick and Hattie Collier Boone. Frederick came to Florida with his mother, my great-grandmother Maribelle Boone. You all might remember her as a nurse and midwife here in town right up until she died in '93. She mostly delivered babies over in the Quarters, but she was known to have delivered a good number of white babies when the need arose. Anyway, Grandmary, as I called her, was widowed young and raised her son up in South Carolina but moved down here when my grandfather Frederick was eighteen. They hadn't been here long when he was arrested and charged with vagrancy. According to Grandmary, he was simply looking for work, same way he had done in South Carolina, by walking from farm to farm and offering his services." Corinne coughed a couple of times and cleared her throat. "I'm sorry, I have a little tickle, I think."

Phyllis got up quickly and poured a cup from the pitcher of ice water by the coffee pot. She placed the cup in front of Corinne and sat back down.

Diane pushed a bowl of mints across the table. "You all right, Ms. Barr? We can finish this some other time if you're not feeling well."

"No, I'm fine. I'm almost done." Corinne sipped the water, cleared her throat again, and went on. "What some of you know, and maybe some of you don't, is the turpentine camps were basically another form of slavery in the Jim Crow era. Blue Creek was a horrible place, run by a man named T.A. Kraft."

LouWanda stiffened and pointed a finger at Corinne. "I knew you was headed there. I told y'all."

"Shhh!" Diane and JoDeen admonished at once.

"My grandfather was sent there as part of his sentence. Now, the odd thing was, wives were allowed at the encampment, as it wasn't an actual prison per se. So, Hattie joined Fred at some point, and got caught up in one of the vilest parts of the system. I'll spare you the details; they aren't something I can speak of easily. Anyway, my grandmother gave birth to my mother about two months before my grandfather was beaten to death for coming to his wife's defense over…well…over the details. After his death, Gramma Hattie stayed on for a couple of months at the camp. It's not clear whether she was held against her will, or whether she couldn't make her way out of the woods and back home on her own. What we know is my mother got sick with the whooping cough and Gramma Hattie convinced T.A. to take her to Mayhew Junction so she could get treatment for her infant. She didn't tell him Grandmary was her mother-in-law; she just said she was a midwife and nurse and could help. He dropped them off at Grandmary's house saying he'd return in a week to pick them up and she'd better be ready to go. For whatever reason—we don't know—he never came back, and they both stayed right there with Grandmary from then on."

Nell Wiggins leaned toward Corinne, reaching across the table to pat as close to Corinne's hand as she could get. "You poor thing. I had no idea things like that happened in our little county. I don't see why we can't put that story in our little book. It has a happy ending, doesn't it?"

LouWanda put her forehead down on the table and moaned.

"Well, it does, in a way, but that's not the end of the story," Corinne said. "I'm sorry, LouWanda, I have to get this out."

LouWanda turned her head to look at Corinne with one eye. "Haven't you said enough? We all know T.A. was a butthead. They's been a'plenty written about it, and it don't do nothin' but bring shame on my family. It ain't our fault he was one of our'n. I don't know why you gotta keep on diggin' up bones that just as well stay buried."

"Well, that's the whole point, LouWanda. There's a part of this story *my* family has talked about for years, and now DNA confirms it. T.A. Kraft was my mother's biological father. Just so you know—I did a search on your family, too. T.A.'s mother and your great-grandfather were brother and sister. That means you and I share a set of great-great-grandparents, Louis B. and Hannah Jane Matthews. I have it all mapped out for you right here." Corinne pushed a piece of paper across the table toward LouWanda. "Looks to me like you and I are third cousins."

"Holy crap," JoDeen said, looking back and forth between LouWanda and Corinne. "You know, now that I think about it, y'all do favor each other a bit."

LouWanda sat straight up and smacked JoDeen Avery right on the arm.

8 - The Proposition

The next morning at the café, Randy Kerner waited for Suvi to get settled, then picked up his own coffee and sat down at Suvi's table without waiting for an invitation.

"Mornin' Suvi, you got a minute?"

Suvi finished the last few sentences of an article he was reading in the Sports section of the Gainesville Sun before he put the paper down and made eye contact with his intruder.

"Randy," Suvi nodded, "how's it going?"

"Good, good, you know, gearing up for the election."

"Do you even have an opponent this year?"

"Not yet. There's still a few more weeks to declare, though. I'm not too awful worried about my seat, but there's some...what's the word...upheaval? Well, let's just call it *concern* with your district."

"My district?" Suvi could not conceal his irritation.

"Yeah, you know Joe Radke is gonna retire, and he's held that seat for a long time, despite the demographic of the district."

"Black, you mean."

"Well, yeah, but Hispanic, too. Ever since the dairy farmers got nervous about hirin' illegals, and that new law team in Live Oak started helpin' 'em get citizenship, it's getting so's we have more minorities voting than ever."

Suvi felt his skin prickle and he sat up straighter. "Is that a problem?"

"No, no..." Randy raised both hands in mock surrender. "I think we *need* some minority representation on the county level. I'm the first to admit y'all have gotten the short end of the stick in a lot of ways."

"Well, Randy, if you feel that way, why haven't you done anything about it? You've been on the commission for years."

"I've been outnumbered for years, too." Randy pulled a napkin out of the box on the table and wiped sweat off his forehead.

Suvi leaned back and dropped his hands in his lap as Sissy placed his breakfast in front of him.

"Okay, Randy, I'm gonna need you to get to the point here. I don't want to eat a cold breakfast."

"I want you to run for office, Suvi. I think you have a voice people will listen to, and it won't hurt at all that you'll be working for U.F."

Suvi snapped to attention. Grabbing the edge of the table with both hands, he pulled himself toward Randy and nearly growled. "That is *not* public news. I haven't even accepted the offer yet. And how the hell do *you* know about it?"

Randy had the grace to turn red. "Sorry, Suvi, word travels fast."

"Look, I have enough on my plate already. There's too much up in the air right now."

"Hear me out, now…I've already thought of all that. We only hold public meetings once a month, and we can Skype you in for any discussions we have in the meantime. Those are all covered by sunshine laws, so they're recorded anyway."

"Why me, Randy? Why is this so important?"

"Because of who's gonna run against you. And if she runs, we're all in for a tough road."

"Why's that?"

"Because she's running as a Republican and is currently unchallenged."

"So?" Suvi knew the answer, but he wanted to hear Randy admit it out loud.

"You know how it is here…" Randy trailed off.

And Suvi did know. As long as he could remember, folks in Fletcher County, like many other rural counties in the South, registered the way their parents and grandparents before them did—as Democrats—even though they voted for the most Conservative candidate on the ticket. This way they controlled who got on the ballot in the primary election, which gave them a better shot at getting the candidate of their choice. So, most candidates ran on the Democrat ticket despite being diehard Conservatives. And most ended up uncontested in the general elections. Newcomers, unaccustomed to local tradition, thought they were voting for real Democrats in these local elections until eventually they learned the truth. Lately, however, more and more people, unhappy with what they called the "Liberal Agenda," switched parties for the first time in their lives and changed their registration to the Republican Party. This upset the apple cart in more ways than one.

"So, you want me because you think I'll be easy?"

"No," Randy smacked the table with one hand. "I want you because you'll be fair."

Suvi stared at his tablemate a few moments longer than was comfortable for either of them. Then he picked up his fork and split his fried egg open, so the yolk spilled out onto the plate.

"Think about it, Suvi," Randy stood to leave. "That's all I ask."

Suvi nodded but did not speak.

Randy reached across the table and picked up the tab Sissy had left by Suvi's plate.

"Hey!" Suvi protested.

Randy laughed and walked away with the ticket.

Moments later, when Sissy came by to refill his coffee, Suvi slipped her his usual ten-dollar bill. "Randy took my ticket," he said softly. "Don't ever let him pay for my meal."

"Got it," Sissy said, and moved on to the next table without further comment and Suvi finished his breakfast in relative peace.

He was almost through with the newspaper, but not quite, when Gabe came in and sat down. Though she was a far more welcome guest at Suvi's table than Randy Kerner, he still shuddered a bit and thought, *here we go.*

"Saw your truck at the Château the other day. How'd it go?"

"My God, I'm going to have to leave this town just to get a little privacy." Suvi followed his quasi-complaint with a sheepish grin.

"Oh, stop," Gabe said. "The front porch of the Château is in almost direct view of my desk. It's not like I was watching for you."

"I know, I know. Hell, you could stand at one end of Main Street on any given day and know what half the town is doing."

"Seriously," Gabe agreed. "So?"

"So, what?" Suvi squirmed in his chair, then caught Sissy's eye and pointed at his cup.

"Don't *so what* me, you know what I'm talking about."

"Well, if you must know, she told me to take the job." Suvi's shoulders sank as he admitted the truth to his friend.

"And?" Gabe asked.

"And nothing. She's done with me, and I don't blame her. Hell, I didn't call her for months and then I show up on her doorstep? She'd be a fool to take me back, and crazy as it sounds, Beatrice Bradsher is no fool."

"I never dreamed she was," Gabe said. "From all I hear, she's a little odd, but a beautiful soul."

Suvi nodded. "That pretty much sums it up. She is a beautiful soul. And I'm an idiot."

Sissy came by with two fresh cups of coffee. She picked up Suvi's used cup and set the new ones down. "Ham biscuit, Gabe?"

"Yeah, but I'll eat it here. Y'all got any bananas back there? I think I need some potassium."

"I'll check for ya," Sissy said, already moving toward the next table.

"So," Gabe grinned at Suvi. "What's next, old man?"

"Guess I'll take the Florida job."

"And?"

"And close the restaurant." Suvi sat in silence for a minute, his head shaking back and forth almost imperceptibly. "I put a lot of time into that place but, truth be told, it's not much of an income for the effort."

"You want me to try to sell it?"

"Naw, I don't think it would fly in this market, if you could even call Mayhew a market. I could lease out the building, and even the equipment I have in there, but I'd just as soon have something to come back to someday."

"Suit yourself, but it seems a little—I don't know—pathetic to me."

"Thanks a lot," Suvi rolled his eyes. "Good to know I can count on you to kick me when I'm down."

"There's a difference between kicking you when you're down and nudging you to wake up. I didn't know you before, but it seems to me you haven't exactly struggled with making decisions in the past. You chose basketball over football so you could play for Florida. You went all the way out west to play pro-ball. You built your house where you wanted it. You bought a restaurant and ran it. Now all of a sudden, you're what? Paralyzed? For crying out loud, Suvi, DO something. Even if it's wrong."

Suvi nodded. "I don't think you understand what —"

"Are you kidding me? *I* don't understand? I was the first black woman to win a PGA championship. I played in clubs where I *still* didn't see a black body in anything but black pants and white shirts. I understand completely what's tied you up in knots, and it ain't got a damn thing to do with a white girl in a square dance skirt." You need to own *that* before you say another word."

Suvi spoke so low and soft Gabe had to strain to hear him.

"Keep your voice down," Suvi whispered. "I'm sick to death of being embarrassed over breakfast."

Gabe leaned in close and spoke so only he could hear. "Then stop acting like a fool. Get off your ass and do something. You want to get over Beanie? Date someone else. You want to work for Florida? Take the job. If it doesn't work out, you can do something different. Look at me. I bought a house I don't even particularly like, but I was damned if I was going to stay in a boarding house all year. The minute something better hits the market, I'll move on that. But I am finally in a position where I have choices in this world, and you can bet your ass I am not going to let *anyone,* least of all *white folk* dictate what I do with my life. Get out of your head, old man, and do what you damned well please."

Suvi's body shook with tension as he placed his hands, both curled into tight fists, on either side of his plate.

"I *am* doing what I please. I am taking the time I need to make a decision about *my* life. Why does everyone presume to tell me what I ought to do with it?"

"Why do you let them?"

Out of the corner of his eye, Suvi noticed Randy drop his napkin in the middle of his plate and grab two tickets off the table beside him.

"Gotta run," Suvi slapped a couple of bills onto the table and was out the door before Gabe could react.

A minute later, Randy stood at the cash register arguing with Sissy over Suvi's tab, and Gabe was left to wonder if she had just ruined a good friendship.

Randy Kerner

They say behind every successful man is a godly woman, and I'm pretty sure that's true. My wife keeps our household running smooth as butter and always has, even when we had kids at home. They're all grown now, with families of their own. The boys anyway. That daughter of mine was the only one to break ranks. She's a marine biologist up in Georgia. Went to school there, too, which like to've killed us all. Her brothers didn't speak to her for a year, not that she noticed. There's one thing I'll give her...she's got focus like the laser scope on my 30-30. She says she's not ready to get married—she's married to her job. I don't think that's sustainable, but she won't talk about it to me anymore. So, I learned to mind my own business.

Anyway, what I mean to say is Suvi Jones needs a wife. Not just any wife, either. A good wife. He needs someone who will elevate his stature in the community even higher than it is. That girl, Gabrielle, for instance. Strong stock. Already made a name for herself like Suvi did. The Bible calls for a man and a woman to be equally yoked. That means no one having to pull harder than the other. Like me and Diane.

I don't know what that little dalliance with Beanie Bradsher was, but I can tell you it'd never work. Now, I'm anything but a racist—I'm encouraging Suvi to run for office, aren't I? Would a racist do that? I want his people to be represented well, and Suvi can do that. We need diversity on the county commission. Would a racist want that? I don't think so. But there's a lot of people in this town who wouldn't cotton to a white woman with a black man, and that would hurt his chances to be on the board. I'm just telling it like it is.

I'm pullin' for Suvi to get himself a wife he can be proud of, and to win this election coming up. And let me tell ya', if I have to sit on a board with LouWanda Crump, I think I will cut my own throat and call it a day. Yes, Sir, Suvi needs to win this election and I'm gonna make sure he does.

9 - Spring Awakening

By mid-April, Mayhew Junction was starting to look like a town in bloom. With contributions from the Atwater Foundation to the Mayhew Woman's Club, which Sweet Lee had been roped into joining, and a matching grant from the state, the downtown area had undergone a beautification project and now sported new signage on every store, flower boxes in the windows, retro-styled lampposts powered by solar energy, and comfortable benches strategically placed. All of the old stores had been repainted, even if they were empty. The store owners were so thrilled, they each updated their window displays and put in extra effort inside the stores to make them feel warm and inviting.

Will Thaxton and Beanie Bradsher were gearing up for the grand opening of La Pâtisserie scheduled for the middle of May. This would put them in a good position for the bridal season; they already had three orders for wedding cakes and several bridal and baby showers booked for cakes and catering. They were not yet officially opened, but they did keep a few pastries in the cases and served walk-ins and guests at The Château.

Dottie Brentwood had gone from working part-time at Sweet Lee's Dress Emporium to managing partner of the store after Sweet and Bubba John won the lottery. Sweet still popped in every now and then and bought all her own children's clothes there to help support the business. The goal was to sell the shop to Dottie if the income was ever enough to support her outright. Until then, she had a stake in the business and every reason to put her best effort into making a profit. So far, so good.

Kenya Green, a high school senior headed for the University of Florida in the fall, worked at the Emporium after school and helped Dottie with displays and purchasing. She had an eye for design and merchandising and planned on studying both in college. She owed Suvi Jones at least a nod of thanks for getting the admissions team at U.F. to look at her application, which almost didn't happen at all. After three requests to her guidance counselor to send Kenya's transcripts to the university, she finally had to hand-deliver them herself and barely made the deadline. Suvi made a few phone calls and Kenya received her acceptance letter shortly afterwards. Her resumé was impressive enough to make it on her own, but she was still grateful to get the help she needed.

She also got a second part-time job waiting tables at The Big Pig, next door to the dress shop, but that was another story entirely. In a few short months, Kenya had amassed enough money to put down on an apartment in the fall—a quad style unit sharing a common living room and kitchen with four bed and bath combinations in each corner. She pinched herself every day to make sure she wasn't dreaming. She was headed for college and she could barely wait.

In the meantime, there was much to do at the dress shop. Prom was just around the corner and there were dresses arriving every day, with alterations being measured and scheduled in the afternoons. This was another thing Beanie helped out with, though Lord only knew how she made time for all of it. Kenya and Beanie arrived at the same time Tuesday afternoon, at 3:30 on the dot.

"Whew!" Dottie brushed a stray hair off her cheek with the back of her hand and heaved a batch of dresses onto the rack beside the dressing room. "Am I glad to see y'all! These guys just arrived, and I need to price them and get them out onto the floor."

"Lord, Dottie, I hope them won't all need alterin', too." Beanie threw her small leather handbag under the counter and headed straight for the back room where the new alteration orders hung.

"I doubt they will," Kenya called after her. "We got those for the last-minute buyers. They're all ready-to-wear. You know—rayon, lycra, jersey—the stretchy stuff."

Beanie reappeared with an armload of dresses. "Yeah, that'll cover a multitude of sins. Come to think of it, don't even offer to alter them things if you can help it. That kind of fabric is a booger to get right."

Dottie laughed. "That's the truth right there. I think we're reaching the cutoff point for alterations anyway, don't you? There's only so much we can do this close to prom."

"Yeah, it'll take me a couple of days to do these, and Will and I are tryin' to get the Patsy open here in a few weeks."

"I love you, Miss Beanie," Kenya wrapped one long arm around Beanie's shoulder and squeezed hard. "You crack me up. The Patsy…"

Beanie rolled her eyes. "I didn't have no say in what Will named the dang thing, but I am not gonna even attempt La Patissa-whatever-it-is. Speaking of which, I gotta get back there now. Dottie, can you grab my bag there and stick it over my arm?"

"Are you walking back with all that? You want me to drive you?"

"Naw," said Beanie. "I got a little wagon hooked up behind my bike. Will found it at the dump for me the other day and I cleaned it up good. It's perfect…got a cover and everything."

Dottie looked skeptical but said nothing. She held the door for Beanie, then followed her outside. *This* she had to see. Sure enough, there was a pull-behind child carrier attached to the seat of Beanie's bicycle. When Beanie unzipped the side panel to load the clothes in it, there sat a large shoebox in the middle of the seat and, if Dottie weren't imagining things, the box was moving.

"What in the Sam Hill?" Beanie thrust the armload of dresses at Dottie, leaned into the carrier and, turning her head sideways, brought her ear close to the box, which was indeed moving. The box lurched sideways and emitted a faint squeal.

"Well, it ain't a snake," Beanie said and grasped the box in both hands. "It's kind'ly heavy."

"Why don't you open it and see?"

Beanie scrunched her mouth one corner and raised an eyebrow at Dottie.

"I'd like to have an idea what it is first," she said. "What if it's a rat?"

The box gave two brief yips.

"I've never met a rat who barked," Dottie said.

Beanie pulled the lid up and looked inside. A tiny white puppy struggled to stand but plopped back into a wad of dirty white terry cloth lining the cardboard box.

"Oh, my!" Dottie draped the plastic wrapped garments over the seat of Beanie's bike and took the box from Beanie's hands. "It's so tiny…what is it, you reckon?"

"Why it's a puppy, Dottie. Anyone can see that."

"No, no, no…that's not what I meant." Dottie grasped the pup with one hand and rolled it over to reveal its smooth pink belly. "It's a girl! Oh, Beanie, how wonderful, you're a mommy!"

"No, I don't think so," Beanie said. "I don't have time to take care of a puppy. You take her home."

"I can't take her home. I have two pit bulls. They'll eat her for lunch."

Beanie winced. "Why do you have dogs like that?"

"Because I live alone, that's why. And I don't have squirrels, or cats, or rodents of any kind with those two in the yard, which is a good thing, but I don't dare bring home anything they might mistake for a meal."

"Well, shoot," Beanie said. "I cain't leave her here. Wait a second...how in the heck did she get in there in the first place?"

Beanie and Dottie locked eyes as it dawned on them both. They spoke in unison, "Useless!"

"Has to be," Dottie said.

"Dadgum his hide," Beanie took the puppy from Dottie and pulled it to her chest. "Cucumbers and squash is one thing, but a puppy is not somethin' you thrust on people like that."

"His truck was parked over at the courthouse when I went out to get the mail. That was a few minutes before y'all got here."

"Yep, it's Useless all right," Beanie said.

"Are you gonna keep it?"

"Of course not! I'll have to find it a new home, though. Golly Ned...how'm I gonna do that?"

Dottie helped Beanie get the dresses situated in the carrier, and the puppy snuggled into the basket on the front of her bike. Beanie pedaled back to the Château taking great care not to disturb her new precious cargo.

***

A few days later, Beanie returned to the Château after a trip to the Dollar Mart to find Will sitting in the middle of the living room floor playing tug-of-war with the puppy and a white crew sock. She couldn't decide which one of them looked happier.

The first day Beanie brought her home, the dog was shivering and obviously terrified of everything. Will and Beanie agreed they did not need another mouth to feed, or the inconvenience of having a yappy breed in a house with constantly changing residents. They agreed they would look for a new home, and they would *not* name her because everyone knows once you name a dog, it's yours. They also agreed they would at least take the dog to the veterinarian for shots and worming and flea medicine, so she'd be ready to go when a home was found. It was the right thing to do. Of course, even the right thing has consequences, as they soon found out.

Beanie called to make the appointment and gave them her own name. But then, when they took her in and Will was filling out the paperwork, Caroline, the receptionist, said, "So her name's Beanie? That's cute."

Will said, "No, that's my...my...*her* name," pointing at Beanie, who held the shivering creature wrapped in an old receiving blanket.

Beanie had been trying to comfort the dog, so she didn't even look up, just kept stroking its head and crooning. "She ain't got a name yet, do ya', baby girl?"

Caroline looked confused, so Will tried to explain. "We're not going to keep her. We can't...so...we really don't want to name her—"

A dog in one of the examining rooms screeched then and the puppy shook violently in Beanie's arms. Beanie tucked her head against her neck and covered her with one hand, "Aw, don't be scared, sugar, ain't nobody gonna hurt you."

The receptionist grinned. "Sugar! Why, that's a great name for her."

Beanie looked up, wide-eyed. "Noooo..."

"You just called her —"

"I know," Beanie interrupted. "But I meant *sugar*, like *honey* or *baby*, you know...like *that*."

"But she's solid *white*," Caroline said. "It's perfect!"

So, here they were today, still trying to convince themselves they were going to find her another home. Will dragged the sock across the puppy's shoulders. As she turned her little head trying to snag it in her mouth, she tumbled onto her back and wriggled madly to right herself.

Will laughed and looked up at Beanie. "Sugar's a klutz."

"I wish you would stop calling her that," Beanie said. "We ain't never gonna get rid of her thataway."

Will pulled the squirming puppy into his lap and kissed the top of her head. "Don't listen to her, Sugar. She doesn't mean it."

Beanie rolled her eyes. "I do mean it. We already said we weren't keepin' her."

"Yeah, well, we said we weren't naming her either, and here she is…Sugar. Sugah-boog. Street name Shaboogie."

"Who are you, and what have you done with Will Thaxton? That's what I wanna know."

Will cocked his head to the side, scrunched his face and thought for a moment. "You know, Bean, that's not a bad question. Marie never wanted a dog, either. Said it was hard to travel with a pet, and we traveled a lot. But the truth is, I *always* wanted a dog, though I did imagine one a bit manlier than ol' Sugar here. A German Shepherd, maybe? Or at least a Lab. But those breeds *really* don't make sense for a B&B. So, maybe *we* aren't keeping her, but if it's all the same to you, I think I am."

Beanie drew her head back and stared at Will for a moment. She wasn't sure how to respond. Lord knows she had no say in the matter. This was his home, not hers. And there wasn't really a "we" to consider in the first place, was there? Except his laying claim to the puppy made her feel very much excluded, and she didn't like that feeling at all.

"Well, alrighty then," she said slowly. "I reckon we got ourselves a dog."

Will grinned and leapt to his feet, tucking the puppy under one arm while hugging Beanie with the other. He looked down at the pup and said, "I told you Mama would come around, didn't I, Shug? She loves you. She just doesn't want to admit it yet."

Beanie closed her eyes and smiled. She wrapped one arm around Will's waist, laid her head on his shoulder and sighed. "What am I gonna do with you two?"

What he wanted to say was, *just love us, that's all,* but he'd already used up his share of courage for the day. "You could go for a walk with us, if you want," Will said.

"That'd be nice." Beanie said. "I got her a collar and leash at the Dollar Mart."

Will laughed so hard he had to sit back down on the floor.

10 - Historical Significance

After a two-month hiatus, the Mayhew Junction Historical Society was gathering again to review the latest version of the *Mayhew Junction: Then and Now* book they'd been working on for over a year. For this meeting, Corinne brought a peace offering of sorts for LouWanda, some bread-and-butter pickles she'd canned the day before, and as much pleasant information as she'd been able to find about LouWanda's family history, which was paltry if she were being honest.

JoDeen Avery made ham-and-cheese pinwheels and Diane brought deviled eggs, which made the church kitchen smell like sulphur, but none of them cared a bit. Diane's eggs were legendary, and the recipe so secret she wouldn't even make them in front of her family. LouWanda, of course, brought nothing at all to the meeting, unless you counted her plentiful sighs.

Ignoring the full pot of coffee Diane had brewed, all five women opted for the sweet tea Phyllis picked up at the local Thriftway. It was dark and syrupy, so sweet it would set your teeth on edge, and that was just the way they liked it.

Corinne bit into a deviled egg. "I swear, Miz Diane, you could make a fortune on these things," she crooned. "When you go'n let go of that recipe?"

"I already told my daughter she'd have to pry it from my cold dead fingers," Diane laughed and shook her head. "You know what she said to me? She says, 'Oh, Mama, they won't be cold.' Can you believe that?"

Corinne popped the last half of the egg into her mouth and savored it before swallowing. "Yes, ma'am, I think I know exactly what she means." She let out a raspy wheeze that passed for a laugh, then wiped her lips with a napkin.

LouWanda sighed and reached for the plate of pinwheels, stacking them one on top of the other in her palm until she had six of them teetering over the tablecloth. As she brought them toward her plate, they took a fortunate tumble and landed in the middle of the intended target.

"Slippery things," LouWanda rearranged the pinwheels into two stacks, then reached for the plate of deviled eggs.

Diane intervened. "Here, let me help you, LouWanda." She lifted the plate of eggs and held them close enough for LouWanda to partake but withdrew the plate and slid it smoothly behind the centerpiece once LouWanda had removed only two.

"Where's Nell?" LouWanda scanned the countertops and nearby coffee table for signs of a cake.

"She's out of town," JoDeen said. "It was a last-minute thing…I think an aunt died or something. She said to tell y'all she's sorry she didn't have time to bake for us."

"Not to worry," Diane piped up. "I asked Beanie to join us and she's bringing something from their new bakery. Said she didn't know what it would be, but it'd be sweet."

LouWanda frowned. "Why's Beanie comin'? She ain't from here."

"What are you talking about, LouWanda? Beanie's lived here all her life." Diane said.

"Why, she certainly has not," LouWanda said. "Her mama came from East Tennessee and her daddy grew up in Suwannee County. They met when he was in the Army, and he dragged her back here, toddler in tow, when he got out. Reba Bradsher hated this town, and she held that over his head till the day he died, and still never forgive 'im. He was a travelin' salesman, you know, and he'd already left her for good when he was killed in a car accident. Ran his car off a bridge and into the Little Pee Dee River up there in North Carolina. So, the widow Bradsher, what'd she do? She took the money she got from the insurance she had on 'im and moved right back up to East Tennessee. Left Beanie with her daddy's parents out there on the river. I don't know where she is now, or if'n she's even alive."

"Lord, LouWanda, how do you know all this? I've been here all *my* life and I never heard the likes."

"Well, you know…people talk." LouWanda sucked at a piece of ham caught in her teeth and sighed.

Diane could scarcely hide her exasperation. "I don't care where she was born, Beanie is a part of this town and has every right to be here. She's bringing us some photos Will found up in the attic of The Château. Says they're well-marked on the back and we may want to include them in the book."

"Whatever," LouWanda said. "I was just sayin'."

62

As if on cue, the reception hall door opened and Beanie Bradsher angled her voluminous skirts through the scant opening, paying careful attention to both the box of pastries she held on one palm, and the small suitcase of photographs clasped in the other.

JoDeen rose quickly to greet her. "What can I take?" JoDeen reached for the box since it seemed the most precarious.

Beanie lifted the suitcase toward her instead. "Here, set these down on the table, wouldja? I'll lay these out over here."

There was soon an assortment of bakery goods displayed on the kitchen counter, the names of which Beanie promptly butchered, but nobody minded. They were good. The cream puffs were light as air, and the macarons, or baby moon-pies as Beanie called them, were soft and sweet on the outside with decadent flavors in the middle. The green ones were filled with lime coconut cream, and the pink ones had a lovely strawberry cream inside. Everyone was impressed, including LouWanda, who tried to sneak two of them into her purse and was promptly busted by Beanie herself.

"Oh, LouWanda, I got some extry little boxes for them things if ya wanna take 'em home. They'll never survive totin' around in your purse."

Corinne could barely contain herself. She covered her entire face with both hands and pretended to have an asthma attack.

Once they finished their treats, the women settled down at the table to view Phyllis's PowerPoint presentation of each page set for the book. The women had managed to create a diverse, sensitive, and accurate story of the town's history. Even LouWanda was impressed.

"Well, that is really somethin', y'all," she said when the presentation ended. "I never even dreamed it would look as pretty as all that."

"Thank you, Miss LouWanda," Phyllis said. "I used the templates the publishing company provides as a guideline. They make it fairly simple, really."

"Simple for you, maybe," LouWanda scoffed. "I don't even know what a template is."

"Me either," Diane admitted. "And the slideshow was amazing. I need to talk to you later about doing one of those things for Randy's campaign."

"So, what're we doin' about the courthouse?" LouWanda asked. "I noticed they wadn't nothin' in there about neither of 'em, and I'm still wantin' to install a monument, whether y'all wanna talk about it or not."

A collective sigh sunk four sets of shoulders at the table.

"Sigh all ya' want," LouWanda said. "I ain't lettin' it go. Matter of fact, I done ordered something to go out in front of the flagpole."

"Now why would you go and do that?" Diane nearly rose from her chair. "I don't remember anybody authorizing such a thing."

"Well, of course not. Y'all wouldn't even talk about it, much less authorize anything. If I waited for all y'all to agree, nothin' would ever get done. I authorized myself so's we could have it by the Founders Day Festival."

"You can't do that, LouWanda." JoDeen said.

"Too bad. It's done. Eustace gave me the name of his cousin up in Georgia and I called him on the phone and placed an order, so there."

The table erupted in protest with everyone speaking at once. Diane got the room quiet again when she placed two fingers between her lips and let out a loud, shrill whistle.

"Well, that's one way to get our attention," Corinne chuckled.

Diane took a deep breath and let it out slowly. "We are not going to derail this meeting over this, y'all. I guarantee you LouWanda hasn't gotten approval to put anything up at the courthouse or Randy would have told me. Beanie, show us what you brought."

Beanie reached for the old leather suitcase beside her chair. "Speakin' of courthouses…"

She scooted her chair back and opened the case to reveal three small boxes of photographs. The first was labeled *Fletcher County Courthouse 1884*. The second box, in the same meticulous handwriting, read *New Fletcher County Courthouse 1910, Edgar C. Hampton, Architect*. The third had no label at all.

"Will found these up in the attic the other day. We was careful not to get these out of order—they's numbered real neat on the back—but me and Will spent over an hour lookin' through the first box the other day. We didn't get through the other ones yet. Look at these here of the courthouse before it was The Château…"

Beanie opened the first box and five heads leaned forward to get a good look. Diane and Corinne both reached for their glasses when squinting didn't work.

Though it was hardly recognizable from the way The Château looked today, the old courthouse, built in 1884, was a large two-story structure made of wood.

"That's The Château?" Diane leaned closer. "That doesn't even look like it at all. And wait…it's sitting where the new courthouse is today. That can't be right."

"That's it, though," Beanie said. "I shoulda brought Will with me. He knows the whole story. He said when they first built it, the courthouse didn't have none of the verandies and such around the top. They put those on when they moved it across the street. See, look at the rest of these."

As they thumbed through the photos, they saw the wooden courthouse in several stages of construction. Occasionally, a photograph would include the blurry figures of dark-skinned workers, always with two white men in the forefront, holding rifles and grinning broadly. Toward the end of the box, there were a handful of pictures showing the courthouse being moved across skids, pulled by two teams of mules and pushed by a row of prisoners in black and white striped uniforms. A series of photos showed the building being turned sideways and set back off the dirt road now known as Fletcher Highway, which finally convinced Diane this was indeed the same building now called The Château.

"This is where they moved it across the street, where it sets now. I don't know why they didn't push it back some. The front porch sets just about right on the road." Beanie said. "But I reckon that was 'cause it didn't have the porch right at first."

"We'll have to decide which of these photos are best for the book. We ought to have an entire section devoted to the courthouses," Corinne said.

"Yeah, especially the one my great-great-grandfather built," LouWanda said. "Is that one in there?"

Beanie opened the second box, placing the lid down beside Corinne.

"*Our* great-great-grandfather, you mean?" Corinne pursed her lips and looked pointedly at LouWanda. "I thought you said he was the architect of the courthouse. Says right here, that was Edgar C. Hampton, and that name doesn't ring any bells at all for me."

Corinne held the box up for LouWanda to read.

"I ain't got my glasses, Coh-rinne. You'll have to read it to me."

"I just did. Says Edgar C. Hampton, Architect. You want my glasses to see for yourself?"

LouWanda looked like she swallowed vinegar. "No thanks, I trust ya."

Corinne rolled her eyes at Phyllis, who shook her head and sighed. "Lord, help," Phyllis said under her breath.

"Well, I know he had somethin' to do with buildin' the courthouse. It's always been known in my family what he done." LouWanda stood up. "I gotta stretch my legs, y'all. I can't sit like this all day."

"Well, look here," Corinne peered at a photo of a man on horseback, a whip clearly visible in one hand. She flipped it over to read the back, then raised her eyebrows and looked straight at LouWanda. "Looks like I found our granddaddy, LouWanda. Says right here, Captain L.B. Matthews, Overseer."

"Lemme see that thing," LouWanda grinned triumphantly and snatched the photo from Corinne's hand.

"Hey, careful," Beanie winced and reached toward LouWanda, but touched only air. "Those things are fragile!"

LouWanda's smile faded as she squinted at the photo. "What the—? Oh, my."

She said nothing else, just set the photo down in the center of the table and lumbered slowly toward the restrooms at the back of the fellowship hall.

JoDeen took one look and rushed to the kitchen to vomit in the sink. Diane tried futilely to fan herself with a paper napkin, and Beanie burst into tears. Only Phyllis and Corinne sat in stony silence with little reaction to the gruesome figure of a black man hanging from the limb of a tree on the courthouse lawn.

11 - The Third Box

Diane Kerner dropped Beanie off at the Château, insisting she would not have her riding through downtown Mayhew Junction with a pale and tear-stained face. She picked up Beanie's bicycle and slid it into the back of her full-size SUV, then guided Beanie to the front seat and told her to stay put.

When she returned to the fellowship hall to retrieve Beanie's things, the boxes of pictures still lay in the center of the table. No one had mustered the courage to remove them. Phyllis was making short work of the cleanup, including bleaching the sink where JoDeen had been sick. Diane offered to help, but Phyllis shooed her away, preferring to expend her negative energy in physical labor. Diane gathered the three boxes, tossed the offending photo into the top box, and placed them all in the suitcase from whence they came.

Once they were on their way, Diane broached the subject carefully.

"Are you okay?" she asked.

Beanie hesitated, then responded. "I don't rightly know if I am or not, are *you*?"

"I'm not sure, either. That was awful."

"Yeah," Beanie agreed. "Awful is right."

"I guess I should have realized things like that happened here, but you know what? I honestly didn't. I'm so used to people around here being mostly upright and church-going folk, it never occurred to me there might be evil in our midst."

"My granddaddy used to talk about the Klan. Says one of his friends tried to get him to go to a meetin' once and he told 'im he wadn't havin' none of it. Says 'is friend told him not to ever say that out loud, 'cause he'd be surprised who their leader was. Told him it'd put Mommer and me in danger. Diddy—that's what I called my granddaddy— he was big on tellin' stories, and you never did know if'n they was true or not, so I always passed it off as a tall tale. I ain't so sure now."

"Did you always live with your grandparents?" Diane asked, curious in spite of her manners about LouWanda's assessment of Beanie's upbringing.

"Mommer and Diddy? Yeah, most of the time. Even when my mama was still around, I spent most nights with them. Except when my daddy came home, then they couldn't drag me away." She shrugged at the memory. "When Daddy died, Mama took off for Tennessee. I was with my grandparents after that 'til they both died, then I was on my own."

"I'm so sorry, Beanie," Diane said. "That's hard."

Beanie took off her hat and smoothed her hair. "I dunno…it was just normal, I reckon. Mommer and Diddy was good to me. I didn't do without nothin' I recall needin'."

"I remember them as fine people. They were Primitive Baptist, right? My grandparents were, too. I think they went to the same church."

"Bethlehem?"

"Yeah, the one east of town. That's right."

"Small world, ain't it?"

Diane laughed. "Small county. I suppose if we look hard enough, a lot of us are related on at least one branch of our family trees." She paused, framing a question in her head.

Beanie pre-empted her thoughts. "I ain't never tried to look up my family tree. Ain't nobody around to ask if I wanted to know. Well…I got cousins on my daddy's side down here, but I try to avoid 'em every chance I get."

"What ever happened to your mother, if you don't mind me asking?"

Beanie stared out the window long enough for Diane to regret the question.

"I'm sorry, Beanie. You don't have to answer that…"

"Oh, I don't mind," Beanie pushed her hat up off her forehead and smiled wanly at Diane. "I was just recollectin' when I last heard of her whereabouts. I reckon she's still alive, but I ain't heard from her since I was twenty."

Diane sat with this information a minute. She tried to imagine abandoning her own daughter and it was simply unfathomable. What kind of woman could do that and still look in a mirror every day? *Sorry* didn't seem adequate.

"Well, I hope she does come back some day, so she can see how pretty you are, and all the good you've done with your life."

Compliments always embarrassed Beanie, so she looked away and covered one cheek with her fingertips. "I ain't done all that much," she muttered.

"I think you have, Beanie, and I mean that. I'd be proud to have you as a daughter."

"You ain't old enough to be my mama," Beanie said, making light of her discomfort.

"True, but I'd still be proud."

By the time they got to the Château, the color was back in Beanie's face and Diane was glad they'd been distracted by talk of family and not the photos. Will was on the porch when they pulled up, so he came out to help them unload the bicycle.

"Are you okay? Did something happen to your bike?"

"Naw, it's fine. Miss Diane just gave me a ride's all."

Diane slid the suitcase from the backseat of the Suburban and held it out toward Will. "I think you may want to take these. I don't want to overstep here, but we had a little upset there at the last of the meeting. I'm sure Beanie'll explain…we were all pretty traumatized."

Will tested the weight of the suitcase. "Did you get all the pictures you needed?"

Diane eased herself into the driver's seat and reached for the handle to close the door. "The pictures were the problem. She'll tell you. Right now, I need to get home and rest myself. Thanks for the pastries, Mr. Thaxton. I can't wait until the Patsy opens."

"It's La Pâtisserie," Will offered lamely, but Diane had already closed the door and was pulling away.

**

Later that evening, Beanie and Will sat at the kitchen table with the boxes of photographs in front of them.

"They lynched a man in front of the courthouse," Will stated the obvious, no question intended. "Now who was this guy, did you say?"

"It's on the back there," Beanie pointed at the photograph, not wanting to touch it ever again.

Will picked it up, winced, and turned the picture over. "*Captain L. B. Matthews.* Who was that?"

"It gets real confusin', Will. The way Corinne Barr explained it didn't make no sense. She said that was her great-great granddaddy, but he's white, so I don't know how that come about. Anyways, LouWanda was goin' on about 'im like he was *her* great-great-granddaddy, and how she had already ordered a statue of him to set there on the courthouse lawn. Lord, Will, you shoulda seen ever'body's faces. It was bad enough she ordered it on her own, but when we all got a look at that hangin', it just went downhill fast."

"I can only imagine."

"I thought I was gonna pass out. JoDeen threw up in the kitchen sink. Everybody was cryin' except LouWanda and she just up and left the room. Took a while to calm down, I gotta tell ya'. Then LouWanda comes back in and Diane walks right up to her, grabs her by the arm and says, 'LouWanda Crump, you just UN-order that thing right now. There is no damn way we are going to put a statue of a murderer in front of our courthouse. What in the hell were you thinking?' And I gotta tell you, I don't think those words've ever been said back to back in that fellowship hall. Not the way *she* meant 'em anyway."

"So, did she cancel the order or not?"

"No," Beanie said, "that's the problem. She said it was already in production and set to be installed sometime before the Founders Day parade. Said it was too late to cancel it."

Will put his head in one hand and shook it back and forth. "What a mess."

"I'll say," Beanie dragged the third box toward her and took a deep breath. "And much as I don't wanna know what's in this thing, I think we'd better go through this whole set 'fore we have any *more* surprises."

Two hours later, Will rubbed at his eyes with the backs of both hands and yawned. "I have to get some sleep, Bean. We've got four guests expecting breakfast in the morning."

"Right," Beanie said, peering at one photograph through a magnifying glass. "We ain't made much progress no way."

"Maybe we can walk over to the library tomorrow afternoon and see if we can find anything. Surely they have some archives, or a historical section of some sort. Somebody took a lot of time to identify the people in the pictures. What I can't figure out is *who* or *why.* Whose collection is this? Why go to all this trouble and then stash the whole set away in the attic? And why not give us some kind of narrative to explain everything?"

"That sounds like an awful lot of work, Will. This is somethin' the Historical Society oughta do, not us."

Will threw both hands up and shook his head. "One would *think,* but you took these to them, and they sent it all back. And from what you're telling me, I'm not sure they even realize what they're dealing with. If they put a statue of a Klan member on the lawn over there, we will have protests like you have never seen."

"Here?" Beanie shot Will a dubious look. "Maybe in Minnesota, they might, but I don't think anyone around here'd get their panties in a wad over it. I don't mean that in a bad way— they's people who'd hate it, but not many who'd speak up one way or the other."

"I'm having visions of Charlottesville, Beanie. You have no idea how fast word travels on social media."

"Social what?"

Will closed his eyes and tried not to look annoyed. "Beanie Bradsher...please tell me you know *something* about social media, you know, like on a computer?"

Beanie pinched one corner of her mouth together and raised her eyebrows. "Well, I use the computer over at the library to put my Avon orders in, but I don't know nothin' about that My Face stuff, if that's what you're referrin' to."

"Doh!" Will bit his bottom lip to keep from laughing. "I think you mean Facebook, but never mind. The point is this could be a real problem. That last set of pictures identified the fathers and grandfathers of half the town as Klan members. I think you and I are going to have to figure out the story behind these pictures before we let them out of our sight again."

"All right," Beanie said skeptically, "if you say so."

"Here's the thing, Bean, whoever captured and catalogued the atrocities in those photos, did so with a purpose. I think it's up to you and me to figure out not just who, but why."

"You lead, and I'll follow. How's that?" Beanie gathered up her latest project and turned out the lamp beside her chair. "I'm goin' to bed. See ya' in the mornin'."

"Sleep tight," Will said.

Beanie yawned. "Don't let the bed bugs bite."

Will sat with the photos for a few more minutes before heading up the stairs to his own very lonely room.

12 - Bad Brain

"You don't understand, Daddy," Bitty wailed. "I *can't* go to school. I can't *do* it."

Sweet stood in the kitchen of her beautiful new home and felt like the walls were crumbling around her. Bubba John lay on his side in the middle of the living room floor, comforting Bitty as she sobbed. Sweet was no stranger to whining children, or temper tantrums, or even raging hormones that turned her teenagers into unreasonable jerks, if she was being honest. But this was the cry no parent ever wants to see in a child—the honest, authentic cry of the heartbroken and helpless. Bitty didn't have a manipulative bone in her body. Sweet couldn't even remember the last time she'd seen her cry in earnest.

"Baby, tell Daddy why you can't go." Bubba John's voice was low and soft as a rule, but Sweet could hear a difference in his tone—something careful about the way he spoke—that revealed his own heightened concern.

"I...just...can't," she choked out between sobs. "It's...too...haaarrrrd."

Sweet resisted the urge to intervene, willing herself to make a pot of coffee she didn't even want to drink. Daisy was already in bed, Tate was in the bathtub and the twins were in their rooms, supposedly studying but likely not.

"Okay, let's talk about this, Punkin." Sweet heard Bubba John say. "Come here and sit in Daddy's lap and let's see if we can get these snuffles out of the way, okay? Then we'll have us a good talk."

"Do I...have to...go to...school tomorrow?" Bitty asked, already crawling toward her father as he raised himself to sit crossed-legged on the floor.

"You do, honey, I'm sorry." Bubba John refused to lie when his children asked a question. It was something Sweet appreciated in him most of the time, but when Bitty's wailing renewed at his response, she cringed and wished he had said something different. Even so, she knew he was the better of the two to deal with this crisis, because she would have made it worse.

Bubba John pulled Bitty into his lap and wrapped his massive arms around her thin body, cupping the back of her head as she buried her face in his neck. He smoothed the soggy red curls away from her cheek and held her tight while she cried.

Minutes later, as she began to relax a bit, he sat her up on his thigh and wiped her nose with the bottom of his t-shirt. "You okay? We can figure this out, baby, but you've gotta talk to me about it like a big girl, okay? Can you do that?"

Bitty sniffed and nodded.

"Now, let's start at the beginning, okay? Tell me what has you so upset. Did something happen at school? Did you get in trouble for something?"

"I always get in trouble, Daddy. All the time."

Bubba John's eyes widened, and he shot a confused glance at Sweet, who raised both hands and mouthed the words, "No idea."

"That surprises me, Bitty-bug." Bubba John wiped a stray tear from her cheek with his thumb. "What do your teachers do when you're in trouble?"

"Mrs. McMinn says, 'Focus, Bitty, focus.' But Mrs. Jessup gets mad and yells at me whenever Mrs. McMinn ain't there, and Mr. Dallas grabs my arm and says, 'I'm tired of you not listening' and makes me stand at the wall. I don't like standin' at the wall, Daddy."

"Well, of course you don't, baby. Who would?"

"Not me."

"Me, either," her daddy answered. "So, can you tell me what you think is happening?"

"I think...I think I have a bad brain."

"Why do you think that?"

"Sometimes my brain thinks an idea and I say, 'no, brain, that's not a good idea', and then I just do the idea anyway."

Bubba John closed his eyes and stifled a grin. When he opened his eyes, he leaned down toward his daughter and said, "I know what you mean, baby girl. I do the same thing."

"You do?"

"Yes," Bubba John said. "I do."

"Do you have to stand at the wall?"

There was no stifling the laugh this question prompted.

"Well, if we were in school, I'm sure Mama would make me stand there at least once a day."

"Oh, Daddy…" Bitty said. "Mama's not a teacher."

"That's true, but I do go to school now. The teachers aren't like that at my school, though, and you know what?"

"What?" Bitty replied.

"I'm not sure they ought to be like that at your school, either. And I don't think you have a bad brain at all, Bitty. I think you have a very, very, VERY good brain, and Mama and I are going to go talk to your teachers about this. But you have to promise me something, okay?"

"What is it, Daddy?"

"You have to promise you'll do your best…you'll go to school every single day, and you'll try your hardest to do your work. And if you do those things, that will be good enough for Mama and Daddy, okay?"

Bitty's eyes filled with tears and she stiffened her body until it shook. Bubba John gathered her into his arms again and kissed her forehead.

"Relax, baby. It's going to be all right, I promise. You have to trust it will be okay. You're not in trouble at home. And sometimes, sweet girl, sometimes you're not even doing anything bad at school. Sometimes teachers are just being impatient, and that is wrong. Bitty, look at me." Bubba John took his daughter's face in both hands and looked straight into her eyes. "I can promise you no one…NO one…is going to grab your arm or yell at you again. And if they do, I want you to tell Mrs. McMinn as soon as you can, and she will call us. Because we are not going to allow anyone to be mean to you. You are a sweet and helpful girl, and you don't deserve to be treated that way, okay?"

"Okay, Daddy," Bitty said, still fighting back tears.

"You have to go to school every day, honey. And Mama and Daddy can't be fighting with you about it every time. It makes everyone in the house unhappy, especially you. So, I want you to do your best, best, *best* to get up and get ready without fussing. If you're feeling scared, you can come get me and I'll help you, okay? We just have to keep talking about it, Bitty-bug. That's what helps us get through it. If you keep those scared thoughts in your brain instead of talking to us about them, your poor ol' brain gets overloaded and just goes *pfffhhh!*" Bubba John threw both hands out, fingers splayed wide.

"It does go poof, Daddy. My poor ol' brain..." Bitty gave a shaky, forced laugh and shook her head.

"It's a good brain, baby girl. A very good brain. I promise."

Later that night Bubba John and Sweet were lying in bed, both too tired to even discuss what needed to be done about Bitty, and yet too worried to sleep.

"Thank you," Sweet reached out and took her husband's hand in her own. "You said all the right things."

Bubba John squeezed her hand and, after a minute or so said, "What time are we going to the school tomorrow?"

"First thing," Sweet replied. "You going, too?"

"Yes, ma'am, I am."

"You know what I love most about you?" Sweet asked, invoking a question Bubba John had asked many a time when they were dating.

"No, what?" he said as if he didn't know the answer.

"Absolutely everything."

Bubba John grinned and rolled toward his wife, and they fell asleep still holding hands.

***

The next morning, Bitty was calmer. She dressed herself as she had for more years than seemed possible to Sweet Lee. Even in the chaos that was the Atwater household of five children, Bitty had a routine. Sweet thought of her life now as BL and AL: Before Lottery and After Lottery. Before the lottery winnings, it was a little more complicated for Bitty to keep her clothes the way she liked them, organized by color and shape. She had shared a tiny room in their mobile home with her two sisters, teenaged B-Kay and toddler Daisy. Now that she had a room of her own, it was easier in many ways, despite having a larger wardrobe. But Sweet couldn't help but think the change alone had been stressful on her quiet, quirky child. There had to be a certain amount of comfort knowing your siblings were near, and change had always been hard for Bitty.

Sweet felt sure there were several factors contributing to Bitty's unusual struggles with school, but there were only two they would focus on today. The first was the classroom assistant Mrs. Jessup. Sweet knew her well and wondered how (and why) she was still in a classroom at all. She had been a presence at the elementary school for as long as Sweet could remember, including when Sweet herself was there. She had to be pushing seventy years old by now, if not more. A stocky little woman, Mrs. Jessup stood less than five feet tall in the two-inch pumps she always wore. Sweet had never seen her in anything other than a knee-length skirt and matching suit jacket, not even at the grocery story on a Saturday. In the classroom, she was efficient, but brusque, bordering on the edge of downright mean. She was a bold authoritarian figure who tolerated no nonsense of any kind. She had clear favorites in the classroom and, though Sweet had been one of them, she remembered being distressed over Mrs. Jessup's treatment of other students. Brusqueness, Sweet could tolerate. Yelling at her child? Not a chance. Same with Mr. Dallas grabbing Bitty's arm. Sweet would homeschool the child before she allowed that to continue.

B-Kay and T-Ray left before the rest of the family this morning. The twins had been more than a little bent out of shape when they'd learned they wouldn't *each* be getting an "after lottery" vehicle. Bubba John had the old minivan detailed and repaired and told them to count their blessings. Sweet loved that about him.

The twins stopped grousing when they figured out they could accommodate two friends each and still have room in the van for their sporting equipment, but they completely embraced their ride when friends christened it the Swag Wagon and covered it with bumper stickers. Sweet started to complain until Bubba John pointed out the car would be too conspicuous for the kids to get into any real trouble without being noticed. She also liked the way he thought.

Sweet called ahead to make sure Mrs. Daniels would be available and requested a visit with the principal at the same time. They dropped Daisy off at daycare and took the older two through the car line before parking in the visitors' space. They didn't want Bitty to know they were staying at the school, as it would be another disruption to her routine. As Bubba John angled his new

Chevy Silverado into the parking space, Sweet put on a fresh coat of lipstick and smoothed her hair in the visor mirror.

"You look pretty, Mama," Bubba John said.

"Pretty old," Sweet tugged at the side of her mouth with one finger. "I'm getting wrinkles already."

"Oh, stop. You are not."

"Worry lines, then."

Bubba John frowned. "Only one way to fix that. Stop worrying."

Sweet opened the passenger door and climbed out of the truck. "Easier said than done."

"I'll give you that." Bubba John took his wife's hand as they walked toward the main office. Minutes later they were sitting in Mrs. Michael's office waiting for Libby Daniels to join them.

"I'm sure she's on her way," Mrs. Michaels said. "She had bus duty this morning."

"No rush on our part." Sweet settled her husband's bouncing knee with one hand. "Despite the fidgeting."

"Sorry," Bubba John mumbled.

"Why don't you catch me up on the reason for your visit today," Mrs. Michaels moved a stack of yellow folders to the side of her desk. "I know you've been working with Mrs. Daniels and Mrs. McMinn on some issues with—Elizabeth is it?"

Sweet stiffened, then willed herself to relax. She was much more comfortable with Libby in the room. "Yes, Elizabeth. Bitty for short.

"And how is that going?"

"Okay, I think. Slow improvement but headed in the right direction."

"So, what brings you here today? Is there a problem?"

"Actually, yes, I mean…not a huge problem, but I just thought…" Sweet trailed off. Mrs. Michaels was hard to read and a little foreboding, and Sweet felt strangely hesitant.

Bubba John waited a bit to see if she would finish her sentence, then stepped in when she didn't.

"Bitty says she has one teacher who yells at her a lot, and another who grabbed her arm…hard, she says. I don't know if you know Bitty or not, but it's not like her to complain. And even if it was like her, it's not okay. And before you even say anything," he held up one hand as Mrs. Michaels started to speak. "I'm willing to talk about raised voices all day long, because I know getting through to kids gets frustrating sometimes, but what I'm not willing to negotiate is a man putting his hands on my child. For any reason."

Sweet reached over and placed one calming hand on her husband's arm and felt him relax back into his chair as if on cue.

"Sorry," he murmured in Sweet's direction.

"Nope," she whispered. "You're good."

13 - Strategies

Libby Daniels entered the principal's office apologizing for being late.

"I'm so sorry. Meltdown in Pre-K." She nodded at her boss's raised eyebrows. "Yep, same one."

"We'll talk about that later, then," Mrs. Michaels said. "Mr. Atwater was telling me about Elizabeth's troubles. Did you know anything about Mr. Dallas grabbing her arm?"

Libby grimaced. "No, what's that all about?"

"Perhaps you can explain further, Mr. Atwater? Do we know what preceded this?"

Once the story started, the floodgates of frustration opened wide and Bubba John and Sweet took turns sharing their struggles with Bitty, and her heartfelt complaints about teachers who yelled or snatched her up by the arm.

"Have you spoken to Mrs. McMinn about this?" Mrs. Michaels asked when they finally took a breath.

"Not specifically," Sweet said. "This came out last night at the dinner table. But she knows we are having trouble getting her ready for school. She used to love school, Mrs. Michaels. And now she doesn't. Something has changed, and we don't know what it is."

"But we know some things," Bubba John chimed in. "And I need to know that the P.E. teacher is not going to yoke up my kid. She has trouble concentrating when there is a lot going on around her, but she's not a bad kid."

"Let me stop you there, Mr. Atwater," Mrs. Michaels said. "I don't even use that term. To me, there's no such thing as a bad kid, only a few troubled ones. But regardless of the name you give it, no child deserves to be treated badly. I have always said that, and I stand by it. I will speak to Mr. Dallas. I want to get his side of the story, but the general rule is, teachers avoid putting their hands on any child unless there is an immediate danger to the child or to someone else. So, I can pretty much assure you this will not happen again."

"Thank you," Bubba John murmured.

"Mrs. Daniels, could you help us put together some strategies to help Bitty participate in gym class and Mr. Dallas cope with her energy?"

Libby Daniels nodded as she made a note in her planner. "Done."

"And as for Mrs. Jessup…" Mrs. Michaels sighed. "I'm going to be honest here. You both know Mrs. Jessup, I feel certain."

Bubba John and Sweet both nodded, and Mrs. Michaels continued.

"I struggle with this. She's qualified and reliable. She knows the kids. She knows the system, and she does a good job."

"And Bitty is terrified of her." Sweet said. "It's a problem for me. I do know Mrs. Jessup, and I survived many a day in her classroom, but Bitty is different. And I want to clarify something: Bitty doesn't complain about the way Mrs. Jessup treats *her.* She is heartbroken over the way she treats other students, and I don't think I have to say out loud which students they are."

Sweet looked pointedly at Mrs. Michaels and watched tension flood the woman's body. She drew herself up in the chair and leaned forward, her hands pressing down on the top of her desk.

"That's both a vague *and* troubling accusation, Mrs. Atwater."

"I can give you direct quotes from Bitty, as well as names if you need them, but I'd rather not. I don't want to risk making Bitty's life at school even more difficult than it is."

Mrs. Michaels raised both hands, palms upward. "Without clarification there is little I can say or do."

Bubba John shifted in his chair, his lips drawn tight. He glanced at the principal, then turned his head and stared at the floor.

"You really need clarification on that?" Sweet asked. "No other parent has complained about how she treats certain kids?"

"I can't discuss what other parents have said. I can only address *your* child and your concerns. So, let me ask you this: what is it you want me to do?"

"Honestly? I'd like for you to take Mrs. Jessup out of the classroom for the good of *all* the students. Barring that, I want you to transfer Bitty to a different reading teacher."

Mrs. Michaels shook her head. "I can't do that. First of all, she's a substitute, albeit a long-term one. Secondly, I'd have to change Bitty's entire teaching team, or hire a new teacher, which is harder than you think."

"But Bitty is not like all the other—"

"Thirdly, I could move her today and she might still end up having Mrs. Jessup as a substitute down the road—*and* I can't make an exception for *any* child, no matter who she is."

"I didn't mean it that way." Sweet was horrified at Mrs. Michael's implication. She looked first at Mrs. Daniels, then at her husband, for backup.

"I know you didn't—" Libby Daniels began, but Bubba John interrupted her.

"I'm not sure where we go from here, but this seems to have gone a little off track."

"I'll talk to Mrs. Jessup," Mrs. Daniels held up a hand when Mrs. Michaels protested. "I'll be diplomatic, I promise. Let me see what I can do, okay?"

Mrs. Michaels shook her head back and forth and looked up at the ceiling. "That's fine, but let's talk about it privately before you do." Without pausing for a response, she turned to address the Atwaters. "We have slightly less than two months until the end of the school year. I don't want you to leave here thinking I've done nothing to help. I cannot and will not change Bitty's class assignment this year, but I will certainly take your concerns into consideration and speak with you personally when selecting her teaching team for next year. It's the best I can do right now."

No one spoke for a long moment, until Libby broke the awkward silence with an overly bright countenance she did not feel.

"So, can we meet back here in a week? I think we can come up with a plan that helps us all manage Bitty better. She's such a love…I don't want to lose her good nature and curiosity. We can figure this out, I just know it. It's a little difficult right now with state tests looming over us, but there are still the evaluations we spoke of last time in progress. In the meantime, I'll work on some strategies to help her feel better about school in general."

Bubba John and Sweet Lee left the office hand-in-hand and stayed that way until Bubba John opened the truck door for his wife.

"Thanks for going with me," she said. "I don't think that went very well, but I'm awful glad I don't have to explain it to you second-hand."

"Wouldn't have missed it." He leaned in and kissed his wife on the forehead, then shut the door.

By the time Bubba John made it around the back of the truck and climbed into the driver's seat, Sweet Lee had made a decision that could change their lives as they knew it.

"What do you think about me homeschooling the kids next year?"

Bubba John's hand froze on the key he'd just inserted into the ignition.

"Are you serious?"

Sweet nodded. "I am."

"Well…" he paused and considered his words. "I think it's something we should consider for Bitty, but Tate would totally freak out, and the twins…wow—"

"No, no, no, not the big kids. Lord, that would just be dumb. But I don't see why I couldn't handle the littles myself."

Bubba John turned the key and started the engine.

"Oh, baby, I don't know…do we really want that kind of commitment? I mean, you were just starting to get some time to yourself."

"Huh!" Sweet shook her head. "I'm not sure I'm cut out for time to myself. Matter of fact, there's one other thing I've been wanting to discuss with you."

Bubba John took a deep breath and steeled himself.

"You know that extra seat at the table?" Sweet asked.

"I knew it." Bubba John dropped his forehead to the top of the steering wheel. "I knew it."

"I'm just talking about fostering, hon, not necessarily adoption for now. We have room."

"At the table and in our hearts—I know." Bubba John repeated what he'd heard his wife say for years. "I know this, Sweet. But can we just wait a little while? There is so much going on right now. Can we get Bitty, at least, settled? I mean, do you really want to start homeschooling *and* take on someone else's child at the same time?"

Sweet tightened her lips, raised her eyebrows, and cut her eyes toward her husband, a comical expression that made him grab his own forehead and moan. "I take that as a yes."

"Smart man," Sweet said. "Let's go home and take a nap."

Gabriella Warren

I've always gone with my instincts. Since I was a little girl, I've trusted that I knew what was right for me better than anyone else. Even my parents figured that out early, and they pretty much left me to my own devices. There's only one time they might have said I'd let them down, but they died never knowing I dated a girl for two years. Which also means before I gave them a chance to weigh in. I rarely regret anything, but I regret not trusting them with the truth.

Oh, I know they'd heard rumors for years, but the rumors were only right once, and they never asked. It's nobody's business but mine who I love. I dislike labels, and I dislike being lumped into any one category even worse. I don't think of myself as gay, or lesbian, or even bisexual, though I think that's probably the best fit. I love who I love. It has never occurred to me to question my own gender, let alone someone else's.

I keep wondering if I'm falling in love with Suvi Jones, but honestly, I don't think so. First of all, he's wishy-washy as hell, always up on some fence over something. Paralysis by analysis. Drives me nuts. Me? I do what I want. Period. It really isn't difficult. I don't trouble myself with what someone else might think or do or say. I have never gotten myself into anything I didn't think I could get myself straight out of if it didn't work. Suvi just wraps himself up in worry, wears it like some badge of honor if you ask me, and that's the one thing about him I don't respect. Because I respect the hell out of that man. I'm going to hate myself for saying this, but he is some catch, as my cousin Dee pointed out. But I'm not fishing for a man. And love is not a sport anyway.

Besides, if I turn this thing into a romance—and believe me, I think I could—if it didn't work out, I'd lose my best friend. That's just not something I'm willing to risk right now. I do not want to be in this crazy place without Suvi Jones. It would be like trying to golf with one arm. Nope. I'm here and I'm happy. I'm not gonna screw this one up.

14 - The Final Decision

When it came right down to it, there was nothing for Suvi Jones to do but accept the job in Gainesville and be happy about it. Gabe was right about one thing—Suvi had never been so indecisive in his life. He chalked that up to Beanie Bradsher. He couldn't remember now who even started the thing—what should he call it? If he was going to accurately portray the six months last year they met in private, and yet oddly public places, they'd had a courtship of the almost traditional kind. They danced on the old railroad trestle over the river and shared their first kiss there.

Suvi had only just felt emboldened to claim the relationship. He'd even begun to think what it would be like to marry her, what their life together might be, he from a neighborhood the town still called The Quarters, and she the cast-off daughter of a traveling man and his discontented wife. He dark-skinned and college-educated, and she the pale hue of her Irish ancestry and raised by farming grandparents with virtually no formal education. It was no wonder it took him some time to commit.

And he'd let it go without saying goodbye, spurred by the all-too-public shaming he'd received by the woman who held his heart in her hands. Unfortunately, at the local Trunk-or-Treat—hosted by several churches and meant to replace the heathen holiday that was Halloween—it was a red velvet cake Beanie held in her hands. He meant to surprise her by showing up at her favorite fall festival. The whole town would know before the rooster crowed the next morning, Suvi was certain of it. But when he arrived, Beanie was cavorting with Will at the cake walk, laughing and flirting like she'd only done with him in private.

He watched long enough to know Will was in love with her, and long enough to realize half the county knew it, too. How could he come in and claim anything? She was *his* girlfriend, not Will's. And that was the sentiment he carried in his entire body…his six-foot-eight frame drawn up an extra half-inch, his trunk-like arms almost bowed with tension and his fists opening and closing with the mantra pulsing through his subconscious brain: *mine, mine, mine, mine, mine.*

Beanie hadn't noticed at first, she'd been so surprised and happy to see him, she almost danced with joy. She chattered like a child as they gathered up the cake she had won. And he, in a jealous rage, had spoiled it all.

Suvi Jones sat up in his big empty bed and wiped his groggy eyes. No use lying here like a lump thinking about what an idiot he'd been.

How could she know what he knew? What would it mean for her if he dragged her into his world? That's why he hesitated. He didn't dare risk their lives when it could blow up so publicly, like a cake to the face, when some nationalist militant with a history steeped in white supremacy decided to take issue with their relationship. He wasn't afraid, but he wasn't stupid, either. It could easily happen, and probably would.

Suvi heaved himself to his feet and lumbered to the bathroom. Maybe a shower would wake him up. The electric razor felt heavy in his hand and when he leaned into the mirror and lifted it to shave, the face staring back at him was almost unrecognizable. His eyes were red and swollen and the skin around his mouth sagged into what looked like a permanent scowl. He put the razor down and splashed cold water onto his face, then forced himself through his routine with all the effort he could muster.

It took him a full half-hour longer than usual to get ready, and he dressed in nice slacks and a button-down shirt, instead of his standard polo, all the while formulating an idea that felt absolutely right—empowering even. Just before walking out the door, he called Randy Kerner's cell phone. To hell with it being only 6:30 in the morning; Randy was probably already on his way to the diner.

"Mornin' Randy," Suvi said when he answered. "I was wondering if you could help me sometime today. I'd like to get my name on that ballot after all."

15 - Make Fletcher County Great Again

"You're doing what?" Gabe reached up and moved the napkin box to the side so she could see Suvi's face better.

"I'm running for the county commission." Suvi lifted a piece of toast and applied a light coating of real butter from a packet on the side of his plate.

"What about the job in Gainesville?"

"Oh, I'm taking that. I already let 'em know. They have a ball team in place already for the upcoming year, so I'll mostly be traveling the state starting next season. I've got time to run for office before I make the transition."

"Dude, that's a lot. I don't mean to be selfish, but I'm thinkin' I might need to get a new golf partner."

"I wouldn't go that far. I'm not actually moving to Gainesville. Yet, anyway."

Sissy plopped a ham biscuit and a banana in front of Gabe. "More coffee?"

"Not yet, Sissy, thanks." Gabe picked a straggling piece of ham off the biscuit and popped it into her mouth. "Man, I love their ham. I gotta figure out what brand it is."

Sissy, already ten feet away, threw over her shoulder, "Smithfield. They got 'em over at the Thriftway. They'll cut 'em into steaks if ya' want 'em."

"She's amazing," Gabe shook her head and picked up her biscuit. "So, does this mean you're keeping your house? Should I take it off the market?"

"Uh, considering you haven't even shown it yet, that's probably a good idea."

"I told you it would be a problem. Truth is, I thought of buying it myself, but I don't know that I'll be staying in Mayhew all that long. I don't want to be stuck with it, either."

"Thanks," Suvi rolled his eyes.

"No offense, old man. Just telling the truth."

"How'd I get so lucky?"

"Lucky about what?" Gabe wiped crumbs from her face with a folded napkin.

"Everybody oughta have a friend who tells them the cold unfiltered truth."

"You're being sarcastic."

"Ya' think?" Suvi glanced at the front door to see Randy Kerner sliding past the line at the register.

Randy scanned the room and stopped when his eyes found their target. Suvi watched as Randy made his way around a booth and two tables to stand beside Gabe, who he nodded to as an afterthought. "Mornin' Ms. Warren. That is great news, Suvi! We can go over to the courthouse right after breakfast if you want."

Suvi squirmed in his seat. "Let's don't announce it to the whole world yet, if you don't mind. I want to make sure everything is in order first."

"Oh, sure, sure," Randy dropped his voice, but it was likely in vain, as the entire population of the round table had already turned to listen.

"What's the announcement?" LouWanda demanded once Randy took his place at the round table.

"Aw, come on, LouWanda," Randy took his cell phone out of his pocket and set it on the table in front of him. "If you heard that much, you heard what Suvi said about it."

LouWanda flipped both hands palms-up and huffed. "He *said,* he didn't wanna announce it to the whole *world.* He didn't say nothin' about not tellin' *us.*"

"Pretty sure that's what he meant, though. You'll know soon enough."

Randy waved Sissy over and pretended to read a text on his phone.

"Don't you tell me he's running for the commission. You know darn good and well my name's already in the hat."

"So? That doesn't mean Suvi can't run, too."

"I figured that's what you was up to, Randall Kerner. That was a dirty trick to play. We've been friends since grade school."

"Calm down, LouWanda. I'm helping him fill out the paperwork is all. I can't help it you live in the same district."

LouWanda glared at Randy, then leaned toward Dottie, who had only recently started coming back to the local table after staying gone long enough to get over being mad at her childhood friend. "Did you know about this?"

Dottie frowned and shook her head. "I didn't, LouWanda, I promise. I had no idea."

"I didn't either," Mac McConnell volunteered. "So, don't even ask."

"Well, I am hurt, Randall. I thought I was a shoe in for that seat. Now all the coloreds'll vote for Suvi. I could lose!"

"LouWanda!" Dottie shushed her friend. "Haven't you learned any better than that?"

"What? What'd I say?"

"You do NOT call them coloreds."

"Why, you called 'em coloreds just the other day. I heard you with my own ears." LouWanda opened a Mini-Moo® and poured it into her empty cup.

"I said *people* of color. There's a difference." Dottie had forgiven LouWanda for the trouble she'd caused last year, mostly because of proximity. It was too hard to work across the street from a lifelong friend and not speak to her at all. LouWanda made the first overture, and Dottie felt relieved. Now, she wasn't so sure it was a good idea. Some people never change.

"That just don't make no sense. Colored people, or people of color. It's the same thing."

"No, it is not the same. When you say "coloreds", you mean people of African descent. But not everyone with dark skin comes from Africa. Just like not every Hispanic person comes from Mexico. It's not difficult to make the correct distinction, but absent the knowledge, it is even less difficult to simply be respectful. People of color includes everyone who isn't Caucasian and there is a big difference."

"Well, you knew what I meant. You said so yourself."

"Whatever, LouWanda," Dottie stood to leave. "I give up."

"Oh, sit back down there. I don't wantcha mad at me again. I don't mean no harm."

"I gotta get to work. I'll see you this afternoon." Dottie's shoulders sagged as she made her way to the car. Every time she thought she'd made progress, LouWanda would open her big mouth and prove her wrong.

And this whole thing of LouWanda running for the county commission was just dumb. Half the town hated her. She minded everyone's business except for her own, and she always offended *someone* in the process.

Dottie made her way toward the side parking lot, head down as she rummaged through her purse for her keys while simultaneously avoiding the buckled walkway running the full length of the restaurant. When she finally looked up to find her car, she stopped dead in her tracks. Plastered across the back of her car were no fewer than five bumper stickers that had not been there when she came in.

An altered Trump sticker, crossing out the T and adding a big red C, was dead center in the middle of her rear window. Another, an oval reading CRUMP 2018, graced the rear trunk panel. Two featuring a bold *Vote Crump!* at the top, and a line below saying *Make Fletcher County Great Again* were sprawled across the bumper. The last, that she could see from this vantage point anyway, read simply *LouWanda Crump for County Commissioner.* This was stuck to the back passenger-side door at an angle that may or may not have been intentional.

"What the...?" Dottie closed her eyes and shook her head and hoped like hell she was dreaming, but she wasn't. She crammed her purse under one armed, stormed across the parking lot and ripped the first sticker off the window. The ones stuck to the bumper were not so easy. It would take a hot washcloth to remove them without leaving residue. That would have to wait until she got to the store, and she was already running late.

"Damn her unruly hide," Dottie said as she slid into her old Chevy Lumina. She hoped no one noticed the stickers as she eased the car out onto Main Street then angled onto a side road to park behind the dress shop downtown.

Suvi Jones noticed, though. He parked right beside her minutes later and grimaced at the sight. Fine, he thought. Fine. I see how this is going to go. He walked straight across the side street to the courthouse, resolved to file the papers with or without Randy Kerner's help.

16 - The Trouble with LouWanda

Sweet Lee Atwater noticed the stickers on Dottie's car, too. She was on her way back from dropping the younger kids off at school when she saw Dottie pull into the parking lot behind the store. It had been a while since she'd popped in to see how things were going, so she looped back around the block and parked next to Dottie's car just in time to see Dottie disappear through the back door.

"Woo-wee," Sweet mumbled when she read the first sticker. She was taking in the full glory of the back of the vehicle when Dottie barreled out the back of the store with a bucket of hot water in one hand and a razor blade in the other.

"Boy, am I glad to see you," Dottie said by way of a greeting. "Can you watch the store a minute while I scrape this nonsense off my car?"

"I was wondering what possessed you." Sweet squinted at the car and shuddered. "Is this a joke?"

"If it is, the joke's on LouWanda," Dottie swooped a steaming wet rag from the bucket and laid it across the trunk.

"Is she really running for office?"

"Apparently so. She mentioned it at breakfast this morning, but I wasn't sure she was serious until I saw these plastered on my car. LouWanda's too cheap to pay for campaign stickers for kicks."

"Good Lord," Sweet said. "I'll go on in and open up shop."

"You sure you don't mind?" Dottie used the blade to pick up one corner of a bumper sticker and removed the offending message with one good pull.

"Positive. I'm in no hurry at all. I'll make us a pot of coffee and we can visit when you're done."

"Thank you," Dottie said. "I'm gonna need it."

Twenty minutes later, Dottie was back in the store, her hair limp with sweat and one finger bleeding.

"I'll get you a Band-aid." Sweet set a cup of strong coffee on the counter and reached beneath it for the first aid kit.

"I've never been so irritated in my life. The nerve of her to plaster those stupid stickers all over my car. Friend or no friend…who *does* that without asking?"

"Boggles the mind, doesn't it?" Sweet shook her head and laughed. "Only LouWanda. That's the answer. Only LouWanda."

"I gotta calm down," Dottie slapped a hand across her chest and took a deep breath. "I feel like I'm havin' a heart attack."

"You're hyperventilating," Sweet said. "Breathe slow, before you pass out."

Dottie took a sip of her coffee and complied, breathing in and out through her nose until she felt better. Sweet pulled up two chairs and sat Dottie down in one before taking the second for herself.

"I don't know why I let her get to me. I was better off when we weren't speaking at all. I felt sorry for her, you know? After that whole Suvi Jones fiasco last year, she actually tried to apologize to him. I say *tried* because it was not much of an apology to hear Suvi's side of it, and I take that man at his word."

"Every single time," Sweet agreed.

"Anyway, I wasn't speaking to her and Suvi wasn't either. For weeks she sat out there in front of her shop and just watched the cars go by. I swore at first she was trying to make me feel guilty, but then I realized, she's just lonely." Dottie sighed. "And Lord knows I know what lonely feels like."

"I knew something had happened between you, but I wasn't sure what it was."

Dottie sighed. "It's always been an on-again, off-again thing. We were inseparable as kids, and good friends in high school, but then I went away to college in Oklahoma and she married Alton Crump. That was the beginning of the end, if you ask me."

"So, what happened? I mean, if you feel like talking about it..."

"You can't possibly have time for all that." Dottie appreciated a sympathetic ear, but she didn't think for a minute Sweet would be interested. "I've kept you long enough."

"I have all the time in the world," Sweet said. "And I know a little about lonely myself."

Dottie couldn't help it. The laugh burst forth from her chest in a single, loud, "Ha!"

"I'm serious," Sweet said, smiling in spite of herself.

"You have five children and a husband. How can you possibly be lonely?"

"Easy," Sweet shrugged. "No time for friends."

"Ahhhhh," Dottie's eyes got moist. "I'm sorry. That was thoughtless of me."

Sweet waved the sentiment away. "I'm fine, Dottie. I have more blessings than I can possibly count. I just understand the need to feel like you have someone to talk to, you know?"

Dottie nodded. "I do know. And I think that's where I was when LouWanda finally got up the nerve to come apologize. She caught me when my guard was down, that's what it was. Suvi and I had a bit of a falling out at the same time, and you were so sick for a while there…I didn't think I had a friend in the world."

"It's a small town. Hard to stay mad at people forever."

"Exactly! And now I'm about to start the feud all over again and I am done." Dottie dropped her chin and cupped her hands over her mouth.

"With LouWanda?" Sweet nudged, after a pause.

"She wasn't always so hard. She had a rough time of it. Married young. Those Pentecostals always do. So dead set on not having sex before marriage that most of them marry the first person who smiles in their direction."

"Wasn't her father a pastor?"

Dottie nodded. "Mayhew Junction Assembly of God. Laying on of hands and speaking in tongues and wives submit to your husbands and all that. But LouWanda was never anything close to meek. I admired her for that. She never cared about what other people thought. I don't know how it was for LouWanda and Alton at first. All I know is, LouWanda married a monster. A pure-D devil in human skin."

Sweet was processing this information when the front door to the shop opened and Suvi stuck his head in and waved.

"Oh, Lord," Dottie said under her breath, and then, "Hey, Suve!"

"I shoulda known better than to get my feelings hurt."

"I was hoping you wouldn't see those stupid things." Dottie shielded her eyes with one hand and stared at the floor.

"Oh, I saw 'em all right, before I went to the courthouse. It's not quite official, but it will be soon."

"Come on in and sit with us. Sweet's here." Dottie motioned Suvi in with a wave of her hand.

94

Suvi scrubbed his boots on the welcome mat and made his way around the dress stand blocking his view. "Sweet Lee! Aren't you a sight for sore eyes? What brings you into town?"

Sweet reached both arms up toward her old friend and he leaned down to kiss her cheek. "Just stopped by long enough to let Dottie get those God-awful stickers off her car."

Dottie groaned. "You *do* know I didn't put 'em on there, right? I'm surprised she didn't nail your truck, too. My God that woman's got balls."

Sweet whooped and slapped her knee, and Suvi doubled over. When he recovered, he wiped his eyes with the back of one hand. "I can think of so many things I'd like to say, but I wouldn't touch that with a ten-foot pole."

Dottie's face reddened. "*Any*way," Dottie tried to get the conversation back on track. "Sweet can vouch for me. I've already said I have no intentions of supporting LouWanda's campaign. Besides, it's not even my district."

"Well—not for voting purposes, it's not." Sweet said. "But the shop is definitely in it."

"Ohhhh..." Dottie raised her eyebrows high as the lightbulb went on. "No *wonder* she's running."

Suvi craned his neck toward the front window. "Speak of the devil. I hate to run, but I don't have the energy today. Okay if I sneak out the back door?"

"Be my guest," Dottie said, and Suvi disappeared two seconds before LouWanda Crump barged in.

"We're back here," Dottie called from behind the clothes rack.

"Who's 'we'?" LouWanda plowed through the hanging dresses and nodded at Sweet. "Oh, hey! How's your legs?"

"My legs?" Sweet shot a "what is she smoking" look at Dottie, who snorted in response.

"LouWanda stood in for you when her church was praying for your recovery. It's a long story."

Sweet nodded. A long story and probably one she didn't need to hear. "My legs are great, LouWanda. Never been better. Please tell your congregation I appreciate the prayers."

"Oh, that's nothin'," LouWanda swatted at the air. "To *God* be the glory. That's what counts."

"So, what brings you over this early?" Dottie was adept at changing the subject before it got out of hand.

"I was wonderin' how you liked the campaign stickers I gave ya'. Pretty snazzy, ain't they? Got 'em done at that new sign shop across from the bank."

Dottie stared at LouWanda and tried to think of something, anything, to say.

"Close your mouth, Dorothy. You look retarded."

Sweet gasped and covered her mouth with one hand. Dottie leapt from her chair and pointed at the door. "That's it, LouWanda. Out! Get out of my store."

"What? What'd I say?" LouWanda looked at Sweet for backup, which was not forthcoming. Sweet shook her head and bit her tongue.

"If you don't know, then I can't help you. I don't care how long we've been friends. I cannot listen to you say things that no reasonable human being would say in this day and age. Seriously … you need to leave."

"You know what your problem is? You are too hung up on bein' politically correct. Have been ever since you came home from college, but it gets worser ever' year."

"Out," Dottie said, pointing again at the door.

"I'm goin', I'm goin'." LouWanda squeezed between two racks and turned back toward Dottie as she grasped the doorknob. "I'll bring ya' some tea later. Maybe that'll sweeten you up."

"Don't even bother," Dottie said as the door clicked shut. "Ooooooo … the things that woman says make me — "

"Breathe, Dottie, breathe," Sweet said. "Don't let her get to you. I honestly don't think she knows any better."

"Lord, help," Dottie sank back into her chair and held her hands out, palms down. "Look at me, I'm shaking."

"It's not worth it, I'm telling you. You know the Serenity Prayer?"

Dottie nodded. "…and the wisdom to know the difference."

"There ya' go. So, finish your story. You were telling me about LouWanda's husband. You've got me curious. Want another cup of coffee?"

"Lord, yes. With a shot of whiskey if ya got it."

Sweet laughed and snagged the two empty cups with one hand and headed for the kitchenette at the back of the store. "Can't help ya there, sister, but I wouldn't stop you either."

When she returned, Dottie was sitting quietly, her elbow on the arm of the chair and her head resting on one fist. She heard Sweet approach and reached up to take her cup. "Thank you."

Sweet sat down, holding her own coffee with both hands. "My fingertips keep going cold. Drives me nuts. So…tell me about your friendship."

"There is no friendship left."

"Then tell me why it matters to you because *clearly* it matters."

Dottie scratched at the back of her neck and gazed off at nothing in particular. "I don't even know where to start. I think I told you, I was dead set on getting out of Mayhew Junction after high school, so when I got accepted to three different colleges, I chose the one in Oklahoma, the farthest one from home. LouWanda and Alton eloped early in my sophomore year, and I didn't even hear about it until a month later. I was busy sampling the smorgasbord of sin that comes with anonymity and freedom, so LouWanda Matthews was the last thing on my mind. Of course, my daddy flew me home from college every time we had a break longer than a week, which was fine at first. I was surprised at how homesick I was, especially given how hard I worked for scholarships so I could get the hell out of Dodge.

Anyway, I came home for the Christmas holidays, which was a few months after they were married. They put a singlewide trailer on her granddaddy's property, and she had it all fixed up. It was cute in a kitschy kind of way. Her mama ran the store she owns now, so there was always an abundance of cheap knickknacks and used curtains at hand, if you like that sort of thing."

Sweet groaned. "Five kids is all the clutter I can bear."

"I'm more of a minimalist myself…but I kind of liked her house. She'd always been a tomboy, and I thought it was sweet. She was trying so hard. You could tell she really wanted to make this man happy. Huh!" Dottie shook her head at the memory. "Fat chance."

"That bad?"

"Yep. Alton was out of town the first couple of days I was home. LouWanda wanted to paint the kitchen to surprise him and I offered to help. We were taping newspapers over the countertops and she told me Alton was preaching in Nashville that week. Now, knowing how much LouWanda loved country music, which she had to hide from her Daddy and Granddaddy of course, I asked her why in the world she hadn't gone with him. You know what she told me? She said Alton didn't like that idea at all. Didn't wanna 'parade his pretty young wife in front of a bunch of men who used church like a singles' bar.' I was horrified—it flung up a slew of red flags for me—but honest to God, I think she was flattered. In all her life, I doubt she'd ever been called pretty."

Sweet winced. "What fool wouldn't want to take his newlywed with him if he could? That doesn't sound right."

"That's precisely what I thought, but I didn't say anything. She seemed so happy. So, anyway, we get done with the kitchen in a couple of days and it looked really good. It was this cheery yellow and she accented it with some cobalt blue glass bottles and plates. We were proud of ourselves—twenty years old and we'd redecorated an entire kitchen on our own, including sewing new curtains.

Then I got busy with family stuff—you know, Christmas and all—and the time got away from me. But I stopped by to see her before I flew back to Oklahoma and it was weird. She came outside when I pulled in the driveway. Said Alton was taking a nap and she didn't want to wake him up. In hindsight I realize she was trying to keep me from coming inside, but I whispered *I'll be quiet* and barged right on in. I could not believe it. That beautiful kitchen…all that work we'd done…was torn all to hell."

"What in the world?" Sweet sat upright in her chair.

"I guess Alton didn't like the color scheme. Said it looked like his grandmother's house. Said he'd been planning on surprising her with a remodel and now she had ruined it. He had ripped the countertops off and started painting the cabinets and the beaded board on the walls this gruesome shade of dark green. He used the new curtains we'd made as drop cloths for painting. I said, '*What the hell, LouWanda?*' And she started to cry and begged me not to make a scene. I may or may not have threatened to go back there and kick his ass, 'cause that's really what I wanted to do. Anyway, we heard him stirring in the back bedroom and LouWanda said 'You have to go,' and I said, oh hell, no, I wasn't going, and she said I'd only make it worse if I stayed. So, I left. And I have hated myself ever since."

"Dottie…why? You didn't do anything wrong."

Dottie's voice was charged with emotion and she spoke through tightly clenched teeth. "I left her. I left her there with no one to protect her from that sorry son-of-a-bitch."

"Oh, no…no," Sweet shook her head in horror. "He hurt her?"

"To this day she won't admit it, but I know damn good and well he did. You don't dislocate your shoulder and blacken both eyes tripping over a laundry basket. I found out a month later from a friend who worked for E.M.S. They had to send an ambulance for her. Alton cleared out before they got there. She told everybody, including me when I finally asked, she was alone when it happened. I didn't believe her then, but it would be almost two more years before I saw it for myself."

LouWanda Matthews Crump

I was born and raised right here in Fletcher County and, aside from a church trip to Orlando which like to've scared me half to death, I haven't gone more'n a county away in all of my life. Some people think that's crazy, but that's just how it was in my family. We're homebodies and we like it that way.

My daddy was pastor of the Mayhew Junction Assembly of God Church, which my grandpa started durin' World War II. Granddaddy used to tell how people'd ask him why he wadn't servin' his country and he'd say, "I serve no one but Christ our Lord." My daddy said the same when Vietnam rolled around, but he got drafted anyway. I was pretty young when he left—I was the baby of the family and the only girl, so it wadn't a surprise to no one I was a tomboy. I'm six feet tall in my bare feet.

Mama tried puttin' me in ballet for a while, but it ain't pretty when you got two left feet and both of 'em's already a size 10. I wore my age for a shoe size right up until I turned eleven. By then I was numb to all the teasin' from the other girls, but that last recital 'bout did me in. I looked at that stupid Yankee Doodle Dandy costume—whose idea was that anyway—and I put my size eleven shoe down on that sparkly black top hat. I told my mama I was tired of bein' the biggest ballerina and I wadn't gonna do it no more. She didn't utter a word, just took the costume back to the dance teacher and I never went back.

Daddy left for Vietnam when I was in Junior High and came home when I was in tenth grade. He was different then, and I learned to tiptoe around him as best I could. He took over preachin' when he got back, and Granddaddy retired. Well, sort of retired anyway. He filled in whenever Daddy took one of his spells, which seemed to get worse before they got better.

All I know is, when it came time to graduate from high school, I had one goal in mind...gettin' myself out of that house. I wanted a baby so bad I could taste it, though I wasn't actually sure how that whole process worked. I just knew it took a husband, and I aimed to find one. That's when I met Alton Crump. Now, I swore I'd never marry a man who wadn't from Fletcher County. I've always had a healthy distrust for foreigners, but Alton Crump was an exception, or so I thought.

Alton claimed to be five-foot-eight, but he was a good inch shy of that, truth be told. But he carried himself like a tall man, head held high, shoulders back, arms almost bowed at his sides. I fell in love with his confidence, I think. He was sure of himself—knew what he wanted—and that included me. I'll never in my life figure out why he chose me. What'd I ever do to get what I got?

He was a preacher like my daddy, but a travelin' one, which is prob'ly the only reason we lasted as long as we did. We married after courtin' only four weeks. He made it clear he wanted to marry a virgin. So did I, for that matter. I think back on all the talkin' we did on my daddy's front porch and I realize he didn't exactly lie to me. He said he was crazy about me, but he wouldn't have "relations" outside of marriage, which I took as a good sign. That was why he said we should elope right away, so we did. Ran off to Waycross, Georgia. Got married by a Justice of the Peace and stopped at a fleabag motel on the way home to seal the deal. What he left out was the two ex-wives he had in Kentucky and Tennessee, but I didn't find out about them 'til he was long gone.

I ain't one to dwell on regrets and all, but I regret ever marryin' that man. Swore I'd never get myself in a fix like that again, and I been true to my word. To the T.

17 - History Lessons

Will Thaxton was on a mission. Unable to find archival documents in the local library, he researched as much information online as he could find from the universities in Tallahassee and Gainesville. He soon realized Tallahassee offered the most geographically efficient collections and started making plans to visit the capitol city. Florida A&M University (FAMU) was the most likely source of pertinent information, holding the Meek-Eaton Black Archives. And for archives, Will knew, it would take preparation and specificity. He needed to know what he was looking for and where he might find it before he made the trip, if possible. The photos provided some information and might be of interest to the university.

Florida history was new to Will, so virtually everything he found was interesting. He couldn't help thinking about the conversation he'd had with his late wife Marie about her sudden desire to move to Florida.

"What do we even know about the South?" Will asked.

"Oh, honey," Marie said, "Florida's not really the *South.*"

But that wasn't true, especially not North Florida, which Will quickly learned was often called South Georgia in jest. But it was no joke when you started looking at the history of the rural area in which they had landed. Florida was indeed the deep South. Most of its residents, in the undeveloped areas anyway, had roots going back many generations, with a clear pattern of migration from Alabama, Georgia and the Carolinas.

Beanie was no help in research. It seemed she had an aversion to the computer. She was, however, very helpful in taking up the slack in the running of The Château as Will devoted more and more time to the historical project. And she was a good sounding board, so their evening routine soon became a discussion of his day's research.

A week before the grand opening of the bakery, set for the first week in May, Beanie was up late in the kitchen perfecting a recipe for maple covered éclairs. Will was seated at the end of the table working on his laptop. Sugar napped at his feet, snuggled in her little red doggie bed which Will moved from room to room whenever necessary.

After a few murmured *ah's* and *wow's* Will looked up over the top of the monitor. "Did you know the governor of Florida committed suicide after the Civil War?"

"Which governor was that?" Beanie asked without really caring to hear the answer. She was more focused on getting just the right pour of the maple frosting down the length of the pastry.

"John Milton. You ever hear of him in history class?"

"Naw, not that I recollect. Our history teachers was always coaches. We didn't talk much about history in them classes. Why'd he kill hisself?"

"Well…there's a few conflicting reports, but I think the gist of it is he'd rather die than set his slaves free or govern Florida under a new set of laws. Something like that."

"I ain't never understood that whole slave thing. What would make someone think it was okay to own a human bein'?"

"Money, mostly."

"That ain't no reason." Beanie frowned indignantly.

"Oh, I agree. I'm just saying that was their real purpose in owning slaves, no matter how they tried to rationalize the brutality or reconcile it with their religion. The whole Southern economy was based on slave labor. It was about money and wealth and social status."

The room went silent as Will studied the monitor, his face becoming more strained as he read.

Beanie carried a tray of éclairs to the table and held it near Will by way of an offer. "Wanna try one?"

"Oh, gosh, Bean … no thanks. I'd never sleep after all that sugar."

The puppy, asleep at Will's feet, startled awake and looked up expectantly. Beanie laughed.

"She thinks you called her. Look at her..."

"Oh, Sugar, no … I wasn't talking about you. I meant the éclair." Will scratched his head and grinned at Beanie. "Why am I talking to a dog like she understands?"

"She prolly does."

"True," Will agreed. "Hey, you wanna go to Tallahassee with me tomorrow? We don't have guests coming until next Friday.

I've got to visit the archive center at the university, but we could still make a day of it. Go out for lunch or something?"

He hadn't meant to make it sound like a date, but somehow it did, so he busied himself by shutting down the computer without saving his research, which created a problem Will was content to ignore for the moment.

"I ain't never been to a college before. Reckon there'll be something there for me to do?"

Will considered the question for a moment. He got tickled when he thought of Beanie strolling the sidewalks of the traditionally black college with her bright ruffled skirts and cowboy boots. He had to take several deep breaths to keep from laughing out loud.

"We'll figure it out when we get there, how about that?"

"It's a date, then," Beanie chirped, then turned to the sink to finish cleaning up.

Afraid he'd ruin the moment, Will didn't say another word, just took his computer and headed up the stairs to bed before the magic wore off.

18 - Who's the Daddy?

After Dottie's revelation, one customer and then another came in and the women had to stop their conversation for a bit. Sweet considered going on home, but she stayed for two reasons. One, because it wouldn't be long before she'd have to pick up Daisy from the daycare anyway and two, because she needed to know the rest of LouWanda's story. She'd lived here all her life and never heard anything about Alton Crump. When you live in a town where everyone knows everyone's business, it's easy to assume you know everything important there is to know. Sweet considered this *important*, even if it was none of her business at all.

When the store was empty again, it was lunchtime, so Sweet walked next door to order salads for each of them. Cherry Allred was at the cash register.

"You're back!" Sweet could barely conceal her surprise, though she tried. "Good to see you, Cherry."

"Hey, Sweet…yeah, Suvi can't hardly do without me, I guess."

That was an interesting way to look at it, Sweet thought. Suvi did have a hard time keeping good help, partially because business was spotty at best, and tips were never reliable. But Cherry was not what Sweet would call "good help." She had a habit of calling in drunk, as Dottie used to say. Prior to Sweet's illness, Dottie was the standard fill-in for several of the businesses downtown. She'd inherited her parents' home when they passed, so she didn't need a huge income to survive, but she liked to help out wherever she could, and she was smart, dependable, and flexible. She stayed plenty busy, and Suvi's Big Pig restaurant was where she had worked most often. Suvi had fired Cherry more than once, but he always took her back. He'd hired Kenya Green, too, but she only worked when she wasn't in school, and she was leaving for college in the fall anyway.

"Can I get two chef salads to go, please?" Sweet forced a pleasant smile at the waitress. No need to be judgmental, she admonished herself. "And two half-and-halfs."

"Comin' right up," Cherry said. "You takin' these home?"

"No, actually, I'm eating next door with Dottie."

Cherry rang up Sweet's order and said, "I thought I seen your car out back all mornin'. You want me to walk 'em over when they're done?"

"That would be very nice, Cherry. Thank you for offering." Sweet added a generous tip to the cash payment. "I don't need any change."

"Awesome," Cherry made change from the register and shoved it into her jeans pocket. "You can get your own drinks if you want. Both the teas are fresh, just made 'em myself."

"Perfect," Sweet said. She filled two large Styrofoam cups with an equal mixture of sweet and unsweet teas, topped them with lids and headed back to the dress shop.

Dottie was touching up her makeup when Sweet returned. The last part of her story had left them both shaken. LouWanda was hard to take sometimes, but no one deserved to be treated so horribly. Sweet didn't know for whom she felt worse, LouWanda for having been abused, or Dottie for carrying so much unearned guilt all these years.

Sweet set Dottie's tea on the powder room counter, then stood in the doorway and watched her apply a soft coat of blush with a brush. "Feel better?"

"Yeah, I think so. It's good to get it off your chest sometimes, I guess. I don't remember ever telling that story before. I guess it felt like an unspoken agreement in a way."

"I'm glad you told me."

"It's kind of hard to abandon her," Dottie said. "And if only that were the end of the story, but God as my witness, Sweet Lee. It's just the beginning."

Sweet leaned her head against the doorjamb and closed her eyes. When she opened them again, she said, "Let's wait until after we eat to finish it. I don't want to lose my appetite. I still haven't gained all my weight back."

"Good idea," Dottie said as the front door chimed signaling the arrival of their lunch.

***

Dottie folded up the plastic container and sat the half-empty cup of tea between her thighs. Sweet still had a third of her salad left, but she was pushing lettuce around the bowl more than she was eating.

"Go ahead and finish the story. It'll take me a while to call myself done."

"You sure?"

Sweet nodded, her mouth now full.

"I didn't see LouWanda for several months after that; I was a little distracted by my own little drama. I was dating a guy I met while doing my clinicals and my daddy wasn't even a little happy about it."

"What kind of clinicals? What was your major?" Sweet wasn't sure she'd ever heard Dottie talk about college before, and she had a fleeting thought to wonder why that was.

"Social work," Dottie said.

"Really?" Sweet squinted her eyes and peered hard at her friend. "I had no idea, though now that I think about it, I'm not as surprised as I think I should be."

"Why's that?"

"Makes sense. You're always helping someone. It's your thing."

Dottie thought about that for a moment, then shrugged. "Well, I didn't graduate, but maybe I got enough knowledge that stuck. At any rate, I didn't want to come home that summer, but Dad insisted. Said he needed help with Mom—she'd been diagnosed with Parkinson's. It hadn't reached a critical point, but if I'm being fair, he really did need the help. So, I came back. By then, LouWanda had gotten a job at the nursing home in town, which is where we took Mom for physical therapy a couple of times a week. It was good to see her, but it was awkward at first. LouWanda seemed to have shrunk in a way, which is significant considering her size. We had lunch together every now and then, but only when Alton was out of town. When he was home, she brought her lunch and ate in the cafeteria. Said she couldn't leave."

"That's odd," Sweet said.

"Yeah...said she had to be on the premises if he called her at work. She worked odd shifts because she had no seniority, so his calls became a topic of conversation among *all* of her coworkers. Apparently, Alton called the nursing home any time he couldn't reach her at home. It didn't seem to dawn on him she might be somewhere else. He would accuse the staff of lying for her if he couldn't reach her at either place. LouWanda's boss finally told her Alton wasn't allowed to call her at work or she'd lose her job. He didn't like it, but he quit calling."

"What kind of lunatic does that?"

"That's what I wanted to know, but you couldn't really talk to LouWanda about it. She would just clam up. Anyway, one day I brought Mama in for therapy and I passed LouWanda leaving from the night shift. She said she was going to go grab some breakfast and did I want to come along? I had about an hour to kill, so we went over to the café—which Edwina's aunt owned back then— and ate some pancakes. I noticed LouWanda didn't eat all her breakfast, which was odd 'cause the girl can eat, I'm just saying. Anyway, when we finished, she said she was going to go help her Mama open the store, then go home and take a nap before Alton got home. He was supposed to arrive sometime before supper, but she wasn't sure exactly when. Long story short—well, kind of— she called me at home a couple of hours later saying something about being robbed, I couldn't really understand. I told her to take the phone outside and wait for me.

"When I get to her house, the living room was the first thing I noticed. There was a huge hole in the paneling, and a heavy armchair was upside down on the livin' room floor. It took both of us to set it right, which I guess in hindsight we shouldn't have done if we were thinking she'd been robbed. Then we went back to the bedroom and saw Alton's suitcase. It was open and partially hanging off the bed, and his clothes were scattered everywhere, some of them ripped to shreds. But his car was gone, so LouWanda thought the worst. She swore he'd been kidnapped or murdered, so she picked up the phone and dialed the sheriff's office. She was talking to the dispatcher when Alton stormed through the front door with fists drawn and accusations flying. Where had she been? Who was she sleeping with? Why hadn't she answered his calls? What was she hiding? I don't think he even realized I was there, he was so focused on LouWanda. She kept speaking softly to him, never raised her voice once. She told him where she'd been and when she got home, but he raged on and on. And when he finally did notice me, he *still* didn't calm down. He started blaming her for letting me see him upset. He kept this up until the sheriff's deputy knocked on the door. And then," Dottie paused for a moment, "the transformation was like magic."

"Hold that thought," Sweet rose and disposed of her salad box. "I'll be right back."

Dottie stood to stretch her legs and waited for Sweet to return from the restroom. When she sat back down, she sighed. "My bladder has no sense of timing these days. Carry on."

"Are you sure? It's such a long story."

"Lord, Dottie, you can't stop *now.*"

"So, Derrick Wallis shows up at the door, and Alton's demeanor completely changes. I'd forgotten all about the phone call, but I guess they heard enough before LouWanda hung up, and they sent a deputy out to check on things. By the time he left the house, Alton had convinced Derrick that LouWanda was hysterical because, you know, it was "that time of the month", and things had just gotten out of hand. But he had it under control now, and no, he wasn't hurt and didn't want to press charges against her."

"For *what*?" Sweet blurted out.

"That's the crazy thing. Alton walks the deputy back to his bedroom and shows him the mess back there and the guy assumes LouWanda did it. So, I'm standing there looking at her like, *why aren't you saying anything*? And she looks at me and says, 'Please…let it go. Please.'

"I don't know why I didn't speak up, Sweet. I was so stunned, so shocked, all I could do was stand in the corner, frozen like a child."

"I don't know that I'd have done any different, Dottie. I swear I don't."

"You know what the real irony is in all this? It wasn't her time of the month at all. In fact, she was excited he was coming home. She'd been waiting to tell him—to tell *anyone*—she was pregnant. When the deputy left, Alton was on edge, but pretty calm. He acted like nothing at all had happened. He sat down in that chair we'd turned back over, looked up at LouWanda and said, 'I'm parched. We got anything to drink?' She almost ran to the kitchen to pour him a glass of tea. When she handed it to him, she said, 'Alton…honey…I've got some great news. You wanna hear what it is?' He kind of sighed like he'd bear it if he had to, then stared at me like he'd really like for me to leave. LouWanda read it the same way and told him she wanted me to know, too. Then she just blurted the news out and waited for us to light up with joy, I guess. But neither of us did. I stood there and glared at Alton. You can't even imagine his face. It was like looking at the devil himself—a dark fury I had never seen before, nor since. I remember seeing this thick vein in his neck pulsing as his jaw clenched and unclenched. 'Who's the daddy?' is all he said."

19 - Lunch Date

Beanie and Will set out early for Tallahassee, even though his appointment with the researcher at the Meek-Eaton Library wasn't until after lunch.

"What is it you're lookin' for over there?" Beanie tucked a set of insulated bags into the back of Will's car and pushed the button to close the hatch.

Will met her on the passenger side and opened the front door. "Trying to figure out the name of the man in the picture, the one they lynched."

Beanie slid into the passenger seat and pulled the right side of her skirt and crinoline across her lap. Will closed the door, tucking her in neatly. She adjusted her skirts again, then buckled her seatbelt while Will rounded the car and climbed into the driver's seat.

"That's gruesome, Will. I don't think I'd wanna know myself."

"It feels like a mystery that needs to be uncovered. And the more I *don't* find answers, the more determined I am to figure it out. Did you know...gosh this shocked me...did you know that Florida had the highest number of lynching's per capita in the whole United States?"

"Remind me what per capita is?"

"Well, it's based on population. So, they did this report on racially motivated lynching's between 1877 and 1950, basically the Jim Crow Era..."

"I know about Jim Crow. Suvi told me."

Will felt the familiar pang in the pit of his stomach but tried to ignore it. "You didn't hear about it in school?"

"Not that I recollect."

"We had a whole chapter about Jim Crow laws in my American History book. That's crazy."

"It *is* crazy. A whole chapter?"

"No, I meant crazy you didn't learn...never mind. Anyway, there were almost four thousand lynching's in twelve states. And we're not talking for things like rape and murder—most of them weren't even charged with a crime. They were killing people for *minor* social transgressions. Not moving off the sidewalk for a white person, sassing your boss, asserting your legal rights. Crazy stuff. Black men were the most likely to be killed for even *looking* at a white woman, but here's the real kicker. Black *women* were beaten or murdered for not submitting to a white man…like, you know, sexually."

Beanie winced. "I don't like talkin' about this. It hurts my heart."

All the more reason *to* talk about it, Will thought. But he said nothing.

The car got quiet after that and Will felt bad about dragging Beanie with him. He'd come too far to turn back now, though. He had a few names, and two which corresponded to the dates of the new courthouse being built, but there was very little information found online that might help him figure out who this man was.

Will wasn't sure what he'd find in Tallahassee, but he had to try.

***

Will and Beanie stopped by a café in downtown Tallahassee for lunch. More coffee shop and bakery than an actual eatery, the menu still offered a few options for lunch. They each chose a chicken salad sandwich served on a croissant, and a pasta salad. Beanie made Will take out his notebook and write down the ingredients as she called them out. Fresh basil and tomato, feta cheese, some kind of peppers—maybe pimento, she thought—and definitely balsamic vinegar.

"This stuff is to *die* for," she said. "They got a little bitta ma'nnaise in there, too, but not too much."

Will took note but hoped they wouldn't use mayonnaise in their version. He was already approaching his highest weight ever on the scales. Not that he was heavy, of course, he just didn't want to push his luck.

The bakery featured cupcakes, which they wanted to serve at La Pâtisserie, so they ordered two different flavors and split them to share. Will preferred the salted caramel frosting and Beanie loved the vanilla latte cake topped with chocolate ganache. Will added to his list a reminder to learn how to make cake pops, which would be an inexpensive draw for parents with children.

When they were finished, he marked his receipt *tax-deductible* and tucked it into his wallet. A scouting trip for business—every little bit helped.

20 - At the Archives

Beanie and Will purchased lattes to go and set off for the Meek-Eaton Black Archives on the campus of Florida A&M University. When they found the historic Carnegie Library building that housed the archives, Beanie unfolded the map Will had printed for her and left to explore the campus, promising to be back in half an hour.

Inside, Will greeted the receptionist and was shown to the office of Gwendolyn Peters, Research Director and Archivist. Will carried in one hand the old suitcase of photos they had found, and in the other, his briefcase. He set the suitcase down to shake the hand of the striking woman standing before him.

"So nice to meet you, Ms. Peters," Will said. "I appreciate you working with me on this."

"It's my pleasure. And let's dispense with formalities. I'm Gwen."

"Gwen it is, and I'm Will."

"Have a seat wherever you like. I'm curious to see these photos you told me about."

Will opened his briefcase and took out a manila envelope.

"There are three boxes of photos all catalogued and in order, but I pulled the section with what I believe to be the most important ones. It's the story I'm trying to unravel anyway."

Will tilted the envelope and twelve black and white photographs, all slightly larger than four by six inches, slid out onto the table.

"Cabinet prints. That'll help us date these." Gwen reached for the photos. "May I?"

"Absolutely," Will said. "But don't worry, the photos are numbered and dated on the back. Whoever did this was meticulous."

Gwen whistled softly as she thumbed through the stack. "I'll say. This is amazing, the clarity of the photos is... Oh my." She stopped at one particular picture, dropping half the stack onto the table.

"Yeah, oh my is right. That's why I'm here."

"If this is what I think it is, you may have the only known record of this event." Gwen winced and took a deep breath. She flipped the photo over and read the carefully printed description out loud. "Fletcher County Courthouse, June 9, 1895. That's it. This is Dell Connolly. How did you…where did you find these?"

"In the attic of The Château in Mayhew Junction. It's the building you see here, the old courthouse. It was moved across the street when the new one was built in its place. I own it now. We run it as a Bed and Breakfast."

"Are you looking to place these photographs with us? I'd like to look through them all if possible."

Will looked stricken. "I don't know about leaving them with you yet. I hadn't really thought that far. I mean, our historical society might be a little… Well, I suppose, technically, I do own them, but still… I don't know yet. I was hoping you could tell me more about the… the event."

"We do have some information on Dell Connolly's murder in our archives, but no photos." Gwen paused and chose her words with care. "You know, we could do high quality scans for your historical society, and of course we would digitize them and make them available to the public, but the originals would always be protected and cared for properly, not left in some attic to deteriorate. Not that you would do that, of course, but someone did. And I have to wonder, I mean… well… honestly, I have to *ask*… You do understand the historical significance, right? Photos like this are rare."

Will nodded. "I understand, yes."

"So why are you here exactly? How can I help you?"

"I… well, I guess I'm just trying to uncover the story, you know, it's like a riddle, kind of? Something to solve? Maybe?" Will caught the expressions washing across the museum director's face and felt awkward and exposed. "I'm sorry, have I said something wrong?"

Gwen took a deep breath and forced a patient, but rueful, smile. "It's a sensitive subject, I'm sure you understand. While I have a professional obligation to the truth, I also have a moral obligation to the family of Dell Connolly. I'm sorry, but I'd like to know your intentions before I tell you what I know about Mr. Connolly. Are you doing research for a writing project or something?"

"Oh, gosh, no. I'm not a writer. We found these photos in the building I own. I think I just want to know if there is a connection to my home. I'm not trying to… it's not just… I would never do anything intentionally harmful with them." Will felt his face flush red and the back of his neck felt soggy at the hairline. "Look, this may be nothing more than morbid curiosity, but I look at these pictures and I just want to know the story. I feel like I should be coming up with something more noble, but I'd rather stick to the truth. I have no ulterior motive, I promise you."

"If I tell you, will you think about donating these originals to the museum?"

"I will, but if you're not comfortable telling me, I'll certainly understand." Will fanned his face with one of the photos.

"Most of what we know comes from a 1941 audio recording of a woman named Nancy Jacobs Wright who, as a child, lived in a farmhouse with her parents George and Susanna Jacobs and her two brothers Thomas and James. It's a fascinating story, but the recording is not good quality despite our best efforts. I can queue it up if you'd like to listen, otherwise I'll just give you the highlights."

"I'd appreciate that," Will said.

Gwen recounted the story she'd gathered from Nancy Wright's recording. On the day of the lynching, Nancy was playing in her back yard when a black man stopped by with a wounded dog in his arms. Based on what she witnessed that day, along with information she'd learned through family stories and newspaper clippings, Nancy told the story of how Connolly had been out looking for his boss's prized hunting dog, which he found tangling with a raccoon she'd treed. On the way home, he stopped at the Jacobs farmhouse and asked if it would be all right if he drew water from their well for both himself and the animal. Her mother refused and ordered him off her property, then pulled Nancy inside and slammed the door.

Nancy had watched from the window as the man laid the dog on the ground and quickly drew water from the well. He'd later told his boss he was more worried about the dog than himself—he thought she really needed the water. Nancy remembered watching the man carefully pour water from the ladle into the dog's mouth. Afterwards, he'd ladled some into his own hand and wet his

116

mouth, then left the yard and walked down the road toward town cradling the dog to his chest. When her mother asked what she was looking at, Nancy told her. She remembered only that her mother had been furious and vowed to make the man pay. Her father arrived home a few hours after Connolly left and, by the time he made it to town to press charges, the story had taken on a life of its own. A posse was formed to deliver justice vigilante style.

Connolly's boss, having been forewarned, gave him a horse and told him to get out of the county, so he did. But not before stopping off at his cousin's house for a few supplies. When word got back to the posse Connolly was gone, the men were enraged. They made their way to the cousin's house and terrorized the man and his pregnant wife, torturing them both before hanging them from an oak tree in their own front yard. They eventually caught up to Dellwood Connolly, too. They brought his badly beaten and bullet-ridden body back to town to string up on the courthouse lawn as a warning to other black citizens who might decide to step out of bounds.

It would be years, Nancy said, before she knew the rest of the story—years before she realized the part she played in the man's death. A simple act of defiance, drawing water from a well, had been conflated into an attack on a helpless woman, a story Nancy knew to be untrue. If only she hadn't told her mother what she'd seen, four lives would have been spared that day and that fact haunted her so much she wanted to set the record straight.

Will felt his stomach go hollow as he listened to Gwen's tale.

"It's hard to hear." Will took a handkerchief out of his pocket and wiped his forehead.

Gwen sighed and arranged the photos into a neat stack. "It's hard to tell."

"I can imagine." Will said. "My wife and I attended some workshops at St. Cloud State... we're from Minnesota... We wanted to learn more about the African American experience, not just for our business, though that was important, but for ourselves."

"Was that your wife I saw with you earlier? Cowboy hat? Boots?"

"No, no, that's just my...that's Beanie. We work together. My wife passed away a few years ago."

"I'm so sorry," Gwen said.

"Thank you," Will waved one hand and changed the subject. "Anyway, we were travel agents. We were also a little bookish... took classes together all the time. We wanted to educate ourselves, especially knowing we wanted to eventually move to Florida. We'd heard stories—you know—about the racism and stuff down here."

"It's a different culture, that's for sure," Gwen said. "I'm from Chicago myself. Well, outside of Chicago, but that's close enough. Anyway, Northerners like to lay blame squarely on the back of the South, but racism exists everywhere. *Every*where."

"Oh, I know. I remember my grandfather telling me a story about a bridge in our town, and how blacks knew not to cross it once the sun went down. I had forgotten the story until Marie and I learned about sundown towns in the workshops we took. I had no idea there was a name for it."

"I'm not surprised." Gwen shuffled back through the pictures in her hand. "Anyway, about the stories. What I want to say, and I think I'm going to be blunt here..."

"Please do," Will said.

"I was raised in a family with tremendous psychic wounds from our own experience with racism in America. I know how difficult it is for some of our elders to hear their stories told. And yet, we recognize the importance of remembering. There are often one or two family historians who are expected to learn and pass on the narratives, but we don't sit around the porch telling them. It's too raw, too painful. So, I get it when you say it's hard to hear these stories. We don't like hearing them, either."

Will nodded and shifted in his chair. "How do you do this job, then?"

Gwen sighed. "With all due respect, white people haven't been the best stewards of our history. The telling of any story is skewed by the perspective of the teller. I'm here because I care about getting it right."

"I promise you, Ms. Peters, I'm here for the same reason. I want to get it right," Will said.

"Well, you brought these photos to the right place. It's a good start." Gwen paused to weigh her words. "I don't want to offend you..."

"You won't," he assured her.

"What is harder still is hearing our stories told by people who have no business telling them. I know how important these photos are to your historical society, but am I right in guessing the leaders of that group are not people of color?"

Will nodded. "For the most part, yes."

"Then I would ask again that you consider placing these photos where they belong."

Will sat completely still for a moment. "I'll bring them back to you soon. You have my word."

Gwen stood and offered her hand, which Will clasped in his own. "Thank you, Mr. Thaxton. You won't regret doing this."

Will couldn't help wondering if that was the truth.

21 - LouWanda Meets the Mouse

The next meeting of the Mayhew Junction Historical Society was held at the Fletcher County Public Library for several reasons. It was a quiet place that would not lend itself to outbursts from anyone, especially LouWanda Crump. It was also a place with access to computers and Wi-Fi, and this was meant to be a learning experience for all those interested. The Outreach Coordinator from the library headquarters agreed to be on hand for technical assistance with computer access and genealogy research. Those members with laptops could work alongside those using the library computers and, with a little luck and a few prayers, they could make progress on some much-needed research. At least that was how Corinne Barr looked at it when she set up the meeting.

And speaking of luck, or the lack thereof, Corinne ended up seated right next to LouWanda. Her prayer was *Jesus help me,* spoken under her breath as she eased herself into the solid wood chair at the table set up by the library staff.

"Is that everybody?" Jody asked as Corinne got settled. "Okay, for those of you don't know me, I'm Jody and I provide technical training for the library. I'm here today to work with you-all on your Historical Society research. Did I get that right?"

Corinne and Phyllis nodded without looking up, each focused on signing onto their laptops and accessing the library Wi-Fi.

"That's right," JoDeen and Diane said simultaneously, then laughed.

"Y'all sound like twins," Nell said.

"I already gotta question." LouWanda raised her left hand and started pushing buttons on the keyboard with her right index finger. "How do you turn this thing on?"

"Whoa, whoa, whoa," Jody extended her arm, but LouWanda was out of reach.

"It's already on. Here let me help you," Corinne covered LouWanda's hand with her own and pulled it toward the wireless mouse on the pad between their computers. "Use this to sign in."

"I signed in at the desk already," LouWanda said.

"Oh, dear," Jody looked stricken. "I was told this would be more of an intermediate group. I'm not sure I have time to start at the beginning..."

"You keep going," Corinne said. "I'll handle this and catch up."

"You sure?" Jody asked.

"Positive." Corinne gave her a reassuring smile.

"What'd I say?" LouWanda demanded.

"Shhh...let me help you so she can get started," Corinne whispered. "Grab the mouse and we'll get you signed onto the computer."

"Grab the what?"

"Mouse...the mouse. This thing. It moves the cursor on the computer."

"Look, the only curser I know is settin' right there, and she cursed in the *church* for crying out loud."

"Extenuating circumstances," Diane Kerner spoke from across the table.

"Ladies..." Jody began.

"Let's start at the beginning," Corinne whispered to LouWanda. "Just listen first, and if you have any questions, I promise I'll answer them.

For the next fifteen minutes, while Jody explained the basics of genealogy to the other four women, Corinne taught LouWanda how to use a personal computer which LouWanda had apparently never done before.

"So," Corinne said, "I want you to think of the computer like it was your office. The keyboard is your typewriter, which I know you can use because y'all had Mrs. Fretwell at your high school. She didn't let anyone come out of there without knowing how to type."

"F-D-S-A...J-K-L-Semicolon," LouWanda intoned in a reasonable replication of their former teacher's very precise and Southern accent.

"We didn't have typewriters at our school," Corinne said drily.

"Well, why not?" LouWanda looked skeptical.

Corinne closed her eyes and shook her head. "So, the keyboard is your typewriter, and the display screen, or monitor, is your paper for now."

LouWanda started to interrupt, but Corinne held up one hand. "Nope…just listen. I'll get there." Corinne covered the mouse with her hand and moved it back and forth across the mousepad. "See that little line waving across the screen?"

LouWanda peered closer. "Oooohhhh, yeah. What's that?"

"That's your cursor. C-U-R-S-O-R, cursor. It like a pointing device. You move the mouse to control the cursor and point at what you want to see. First, we are going to sign into the Library system. You have to think of this as opening the library doors. You want to go in and access their books and files and programs, so you have to sign in, just like you did at the desk, but to access the computer files. Does that make sense?"

"Well, sort of," LouWanda grumped.

"So, I'm going to sign in for you to save time. Next time you come in, Miss Janice will help you if you don't know how. So now, look at the screen…see all those boxes up there? Those are called icons, and this is called your desktop. And you can think of it like the desktop in your office. On your desk, you might have a dictionary…" Corinne wiggled the mouse and pointed to an icon for Webster's Dictionary. "On this desktop, that's right here. You click on that to open it. Here, you try it."

LouWanda picked up the mouse in two hands and aimed it at the computer screen. Corinne stifled a laugh. "It's not a remote, LouWanda. Put it down on the pad."

"Oh," LouWanda said. "Right."

"It has two buttons…see, right here. The left button is the one you use most. You click with your pointer finger when you want to open one of the icons, like opening a book. The right button is more like turning to an index in the book you're using."

"I'm confused already," LouWanda looked hopeless.

"It can be confusing," Corinne nodded. "But let's play with it a while and you'll get the hang of it. It's not as hard as you think. It just takes practice."

For the next thirty minutes, Corinne had LouWanda opening applications like the card catalog and the digital microfiche files and exploring websites like the one for newspaper archives. She explained how all of these were like files she might keep in her filing cabinet in her office, except these could be accessed with a click. As obtuse as LouWanda seemed, she picked up the concepts fairly quickly under Corinne's careful tutelage. And by the time Jody got through with her presentation on using genealogical resources, the pair were ready to tackle the ins and outs of Ancestry.com together.

22 - Road Trip

LouWanda Crump decided she very much liked learning how to use a computer. She started closing her shop for a full two hours at lunch so she could go over to the library and putter around. Every now and then she called Corinne and asked if she'd meet her and show her a few more things, and Corinne agreed, not because she was trying to cozy up to her cousin, but because she was a firm believer in keeping your friends close and your enemies closer.

On the Friday before the next historical society meeting, LouWanda asked Corinne to help her with an online order, though she didn't tell her up front it was for the monument. LouWanda didn't think Corinne would mind, seeing as how they shared that ancestor in common, a fact that didn't really bother LouWanda so much anymore. Especially since she had realized it was *her* blood that ran through Corinne's line and not the other way around. *Not that it should matter*, LouWanda told herself. *Far be it from me to be racist. I'm just trying to be a good Christian, that's all. The Bible makes it clear about mixing races. I can't help what my ancestor did, but it'd be a hard pill to swallow if my own blood was mixed. But that doesn't make me a racist, does it? Of course not. Just a good Christian, that's all I am.*

Corinne was already seated at a computer when LouWanda walked into the Fletcher County Library. She waved at the girls behind the counter and failed to notice that two of them instantly made themselves scarce. One went to clean the bathrooms and the other to shelve the ten books that had come in that morning. Anything, *anything* but having to help LouWanda Crump on a computer.

"Hey, Cousin," Corinne teased. She knew how much it bothered LouWanda and she had no intentions of letting her off the hook.

"Oh, stop," LouWanda groused. She was in no mood today. A pipe had burst in the back of the store and wiped out a whole rack of National Geographic magazines, plus a stack of LPs she'd had sitting in a box on the floor for over a year. She'd intended to go through them before putting them out for sale. There were some real golden oldies in there, Roy Acuff and Kitty Wells and even a couple of Little Jimmy Dickens. She didn't even own a record player anymore, but she thought surely she'd get one in at some point and could play some of her old favorites again. Anyway, it was a mess and they were all ruined now.

Corinne pulled out the chair beside her and LouWanda lowered herself into it with a whump.

"What's wrong?" Corinne asked.

"Oh, just everything." LouWanda picked up the mouse and swiped it back and forth across the mousepad a few times, peering closely at the computer screen to find the bouncing arrow.

"Did you forget your glasses again?" Corinne stilled LouWanda's hand with her own. "Stop. It's right there."

"They're in the car, I think. Or maybe on my bedside table, who knows? That's the least of my worries today."

"What's the most of them?" Corinne went back to her own laptop, bookmarking an article she wanted to read later.

"Busted pipes, ruined records, the sales tax people breathin' down my back, and my monument stalled at the factory, so's we may not get it in time for the Founder's Day parade. That's what I need your help with."

"I thought we all nixed that idea, LouWanda."

"Too late, it's already paid for."

"Well, if it's delayed, it's not made, so you can still cancel it, can't you?"

"Look, I didn't ask you down here to argue about the monument. I need you to help me figure out where it is."

Corinne rubbed at her forehead and pushed her own glasses back up on the bridge of her nose. "I swear," she said under her breath.

"What'd you say?" LouWanda was still leaned in close to the screen.

"Shhhh…" said Miss Janice from the circulation desk.

"Sorry," LouWanda called out without lowering her voice at all. Miss Janice shook her head and went to get a cup of coffee.

"You go'n get us kicked out of here one of these days, Cousin. Mark my words." Corinne scooted her chair over and took control of LouWanda's mouse. "Where are we looking?"

"Well, the company is called Monuments something. I think it's in Alabama. That's one of the things I wanna find out."

"Did you try calling them?"

"Well, of course I did, but they don't never call me back. That's why I'm tryin' to look on the computer."

It took a few minutes to find the company. It was in Georgia, not far from the Florida line. Corinne pulled it up on a map and showed LouWanda how to get a street view of the address. It was an old gas station close to downtown Ellaville—paint peeling with a hand-lettered sign that read Monuments R Us centered over the top of what was once a two-bay garage. A grassy area beside the pavement held about ten different styles of headstones and the rest of the lot was covered with an assortment of concrete statues, birdbaths and metal sculptures, the largest of which was a giant chicken, standing at least ten feet tall.

"Are you sure this is it?"

"Pretty sure. That's the phone number I been dialin'," LouWanda said. "They got a lotta stuff, don't they?"

"I'll say. How'd you find these guys?"

"Oh, I asked if anybody knew of a place that did Confederate statues and Eustace Falwell said he had a cousin did 'em and he give me the number. I wanted bronze, but that was expensive, so I ended up gettin' concrete for the statue—they said it polishes up real nice—and a granite headstone for the memorial."

Corinne pulled a handkerchief from her purse and wiped her face several times.

"LouWanda, I think you should have waited on this. I don't think this is going to be well-received, if I'm being honest."

"So, what else is new?" LouWanda said, scraping her chair back from the table. "Nobody likes anything I do. I learnt long ago it's better to get forgiveness than permission. Now are you gonna help me or not?"

"I just did. There's the place. It's…" Corinne typed a couple of keystrokes and hit enter on the keyboard, "about an hour from here. My suggestion is you go up there and see for yourself where your order is. They can't hang up on your face."

"I don't wanna drive all the way up there by myself. What if my car breaks down?"

"That is not my problem, dear cousin. You the one wantin' the memorial. You go get it."

126

Corinne packed up her computer and stood to leave with LouWanda sitting there fuming. She was about to walk out when LouWanda reached for her arm.

"It's real important to me, Corinne. Would you please go?"

Corinne Barr felt her eyes roll so far back she thought they might actually get stuck. She sighed and shook her head like she didn't even believe what was about to come out of her own mouth.

"I'm sure I'm going to regret this..." she began.

"Oh, yay! I *knew* you'd say yes!" LouWanda clapped her hands together.

"Shhhhhh!" Miss Janice said.

"Sorry!" LouWanda hollered.

"Lord, help," said Corinne.

"We'll go tomorrow," LouWanda said in a stage whisper. "You're drivin'."

***

LouWanda opened the back door of Corinne's Cadillac and deposited a soft-sided cooler slightly larger than a lunchbox onto the floorboard.

"I brought sodas and some muffins from the Jiffy Store."

"I've already had breakfast," Corinne said as LouWanda lowered herself into the front seat with a groan.

"Oh yeah, me, too," LouWanda huffed. "I figured we might wanna snack."

"That was thoughtful of you, Cousin."

"Why do you insist on callin' me that, is what I wanna know?" LouWanda shoved her purse underneath the seat and fiddled with the seat belt.

"Because it gets under your skin," Corinne admitted drily. "And because we're cousins. Are you ashamed of that?"

"Why, no," LouWanda snapped. "I think it's silly, that's all."

"Then we're even. I think this monument is a silly idea, and I think it is going to cause more problems than it's worth.

"Well, I would think you'd appreciate it a little more since it's your great-great-grandfather, too. He built the courthouse, for cryin' out loud."

Corinne gave a side-eyed glare and pursed her lips. "You saw the photo, Cousin. He hung a black man in front of that courthouse. And he didn't build it. He was the overseer. Big difference. Black people built it. I'm just sayin'."

"Whatever. Are we gonna fight about this all day? 'Cause if we are, you can turn this car around and take me home. I don't wanna— What are you doin'?"

LouWanda flattened her hands out to her sides, with one landing on the inside of the door and the other on Corinne's upper arm.

"I'm turning the car around," Corinne said.

"You're gonna get us killed drivin' thataway. Lord Jesus..."

"Since when do you take the Lord's name in vain?" Corinne forced herself to look stern when everything in her wanted to laugh out loud.

"Since you nearly killed us, that's when. Now wait a second...I don't wanna fight, but I don't wanna go home neither. Just git us turned back around and we'll start over."

"You gonna behave?" Corinne asked.

LouWanda sighed loudly. "Yes, I'll behave."

Corinne found a pull-off and turned the car back around more slowly this time. She'd made her point and didn't expect to have *much* more trouble the rest of the day.

When the two women made it to Ellaville, Georgia, they were chatting like old friends. Turned out each had plenty of family stories to tell that made them both laugh.

"Can we stop before we get to the monument place. I gotta pee," LouWanda said.

Corinne didn't answer, just pulled the car into a burger joint and parked in the shade. "You go ahead, I'll go when you're done. I don't want to shut the car off."

When LouWanda got back in the car, she noticed Corinne had put on a fresh coat of lipstick.

"My mama used to get all over me about wearin' lipstick." LouWanda said. "Said it was of the devil, but I liked it. I thought it made me look pretty."

"I don't think I've ever seen you with makeup on at all," Corinne turned to face her, "much less lipstick."

"Oh, I don't wear it now at all. I ain't worn makeup since Alton told me I looked like a fat ol' whore in it."

Corinne looked horrified. "He told you *what*?"

"I know, I know, it's awful, but there it is. I threw out everything I owned and never bought another tube of lipstick in my life. Beanie puts her Avon books in my store, but I don't even look at 'em anymore."

Corinne found herself absolutely speechless. She got out of the car without saying a word and went inside to use the restroom. She was still mute when she slid back into the driver's seat.

"What'sa matter with ya?" LouWanda asked.

"I—" Corinne shifted her entire body so she could face her passenger. "I'm sorry for you, that's all. That was a hateful thing for him to say, and I'm sorry he hurt you like that."

LouWanda dismissed the sentiment with a wave of her hand. "Oh, he was always like that. Water under the bridge now. Nothin' to be sorry about."

Corinne looked at LouWanda long and hard, narrowing her eyes as she tried to read her expression.

"Well, I *am* sorry. No one should be treated that way, Cousin. No one."

For the first time since learning they shared a common ancestor, LouWanda found the term *cousin* a comforting thing.

23 - Nothing to Crow About

Monuments R Us looked even worse in person than it did in on Google Maps. The lot next to the garage was unmown and the grass was higher than half the headstones there. On the paved section in front of the building, several birdbaths had tipped over and lay in pieces. The ten-foot chicken was still there, which made the place easy to find. There were a number of strange sculptures made from engine parts, and a row of garden gnomes in front of another row of angels, all made from concrete. A tattered rebel flag hung beneath a faded American flag from a flagpole more rust than metal.

Corinne found a parking space on the street beside the building, and they could hear a cacophony of sound emanating from the open doors of the former garage as they approached.

"Hey, Rooster," one young man in overalls shouted as the women wound their way through the merchandise littering the front of the building, "we got comp'ny!"

Corinne turned to look at the gigantic bird standing guard at the corner of the sidewalk. "Ahhh," she nodded, noticing the spray of tailfeathers and the faded red metal crown and wattle. "It's not a chicken, it's a *rooster*."

LouWanda followed her gaze. "Sure 'nuff is," she said.

They both turned in time to see a small man slide out from behind a canvas tarp strung from the ceiling inside the garage. "Shut 'er down, Lonnie," he hollered over the rumble of an air compressor, and the man in the overalls complied.

"What can we do ya' for, ladies?" the man swiped at a coating of white sand lodged in his Fu Manchu mustache, then stuck his hand out in greeting. Neither woman offered her hand in return and he dropped it quickly, smacking sand from his leg like that was his intention all along. "Sorry 'bout the dust. I'm blastin' a monument right now. I'm the owner here. You can call me Rooster."

LouWanda found her voice first. "I been tryin' to call you all week. You're s'posed to be doin' a memorial for the Fletcher County Courthouse, and I ain't heard a peep from ya."

"Miss LouWanda? Oh, yeah, I keep missin' your calls, we been so busy and all. Matter of fact, I'm blastin' it right now. Takes forever gettin' some of this granite in. They always wanna ship it across the country, 'stead of gettin' it local. Anyway, I'm 'bout done with it, you wanna see?"

"Yeah, where is it?" LouWanda scanned the cluttered shop, trying to make sense of the piles of debris, none of which looked like monuments of any kind.

"Oh, come this way." Rooster waved a hand to follow him. "It's back here behind the tarp. I been workin' on this thing all day."

LouWanda scooted around a garbage can filled with pieces of rubber stencils and stepped over broken pieces of concrete scattered across the floor.

"I'm gonna stay over here," Corinne said. "This looks dangerous."

"Oh, come on ya big baby," LouWanda groused. "If I can make it, you can."

Rooster pulled the tarp back and waved them in with a flourish. LouWanda pulled the tarp aside and gasped. "It's beautiful!"

Corinne peered over her cousin's shoulder. "Oh, good Lord," she said. "What in the world have you done?"

LouWanda ignored the comment and clasped her hands in delight.

Rooster grinned and pulled himself up to a full five feet. "I got your statue in this week, too. I gotta polish it up for ya, though. The Confederate soldier, right?"

LouWanda's eyes got wide and Corinne's got wider.

"What Confederate soldier?" Corinne demanded.

"I been meanin' to tell ya…they's just kinda one statue to choose from and, depending on what colors you paint it, it can be Confederate or Union. You know…multi-purpose."

"Since when was L.B. Matthews a Confederate soldier?"

"Well, I assume he had to've been. You called him Captain Matthews yourself."

Corinne rolled her eyes. "They called *every* overseer Captain. It doesn't mean he was military."

"Don't mean he wadn't, neither."

24 - Stormy Weather

By the time school let out for the summer, Bitty had settled into a reluctant truce, buoyed partially by blatant bribes: go to school every day and Sweet would take them to St. George Island for a weeklong vacation. The beach was Bitty's favorite. She could collect all the shells she wanted and line them up on the shoreline by size, shape and species. What she didn't know, she looked up in the tattered book she kept on her own bookshelf: *Audubon's Field Guide to North American Seashells.*

This year they rented a house right on the beach. It was a far cry from previous summers when they would get up before sunrise and drive the two hours to St. George for the day, or the Sunday afternoons at Keaton Beach one county away. Tiny Keaton in the Big Bend of Florida didn't have the white sand beaches and clear blue water like St. George Island in the panhandle. And they had never stayed an entire week at either beach before.

The twins convinced Sweet to let them drive the Swag Wagon just in case they needed two cars for "you know, *whatever"* was how they put it. Once they'd accomplished that feat, B-Kay and T-Ray lobbied for each bringing a friend, which meant she'd have to let Tate bring one, too. Bitty preferred playing alone, and Daisy was still too young to care, so at least it was only three extra mouths to feed. She put her foot down when T-Ray asked if he could bring his new girlfriend.

"Have you lost your mind?" Sweet glared at her son, who struggled to maintain an innocent expression.

"What?" T-Ray threw both hands up beside his shoulders.

"You know exactly what," Sweet said. "Don't make me say it in front of the babies."

"Who's a baby?" Tate protested. "I ain't a baby."

"I am not having this discussion right now. Y'all can each bring one friend...same gender...that's it." When Sweet saw T-Ray look at his sister with raised eyebrows and a conspiratorial grin she added, "And no, she cannot bring your girlfriend. Don't try me, son. You'll be on your own out there."

"Don't bring me into this, Mama, I wouldn't have brought her anyway. She looks way better than me in a bathing suit." B-Kay looked up from the knitting loom stretched across her lap. She'd found a new hobby and was already working on Christmas gifts.

"Oooo, somebody's jealous," T-Ray smirked. "I'll tell her you said so."

"Oh, don't worry, Tee, she already *knows*."

T-Ray curled his fingers into claws and hissed like a cat.

"Better feline than canine, brother." B-Kay added a tiny woof for emphasis.

"Y'all stop," Sweet said, stifling a smile over the always-interesting banter between the twins. "Little pitchers have big ears."

* * *

When the day finally came to leave, Sweet, not quite yet accustomed to having enough money to eat out whenever they wanted, packed the usual bevy of coolers. Bubba John drove separately with the loot in the back of his truck. He would stay a few days and go back home to study for the state boards for his contractor's license.

The twins left early to pick up their friends and promised to meet Sweet at the Walmart in Perry, where they would get a few more supplies. Four hours later, the Atwater caravan pulled into the driveway of the three-story house that would be their home for the next week.

Sweet rode up on the elevator with the youngest four children, and Bubba John rounded up the teens to help him unload the supplies. All of the kids were clamoring to go beachside, but Sweet stood her ground. Unpacking first, then lunch, then sunscreen, then the beach. After much groaning, the tasks were complete, and the expanded family trudged across the boardwalk protecting the dunes and spilled out onto the gleaming sand of St. George Island.

Bubba John and B-Kay tackled the new sun canopy, while T-Ray flirted with his sister's friend Luciana. T's friend Dylan sat at the water's edge with Daisy and Bitty and helped them start building a sandcastle, which endeared him to everyone, especially B-Kay and Sweet. Once they settled into beach chairs beneath the tent, both Sweet and Bubba John let out deep sighs and sipped their red plastic cups of sweet tea and Budweiser respectively.

After teaching Tate and his best buddy Evan how to use their new boogie boards, the teens decided to walk down to the public park where there was likely a game or two of beach volleyball in progress. Daisy eventually tired of sandcastles and, still wary of the lapping waves, curled up on a beach towel beside her mama and took a nap. Bitty splashed in the shallow waves for a while, collecting her usual horde of seashells and bringing the occasional specimen to show her parents.

"Mama, look," Bitty plodded through the thick sand, hand held straight forward with a seashell rocking in her upturned palm. "Did you know a spotted slipper shell is in the family *crepidula*? It looks like a boat. I have five of them so far, but this one's the biggest."

"Nice one, Bitty-boo," Bubba John said.

"Amazing," her mama echoed.

Satisfied, Bitty went back to her pile of shells and scooped them into the circle of her crossed legs.

Sweet reached over and patted her husband's arm. "Look how beautiful she is."

"Who, Bitty?"

"Mmm-hmm," Sweet nodded.

"She is. I'm starting to see what she'll look like as an adult. She's lost the baby look."

"They're growing up fast, Daddy."

Bubba John sighed again. "Tell me about it."

After a few more minutes of peaceful silence, Sweet spoke again. "They want to test her for autism this summer. Miss Daniels called me last week. They want to see whether she has ADHD or autism or both."

Bubba John sat forward in his chair. "Last week? You haven't said a word about this."

"I know," Sweet said. "Just waiting for the right time. Had to process."

"What will they do?"

Sweet leaned down and swatted a fly from Daisy's forehead. "I don't know. I haven't signed the papers for them to do the testing yet. Wanted to talk to you first."

"Autism, Sweet? Really?"

Sweet shook her head and both corners of her mouth turned downward. "Libby Daniels doesn't think she's autistic. Maybe on the spectrum, but only mildly, like Asperger's Syndrome, I think she called it."

Twenty feet from them, Bitty sat placidly on the smooth sand left by the receding tide, sorting seashells by shape and size.

Bubba John felt a catch in his chest that made it seem hard to breathe. "What does that mean?"

"I'm not sure I *want* to know what it means, hon." Sweet held her hand out to him, palm up, and he took it. "I don't know if we should even let them test her."

Bubba John said nothing.

"Really, honey, what will it change? She's Bitty. She's different. She's unique. She doesn't need a label following her around all her life. Whatever it is…is part of her. And what good would a label do her? What would it get her? If she needs therapies or special services, we have the money to get them for her. We don't need a diagnosis; we just need a strategy to help Bitty be her best self."

Sweet didn't expect her husband to respond. He often didn't. He thought. He processed. He listened. That was his way.

Sweet stood and walked down to the water's edge. Bitty had arranged the shells into a symmetrical shape, with crossed lines and decorative points that formed a circle.

"What a pretty flower," Sweet said.

Bitty said, "It's a mandala. We learned about them in art class. Did you know a mandala is a circle *and* a square? A mandala is a geometric sign for symmetry. That means balance. I like symmetry. Symmetry is beautiful. Don't you think so, Mama?"

"I do think so, baby. Very beautiful. Just like you."

"Thanks, Mama," Bitty said without looking up.

Sweet stared out across the waters of the Gulf of Mexico, so vast she felt insignificant and small. The waves were rolling in steady, not crashing hard yet, but not the simple swells they often saw in calm weather. In the distance, to the east, the skies were bright blue with white cumulus clouds forming giant faces tilted upwards. To the west, the sky was dark, and a wall of gray haze connected clouds to water. A storm you could see, but not feel. A storm of significant size, and no way to know yet where it was heading.

Sweet felt Bubba John before she heard him. He stepped up behind her and wrapped his arms around her midsection. She covered his hands with her own and laid her head back against his chest and they stood that way for a while.

Then he kissed her cheek and said, "Looks like a storm out there, Mama. You ready to go in?"

"Let's give it a little bit and see what it does. It'll be a fight to get those boys in before it's even thundering."

"Want me to call the twins?"

"Nah…let 'em go. They know how to get out of trouble if they need to."

"You feelin' all right?" Bubba John turned Sweet to face him and peered at her, worried.

Sweet laughed. "Am I that bad?"

"Well, I didn't wanna be the one to tell you, but…"

"I know, I know…too controlling."

"I didn't say it." Bubba John backed away protecting his face with both hands.

"Oh, stop," Sweet laughed again. "But, you're right, and I have finally found something I absolutely cannot control. I'm trying to adopt the vacation mentality here. You can't hold back the tide, so you might as well go with the flow. How's that?"

"Works for me. But you are not a go-with-the-flow kinda girl."

Sweet smacked him on the upper arm and trudged back through the sand to the tent where her sleeping baby was waking up.

"Ten more minutes, boys," Sweet called out to Tate and Evan. "Storm's brewing."

25 - It's Getting Hot in Here

Summer found The Château's business booming. Will's attention to social media brought double the number of guests they'd had the year before, so they hired Sissy Coleman to take up the slack in housekeeping, which she worked in around the busy hours at the café. The addition of an ice cream station in the bakery kept their doors swinging so regularly, they had to add a wall unit air conditioner to keep the room cool enough for the frostings not to melt. Will hired Kenya Green to help out in the bakery and Suvi Jones' old line cook Jesse for the weekend breakfast crowd. Kenya would leave for school at the end of summer, which worked out well for everyone. The real coup was Nell Wiggins, who actually walked in and applied for a job.

Beanie was standing in front of the display case, checking to make sure it was level and evenly spaced, when the door clanged open. Beanie did a double-take.

"Hey, Miss Nell." Beanie didn't mean to sound as surprised as she was, but Nell's cakes were famous in town. What could she possibly want to buy from The Patsy? "How in the world are ya'? I haven't seen you in ages."

"I'm doing pretty good. Cecil's been down in his back for a while, but I think he's just milking it now. He's got used to me waitin' on him hand and foot."

"Don't spoil him now, Miss Nell. He won't be good for nothin'." Beanie laughed as she said this, but Nell meant business.

"I'm afraid it's too late. The damage is done. And now I need to teach that man a lesson. I'd love to come to work for you, if you'll have me. I'll do anything you need. Bake cakes, work the counter, sweep the floors. I don't care, Beanie. If I don't get out of that house, I'll go crazy. It was fine before Cecil retired—I could do whatever I wanted. But now he's got me feeling like a puppet on a string. 'Do this, Nell. Bring me that, Honey. Why don't you put down that sewing and come talk to me?' I swear I'm either gonna divorce him or kill him, and my reputation can't take either one."

When Nell stopped to take a breath, Beanie patted her on the back.

"Sit down, Miss Nell. Let me get you a cup of coffee and a muffin. I got Morning Glories right out of the oven."

Nell did as she was told and sat down feeling like she'd released a mountain of weight. Beanie came back minutes later with two cups and two muffins reasoning that nobody likes to eat alone.

"I'm gonna be big as a barn if I don't stop this," Beanie said as she sat down. She instantly regretted it, given that Nell Wiggins had gone soft over the years.

"If I had to give up my baking to stay skinny, I'd keep the cakes. Hands down. Cecil used to complain I'd let myself go, but he never once complained about eating my food. And he didn't say a word when I'd buy him six pairs of pants a size larger. He probably never even noticed the weight he gained. You know what set me off now, Beanie?"

Beanie had a mouthful of muffin, so she shook her head and waited.

"I had to go out of town to help my sister out after her surgery, and I went and bought my husband a bunch of frozen dinners, 'cause Lord knows the man hasn't cooked a whole meal in his life. I set them all up in the freezer, showed him how to heat them up in the microwave, and even cooked a few meals to leave in the refrigerator so he wouldn't starve while I was gone."

"That was awful sweet of you. I'm sure he appreciated it." Beanie was grasping at straws now. What do you say to a woman who is venting her heart out?

"That man appreciates nothing," Nell said, her eyes growing instantly shiny with unspilled tears. "I asked him what he wanted for supper last night and you know what he said? He said he'd have one of those frozen dinners, 'cause they were delicious."

Beanie looked a bit like a deer in headlights. She couldn't for the life of her figure out a reasonable response, so she said, "Awww, I'm sure he—"

Nell plowed on, almost wailing, "I've spent more than thirty years cooking gourmet meals for a man who thinks frozen dinners are delicious! It's the last straw, Beanie. The very last straw. I need a job where I'm appreciated. Can I come work for you?"

"Well, we could sure use the help, Miss Nell, and Lord knows we'd appreciate your skills, but you're our only competition in town. How's that gonna work?"

Nell waved the notion away. "Pfff, there's not a cake I make you can't find a recipe for on a half-dozen websites with one search. What makes my cakes good is butter, and lots of it. I don't skimp on anything and I don't care how many calories are in it, long as it tastes good. I'll make 'em for you to sell and be happy with fifteen dollars an hour. I've been making $40 to $50 per cake for years now, and that's without extra decoration. And I promise I won't make any on the side, long as I'm working for you."

"Sold." Beanie knew a good deal when she saw one.

***

Later that evening, Beanie and Will discussed Nell's visit after a supper Will cooked for just the two of them.

"I felt so bad for her, Will. What could I do? I told her of course she could come work for us."

"Oh, I agree," Will said, stacking their used plates and utensils in the center of the table. "I'm a little worried about $15 an hour, but that's because we're just starting out."

"Well, it's not full-time, and we'll make it up in the business she brings with her. Honestly, Will, I think she just wants to get out of that house. I don't really expect her to stay forever, but I couldn't tell her no. I just couldn't."

"You did the right thing." Will said. "Truth is, I'm betting we can both learn a thing or two from her."

Will was right, of course. But it was more than baking Beanie would learn.

26 - Special Delivery

The Big Pig Barbecue was officially closed and Suvi spent half his time on the road to Gainesville every day. It didn't leave him much time for campaigning, but he wasn't too worried. Given the choices, if he couldn't win the election based on his own reputation, he figured he didn't need the job anyway. Truth be known, the more time he spent away from Mayhew Junction, the more he remembered how much he liked it. Being away, that is. He was starting to feel like his old self again. He'd even started working out on a regular basis, something he hadn't done for years. He stayed close to home on the weekends, though, and managed a game or two a week with Gabe. Their friendship had become easy, familiar, and they spoke every day by phone and ate dinner together at least once a week. They were seen together so often, tongues were wagging in town, but neither of them noticed.

Dottie started carrying a line of sporty bathing suits, and shoes designed for the water. Given that it was the only clothing store in town, her business picked up exponentially with the increase in traffic at the Château. Mayhew Junction typically fell into lethargy in the heat of the summer, but this year seemed different. Even LouWanda Crump's business was better.

Of course, she used this to her complete advantage, decorating the entire store with campaign signs and patriotic trinkets. LouWanda was consumed with the details of the Founders' Day festivities, volunteering to serve on any committee that would take her, including the one appointed to hire musicians for the event.

Her first choice was the youth band from her church, reasoning that Christian music was always appreciated in town. And it was. And with any luck, the youth would rise to the occasion. Her second choice was a volunteer from the round table. Eustace Falwell piped up and said he'd be happy to host a karaoke tent with his new three-hundred-dollar state of the art karaoke machine from Costco. Done and done, LouWanda thought. The more the merrier. She made sure his tent assignment was by the courthouse, so she'd have a microphone to introduce the new memorial statue and monument, which was set to be installed in a place of prominence in front of the flagpole after the Founders' Day parade.

The *Mayhew Junction: Then and Now* book had already been sent to the printer, though LouWanda had been, for all practical purposes, barred from participation in the final entries. Diane Kerner and Corinne Barr had announced they would form a committee to finish compiling the information and perform the required formatting. LouWanda was taking preorders for the book at her shop, but so far only three people had signed up.

School was set to start in mid-August, which meant September was just around the corner. Founders' Day was always held the first weekend in October, so LouWanda felt a keen sense of urgency to be prepared sooner rather than later. On August 4th, she got a call from Rooster saying everything was ready to be picked up, or delivered for an extra $200, if she'd rather. As much as she wanted to see the monument, she decided it would be better to have them deliver it the day of the event, just in case someone still had their panties in a wad over it all.

"That's fine and dandy, Miss LouWanda," Rooster said. "And for an extry hun'erd, I can bring a Confederate Color Guard and do a little ceremony for ya'. We got a little group called the Sons of the Confederacy over here and we all the time doin' re-enactments and such. It'll be great."

"Perfect," LouWanda said. "I'll call ya tomorrow and work out the details."

LouWanda hung up the phone feeling exceedingly proud and anticipating a glorious celebration for the entire town.

27 - *Be Careful What You Ask For*

In early September, a reporter from the *Tallahassee Times* showed up in town and started asking questions. As luck would have it, she stopped at the café for breakfast first.

Marley Ann Maxwell was still in FSU's journalism program and was interning with the newspaper during her junior year of college. In her backpack was a laptop computer, two recording devices, and one extra camera lens. The camera itself she kept on a strap hanging off her shoulder.

Eustace Falwell was the first to strike up a conversation.

"Whoo-wee! That's some fancy equipment you got there."

Marley looked up from the menu she was studying, flipped a long strand of dark curls over her shoulder and gave the interloper a half-smile. She followed his gaze to the Nikon D5 she'd placed on the table in front of her. "I guess you could call it that."

"Mind if I take a look?" he asked, his hand already reaching for the camera.

Marley moved faster, clasping the strange man's hand in her own. "Nice to meet you. I'm Marley." She gave his hand one last firm squeeze and pushed it away from the table. "And you are?"

"Oh…oh yeah, right," Eustace snickered. "I forgot my manners. I'm Eustace. We don't get many strangers comin' in this early in the mornin'—'specially not pretty ones with fancy cameras. What brings ya' here?"

Marley pulled the camera to her right, tucking it in beside the napkin holder. "Oh, I'm just trying to grab a quick breakfast before I get to work."

If she thought Eustace Falwell would take the hint, she was sorely mistaken.

"You workin' somewhere 'round here, or you just passin' through?"

"Neither. I'm in town for the day."

"Oh yeah? Who you workin' for? You doin' a photo shoot or somethin'?"

142

"Working on a story, actually. For the *Tallahassee Times*."
Marley caught Sissy's eye and wiggled the menu in her direction.
Sissy made a beeline for the table. She knew a distress signal when
she saw one.

"Okay, Useless, time to head back to your own table. I think
this lady wants some breakfast." Sissy angled her body between
Eustace and the table and flipped open her order book. "What can I
getcha today? Want some coffee? I just brewed a fresh pot."

Eustace shuffled back to the round table muttering to himself.
Marley breathed a sigh of relief and gave Sissy a grateful smile.
"You are officially my hero. Coffee sounds great. With cream,
please."

"Sorry it took so long. You hungry?"

"Could I get an egg white omelet with spinach and cheese? I
know it's not on the menu, but..."

"No problem. If they ain't got spinach back there, I'll run across
to the Dollar Mart and grab some."

Marley's eyes widened. "Oh, please don't go to any trouble...if
you don't have spinach, they can make it a western omelet and
that'll be fine. Just no yolks, if that's okay."

"Ain't no trouble, really. We prob'ly got some spinach in the
freezer." Sissy flipped her book closed, then brought it up beside
her mouth and lowered her voice, "And don't pay no mind to
Useless. He's just nosy. He don't mean no harm."

"Thank you," Marley said. "You never know about some guys.
I've learned to be careful."

"I'll be right back with your coffee. If you need anything else,
I'm Sissy. Just holler for me. Everybody else does."

Marley watched Sissy make her way back across the room,
barely stopping to swipe a tip off a table and scoop up the dirty
dishes before heading back toward the kitchen.

Moments later Marley watched Sissy dash across the street,
enter the Dollar Mart, and come back swinging a plastic bag from
the crook of her elbow. The entire transaction took less than three
minutes. Her food was out in another ten, and Marley counted
herself lucky the service was so fast. She did, indeed, have work to
do and she wasn't sure where she should start.

Had she known the very source of her story sat four tables over, she might have stayed a while. Lacking that information, Marley decided to stop in at The Château first.

***

Will Thaxton greeted Marley warmly at the door and invited her into the kitchen where Beanie was filling a batch of cream puffs and waiting for cupcakes to cool so she could frost them. Marley refused the cup of coffee Beanie offered and pulled a bottle of water from the side of her backpack.

"How 'bout one of these cream puffs?" Beanie held out a gloved hand with a golden pastry sitting flat on her palm. "They're good'n fresh."

"Looks delicious," Marley said, "but I'll have to pass."

"Cupcake?"

"No, thank you. I had breakfast at the Mayhew Café."

"I'll take a cream puff, Bean." Will said, not because he was hungry, but because he thought Beanie's feelings might be hurt.

Will took his usual seat at the end of the table. Sugar, who generally followed Will from room to room throughout the day, settled into her red doggie bed beside his chair.

"Thank you for agreeing to talk with me this morning." Marley placed a small digital recorder on the table and pushed the "on" button. "Do I have your permission to tape this conversation?"

"Fine with me, how about you, Bean?"

"Don't matter none to me. I'm gonna be bakin' anyways." Beanie picked up the pan of filled cream puffs and slid it into the baking rack with a little more force than necessary.

Will winced. "Why don't you sit down and talk with us for a minute, Bean? I'll help you frost those cupcakes when we're done."

"Suits me." Beanie peeled off her plastic gloves, rinsed her hands under the faucet and dried them on the towel she wore on her shoulder. She took a seat at the table, next to Will and across from their guest.

"Ready to begin?" Marley opened a ring-bound folder and picked up her pen.

144

"Um, sure, but…" Will hesitated, still forming the question in his mind.

"Is there a problem?"

"I hope not. I was just wondering what this was all about. You weren't really specific when we set up the appointment, so I've been curious… you know… why us?"

"Oh, of course. Well, it's basically a human-interest story about the history of the town. We got an anonymous lead about the Historical Society and I suppose my editor thought it was an interesting line to pursue, so—here I am." Marley laughed like the joke was on her, then added soberly, "I'm an intern."

Marley first asked about the history of The Château and Will provided the details he knew, including moving the building from its old site when the new courthouse was built. Will didn't mention the photographs he had. Why borrow trouble?

She was interested in Will himself and how he came to own The Château, which Will was uncomfortable discussing, truth be told. He preferred to keep his private life private. But then he thought about how Marie would have handled an interview like this—she'd have been in her element, holding back nothing at all. So, to honor her memory, Will told the difficult story of losing his wife to cancer, and how he was carrying on with the dream she had for the Bed and Breakfast she'd always wanted to own.

Of course, that led to the awkward question of his relationship with Beanie.

"Oh, we're partners, is all," Beanie chimed in when Will struggled for the right words.

"Partners like *partners*? Or just business partners."

"Business," Will said a little too quickly.

Silence hovered over the kitchen long enough to make the oven timer sound like a car horn and all three of them flinched. Beanie got up to take two dozen Morning Glory muffins from the oven, then started a batch of butter cream frosting for the cupcakes.

Will took a sip of cold coffee, then reached down to stroke his sleeping puppy's head. In typical Chihuahua fashion, Sugar growled at the intrusion, but offered her belly with a sheepish glance when she realized her mistake.

"So," Marley was the first to speak, "I've been told you have some knowledge about the Dellwood Connolly murder back when

The Château was being moved. You've found pictures or something?"

If Will was tentative before, he was downright suspicious now.

"I knew there was more to this than you were saying," he began.

Marley's eyebrows went straight up.

"I…is this okay? I didn't mean to catch you off guard."

The whir of the Kitchen Aid mixer made Will raise his voice almost to a shout.

"It would have been helpful if you'd told me from the start you were interested in the pictures."

Marley considered her words for a moment before deciding honesty would be the best course of action. "Would you have spoken with me if I had?"

"Probably not, and I don't appreciate being misled."

"With all due respect, Mr. Thaxton, I told you the truth. It's a human-interest story about the history of the town."

"Tough time to be telling stories like this, don't you think?"

"All the more reason to tell it," Marley countered.

"And you're just an intern?"

"I graduate next year."

"Looks like you're off to a good start then," Will said. "But I'm not ready to go public with the photos. You can get copies of them when I turn them over to the archives at Florida A & M."

"May I see them now, though? I'll turn my camera off."

Will stood reluctantly, exited the kitchen and returned a few moments later with a stack of photos, which he slid onto the table in front of the journalist.

"Once they are at the archives, I won't have any say over what happens to them, but I'm not willing to make decisions about their use now. I don't want that on my conscience. You can see this set, which includes one photo of Dell Connolly, but you'll have to wait until they are made public to see the rest."

"Fair enough," Marley said, thumbing through the photos. "But I will be writing about them. Is that o—oh, gosh. That's awful."

"Exactly." Will poured himself another cup of coffee. "So, I don't think I can stop you from writing about them. Clearly you knew they existed before you came here."

"I'm just doing my job, Mr. Thaxton. It's nothing personal. It would be helpful to have your consent."

"I would prefer you leave me out of it," Will said. "I have a meeting in five minutes, so I'm going to go ahead and say goodbye now, Miss Maxwell. I appreciate your interest in The Château and wish you the best."

After Will retrieved the photograph and took his leave, Marley turned to Beanie, who was ladling butter cream into a piping bag with a spatula.

"I didn't mean to upset him."

"Who, Will? Oh, don't worry about that. He don't like talkin' about those pictures, that's all."

"Do you have any suggestions for who I might speak with next?"

"I dunno," Beanie twisted the end of the bag and squeezed a perfect mound of frosting onto a double chocolate cupcake. "I reckon you might oughta talk with somebody at the Historical Society. LouWanda Crump is somehow related to the man on the horse, and Corinne Barr is, too. I don't know how to get a'holt of Miss Corinne, but Miss LouWanda is over at her shop by now if you wanna run by there on your way outta town."

"Perfect." Marley shut down the recorder and packed up her bag to leave.

"You sure you don't wanna try one of our cupcakes?" Beanie tried one last time.

Marley prided herself on her intuition as a journalist. "I'm still not hungry, but I'll take one for the road, if you don't mind."

Beanie Bradsher had no idea how beautiful she was when she smiled, but Marley noticed. She pulled her camera off her shoulder and snapped a picture of her, beaming as she held a freshly frosted cupcake out toward her guest. And that was the picture that ran on the front page of the *Tallahassee Times* Life section. It was an ironic photo for the story Marley told, and one that would bring its own set of problems to town.

Sissy Coleman

Sometimes I wish I could change my name. It's all I hear, all day long. Sissy, order up! Sissy, more coffee. Sissy, my eggs ain't right. Sissy, you got change for a dollar?

My name ain't really Sissy, but Lord, if I had to hear Bernelle all day, I'd rip my hair out. Who names a baby Bernelle? You'd think my daddy's name was Bernie or somethin', but Mama says no. She won't tell me what it is, though, only what it ain't. I never met my daddy no-ways.

I decided two things a long time ago. One: Mama don't know who he is, or just ain't real sure. Two: I don't need to know who he is either. Any man who don't claim his kid ain't worth knowin' to begin with. There's also two things I don't need, a man or a baby. I get along fine without either of 'em.

I still live with my mama. I mean, I still live in her house and take care of her dogs and her chickens when she ain't there, which is most of the time. That's the difference between me and her—I don't care to be with a man, and she don't care to be without one. Or two. Mama gets around, I'm just sayin'.

I been workin' two jobs since I can remember. Mornin's at the café and house-cleanin' in the afternoons. I clean for Randy Kerner's wife Miss Diane, and Miss JoDeen Avery, and Miss Eleanor Moses twice a week. She's got a big ol' house and more money than God. I do Suvi Jones's house once a month—he don't mess much up—and I stop by and do laundry for Miss Hazel Pruitt every now and then, but I don't let her pay me. She's had more'n her share of struggles and she don't have a pot to pee in. She makes me peanut butter cookies, which I can't eat, and peach jam, which I can. Course, I gotta pick the peaches off her tree and haul 'em inside first. Miss Hazel's been down in her back for years now, but she gets around pretty good for bein' close to a hundred.

Anyways, I get by okay. I'm used to workin' hard and fast. Git 'er done...that's my motto. I'm all the time thinkin' I'm gonna up and quit waitressin', but I just don't know what Edwina'd do without me. I've tried to quit, but these people run all the new girls off with their "get me this" and "bring me that" and hardly tippin' at all. Every now and then we get people passin' through who tip pretty good, and Sundays are okay since I stay through the lunch hour. But Lord, they run me ragged, I gotta tell ya'.

I don't know if I can make it through another election season. Lord at the drama. Miss LouWanda runnin' against Suvi Jones, and now some reporter shows up in town? They's somethin' bad fixin' to happen, I can feel it in my bones.

28 - Twin Troubles

Sweet should have known letting the twins bring extra friends to the beach was a bad idea. Teens naturally come with a heavy dose of drama, but twin teens are double trouble, especially where summer romance is involved.

After the beach trip, T-Ray had three issues to deal with: a scorned ex-girlfriend, an irate sister, and a new girlfriend who was way too good for the likes of *himself*. But B-Kay didn't have a whole lot of room for talk. Truth was, she'd fallen for her brother's friend Dylan. How she justified being angry at T-Ray for taking up with Luciana, Sweet would never know, but she was determined to stay out of the fray.

Thank God for cell phones was all she could think. Back in *her* day, all the drama would have taken place over the family phone. She remembered her own parents grousing about the number of times Bubba John called. She would rip the phone out of the wall if she had to put up with that nonsense.

When they first got phones, Sweet made the twins turn them in at 9 p.m. But after the beach trip, the house phone started ringing at all hours, so Sweet extended the time to midnight. She promised the twins if one of their friends called the house after that time, they'd both lose their phones for a week, no matter whose fault it was. Thus peace, of sorts, was restored to their household. The rest of the summer rolled by slow and heavy, like the humidity that hung in the air around them.

Bubba John spent the summer alternately studying for his general contractor's license and building a pool house to go with the large above-ground pool they'd had installed in early March. The farmhouse had been set back far enough from the river that it always stayed high and dry, but Bubba John had the pool house designed to be built on pylons one story up, just in case. This would create a nice shady spot underneath for an outdoor living space and protect the inside from flood damage if the river ever rose that high. Before summer was over, the Atwater kids were two shades darker and the foot traffic in and out had worn Sweet to a frazzle. She didn't mind. She'd rather have a house full of kids than to wonder where her own were and what they were up to.

With Bitty, Sweet broached the subject of the new school year more cheerfully than she felt.

"Are you excited for school to start next week, Bitty-boo?"

Bitty looked up from the book she was reading. She'd discovered *Junie B. Jones* and *The Magic Tree House* and was flying through them as fast as Sweet could get them from the library.

"I'm going back to school?"

"Yes ma'am, next Monday." Sweet forced a smile.

"Whew!" Bitty flipped the book page-down over her leg.

Sweet froze and looked at her daughter sideways. "You happy about that?"

Bitty nodded. "Oh, yeah, Mama. I think I'm gettin' dumber without school."

"Well, I don't think that's possible, but I'm glad you're excited. We're going to meet your new teacher in the morning. Mrs. McMinn thinks you'll like her. She said she chose her especially for you! Isn't that cool?"

Bitty's eyes narrowed and she said nothing.

She's on to me, Sweet thought. And it *was* a bit of a stretch. Bitty picked up her book again, leaving Sweet standing at the kitchen counter reflecting on her meeting with Delia McMinn.

***

What Delia had said when they met the week before was that Bitty was an extra consideration when they'd hired the new teacher over the summer. She was new to the area, moving south from Maryland when her husband took a job overseeing the state prison housed in the county.

"She's far more qualified than we can afford," Delia had said. "She has a Master's in Early Childhood Development, with emphasis in children with sensory processing issues and autism. She doesn't want to work in that field but wanted to be well-rounded as a teacher."

Sweet had not been prepared for the A-word to be thrown out so casually.

"Bitty's *not* autistic."

Delia's eyes got wide, but she walked back her own reaction and spoke carefully.

"I didn't mean to imply anything, Mrs. Atwater. I meant to say we were excited to get a teacher of this caliber, and we think Bitty will do well in her classroom. And that will give us time to start the testing."

"I don't think we want to do that testing right now."

"Okay," Delia used the most reassuring tone she could muster. "I guess I'm a little confused. I thought we were on a different track."

"I'm sorry," Sweet dropped her head and stared at the floor. "I just… My husband and I decided we don't want any labels put on Bitty right now and I'm a little sensitive about it, I think. We'd rather give it some time before saddling her with a diagnosis that follows her all her life."

"I have to be honest, Sweet," Delia reverted to the familiar first name despite her training, "I'm inclined to agree with you on one hand, but I want to make sure you've really thought this out."

"I just want to give Bitty some time, that's all."

"I support you on that. One hundred percent. My hesitation is that testing would identify any eligibilities for exceptional student programs, including classes for gifted students, for which I'm almost certain Bitty would qualify. Of course, they would identify any other issues as well."

"Such as?" Sweet frowned.

"Well, you know, if she's on the spectrum at all. The designation would make her eligible for programs that could help."

"And the school would get funding to cover those costs, right?"

"Yes," Delia acknowledged with a firm nod, "we would."

"I don't mean to sound ungrateful, but my decision will not be based on what's good for the school. It's my daughter I'm looking out for."

"Of course you are, Sweet. And I'm looking out for both."

"I don't— We're not ready for testing yet. I'm sorry."

Delia McMinn closed the manila folder she'd had open on the table and reached out to cover her friend's hand with her own.

"Then we won't test yet. It's your call. In the meantime, when the new teacher arrives, we'll see if she has any recommendations you might implement through outside sources. I know you have the means. I mean, I know about the lotto thing…so you may be able to avoid the stigma of an educational label, if that's your main concern."

They had ended their meeting shortly afterwards, but the comment stuck in her mind, plucked away at her conscience. How many parents had the options she had now? She felt grateful and unworthy at the same time.

***

The back door slammed, shaking Sweet from her thoughts.

"I'm tellin' Mama," B-Kay stormed through the living room with Daisy on her hip and her twin on her heels.

"Go ahead, ya big baby," T-Ray's voice boomed. "I'm callin' it like it is. She's a bitch and she needs to leave me alone."

"Whoa, whoa, whoa," Sweet said. "Language, please. Your sisters are right here."

"They've heard worse," T-Ray headed straight for the refrigerator. "Probably from *you.*"

Sweet caught her son by the arm and spun him to face her. "Hey! No, sir!"

T-Ray gave his mother the withering look to which she'd become accustomed but said nothing.

"What is the matter with you?"

"I'm pissed, that's what."

"I get that," Sweet said. "But you still don't get to speak to me that way…"

"Whatever," T-Ray pulled his arm from his mother's grasp and wrenched the refrigerator door open.

"B, could you please take the girls back to your room for a few minutes?"

"Anything to avoid the blithering ass-hat," B-Kay flipped her head in her brother's direction.

"Could y'all stop with the name-calling, please?"

"It's okay, Mama, I'm going." Bitty stood and, with her book still open in front of her face, headed off down the hallway. B-Kay and Daisy followed.

"Now," Sweet turned to face her son, who stood in the door of the refrigerator drinking orange juice from the carton. "Oh, my Lord, T, really? Give me that."

T-Ray popped the center of the spout closed, tossed his mother the now-empty carton, and shut the refrigerator door with his foot. "It was almost gone. Besides, I saved you from washing another glass. You're welcome."

That was it. Sweet could take a little raging, the occasional potty-mouth, a few stink-faced looks, but this was a line no child of hers was going to cross. She slammed the empty orange juice container onto the center island and moved toward her son.

"What did you say to me?"

T-Ray's eyes got wide and he flattened his back against the narrow freezer door. Something about her tone was different.

"God, Mom, it was just a...ow!"

"Let me tell you something, Mister," Sweet had the bottom half of her son's face in one hand, her fingers and thumb pressing so hard his lips splayed outwards as she pushed his head back against the stainless steel door.

"Ow, ow, ow...shtop!"

"No, *you* stop." Sweet said, pressing harder. "Don't you ever—*ever*—say anything like that to me, or to any other woman for that matter. Do you hear me?"

"Yesh," T-Ray's eyes filled with tears, but he didn't move.

"Yes, what?"

"Yesh, ma'am," he grunted.

She let go of his face with one last squeeze and backed up. T-Ray wiped at his eyes and rubbed at the red spots on both cheeks.

"Jeez, Mom, that hurt."

"I meant for it to. Sit down."

"You bruised me."

"I'll do worse than that if you don't change your attitude. I am not your personal maid, and I am not going to be taken for granted. And I am, *by God*, not going to be spoken to that way, not by anyone, let alone a son who has far more advantages than he has earned. Now, sit down and tell me what this is all about."

T-Ray did as he was told, pulling a stool up to the other side of the island out of his mother's reach. He sat silent, still rubbing at his cheeks and fighting back tears.

"First of all, Luciana's mad at me 'cause of something Hannah said. But it's a lie, and Hannah's telling everyone. She's such a bitch. I don't know why I *ever* liked her."

"What's the lie?"

"It's too embarrassing, Mom. And besides, she made it up. I mean, like out of the blue. Who does that?"

"You know what? I can't answer that. Maybe she's just mad. Maybe she has *reason* to be mad, I don't know. What I know is, I'm raising you to be a gentleman— Right, roll your eyes all you want. I am. And it doesn't matter what she says or does. You are going to take the high road."

"What does *that* mean?"

"It means you say nothing. Don't talk about her. Don't call her names. Two wrongs don't make a right. And, by the way, you committed the first wrong and you know it. You were still dating her when you started flirting with Luciana. So, let it go. She's mad. It'll blow over. Don't make it worse."

"Mom, she's got everybody believin' there's something wrong with me. And besides, she's never even seen my...you know...she's never seen...I swear Mom, never."

"Your penis? She's talking about your penis?"

"Yes! And now everyone thinks..."

"Okay, stop. Stop right there. It doesn't matter what anyone thinks, T. You know the truth."

T-Ray dropped his head onto the island countertop and groaned. "I'll never live it down. My life is ruined."

"Your life is not ruined, Son, but listen. Look at me."

T-Ray lifted his head and looked mournfully at his mother. "What?"

Sweet bit her bottom lip and fought to keep a straight face. "You have to promise me you won't start showing it to everyone to prove her wrong."

T-Ray grinned. "I already offered to show Luciana. She respectfully declined."

"Best news I've heard all day."

Sweet rounded the side of the island, reached out and brushed T-Ray's hair from his forehead. "You okay?"

T-Ray nodded and rubbed the cheek where his mother's thumb had squeezed the hardest.

"Still hurting?" Sweet asked.

"You squeezed hard." T-Ray's voice had just enough of a catch in it to break a mama's heart.

"Want me to kiss it better?"

She meant to make him laugh, to ease the tension. But T-Ray lifted his chin and offered his throbbing cheek to be kissed.

"Awww...baby, I'm sorry." Sweet gave him three quick smacks and wrapped him in her arms. She hugged him to her chest, kissed the top of his head, then took his face in both hands and pushed him back to look directly into his eyes. "But if you ever sass me like that again, I'll make ya' bleed."

"I thought you already did. You got, like, Popeye-hands or somethin'."

They were still laughing when Bubba John came through the back door with Tate in his arms.

"I found this little guy sound asleep in the pool house. Did y'all forget he was out there?"

"Naw, Dad, we left him playing video games. He didn't want to come in."

"What were you doing in the pool house?" Sweet asked Bubba John.

"Oh, I took some firewood out there and a little surprise for the kids."

"What'd you get, Dad?" T-Ray forgot all about the stinging cheek.

"Go see for yourself," Bubba John said. "I gotta put this one down."

T-Ray was out the door before his father finished speaking.

"Put him in bed, not on my couch with those nasty clothes still on." Sweet scratched the back of her head and looked around her beautiful new kitchen. "I have got to figure out what to cook for dinner here."

Bubba John was back in a few minutes. He washed his hands in the sink and reached for his wife, who was leaning into the refrigerator hoping something would jump out at her. He pulled her back into his chest and wrapped both arms around her midsection. She relaxed into him and cupped her hands over both of his, sighing loudly.

"Rough day?" Bubba John asked.

She shook her head, rolling it back and forth across his chest. "Not really. Rough couple of minutes is all. You missed the fireworks. Thought I was gonna have to kill your boy."

"T?"

"That's the one."

"What'd he do now?"

"I'll tell ya' while we cook. I think I have some hamburger patties in the freezer."

Bubba John headed for the freezer as T-Ray bounded through the door hollering for B-Kay.

"What'd you get them? Two seconds ago, he wasn't speaking to his sister," Sweet said.

"Aw, just some new chairs they wanted for playing video games. I got a few bean bag chairs while I was at it."

"Please tell me you got vinyl." Sweet wrinkled her nose at the idea of wet bodies on cloth chairs.

"Aw, crap," Bubba John said. "Denim. Is that bad? They said they're washable."

Sweet scoffed. "Yeah, once you remove the beans."

"Shoot, I thought I was doing good. They can move them wherever they want without scratching up the floor."

Sweet took his face in both of her hands and kissed him squarely on the mouth. "You did great, baby. I'm being a spoil-sport. Denim is great. More comfortable anyway."

Seconds later T-Ray came back down the hallway dragging his sister by the arm. "You gotta see these things, B. They got cup holders and everything."

Sweet shot her husband an incredulous look. "Bean bag chairs with cup holders?"

"No, no, no...I got gaming chairs, too. You'll have to see for yourself. Too hard to describe."

"I'll take your word for it. I gotta get these burgers going."

Thirty minutes later, the clan was assembled at the long pine table Sweet loved. Tate managed to eat two burgers despite being groggy from his nap. The twins were back on speaking terms and Bitty managed to eat most of her french fries without sorting them by size. Sweet couldn't help but smile. Maybe everything would be fine after all.

29 - *Heading for a Fall*

September was a flurry of activity preparing for the Founders' Day Parade. Will and Beanie decided to have a parade entry to advertise the new bakery. It was Beanie's idea to push a rolling cart full of bakery treats. While Will pushed, Beanie would throw handmade caramels and fudge, wrapped individually of course, into the crowd. Each had a tag with the name and logo of La Pâtisserie, and random tags had an additional coupon for a free pastry, which could be claimed at any time, even during the parade. Nell Wiggins volunteered to watch the bakery during the parade, saying she'd seen enough sequined toddlers shaking hips and waving batons to last a lifetime. Beanie couldn't imagine what Nell had against sequins but appreciated the help nonetheless.

Will found the entire plan brilliant. Well, everything but the cake hats Beanie made and was determined they'd all wear. Will had no idea how she did it. She managed to flatten the brims of some old hats and built cakes that looked almost edible using fabric and stuffing and a variety of silk petals.

Will convinced her they'd be able to wheel an entire cake down the parade route. Not enough to feed the whole town, but big enough to make a statement. There were festivities after the parade, and B-Kay could sell slices of the cake from the cart outside of The Château once the parade was over.

Will made the oversized cart out of reclaimed wood and a pair of wagon wheels he found at the flea market. Beanie liked that Will was so handy. She drew out a rough idea for a cart and he made it happen in a matter of a week. They were becoming quite the team, both of them thought and neither mentioned.

***

Suvi Jones had six signs made for his campaign. Each four feet tall and six feet wide. He placed them in protected spaces around his district so they would be well-seen, but not obnoxious like the rows of yard signs with which LouWanda Crump and several other candidates littered the county. He took out one quarter-page ad in the weekly newspaper and got himself invited to Rotary and

Woman's Club meetings and several men's breakfasts at churches in his district, and that was the extent of his campaigning. He spoke plainly and openly about the things he'd like to see happen in the downtown area and surrounding neighborhood. He opted not to speak of his opponent at all, figuring she could dig her own grave or build her own castle, whichever the case may be. His strategy was *no* strategy—just be who he was and say what he thought. If that didn't work, nothing would, to his way of thinking.

LouWanda Crump, on the other hand, made a spectacle at every opportunity, including surrounding all six of her opponent's signs with at least ten of her own. She plastered everything she could with bumper stickers and signs and often sat outside her shop with a MAGA hat and a hand-lettered sign reading HONK IF YOU LOVE JESUS – VOTE CRUMP IF YOU LOVE YOU'RE COUNTY. Unfortunately, no one who caught the grammatical error had the intestinal fortitude to point it out.

That is, until Dottie got sick of the blaring horns of passing trucks and hot-footed it across Main Street to confront her friend.

"For crying out loud, LouWanda, could you manage a tiny sense of dignity here and stop this? Nobody wants to hear horns honking all day."

"Hmmph," LouWanda snorted. "They don't seem to mind it in New York City."

"Well this is *not* New York City and I mind very much. I just spilled coffee on a whole stack of t-shirts."

"Well, what were ya' doin' drinkin' coffee over top a' the merchandise?"

"I wasn't! That last horn startled me so bad I threw my whole cup in the air."

"Lord, Dorothy, I don't believe I'd admit to bein' that twitchy."

"I'm not twitchy. I'm tired. Tired of horns going off, and tired of looking over here at a freaking circus sideshow. Can't you give it a rest?"

LouWanda heaved a sigh and sat down in the plastic chair she always left by the door to her shop.

"Sure, I can give it a rest," she said, chortling at her own joke.

"Not funny, LouWanda. Put the damn sign down."

"You don't have to curse at me—"

Whatever she said next was drowned out by the blast of another car horn, during which Dottie seized the opportunity to wrench the offending sign out of LouWanda's hand. At this point, Dottie looked at the sign.

"Oh, for God's sake," she muttered, shaking her head.

"What?"

"You can't even spell right."

"What?" LouWanda repeated. "What'd I get wrong?"

"You know what that says? That says *Vote Crump if you love YOU ARE county.*"

"Why, Dorothy, you have gone off your rocker. I'm lookin' right at it and it clearly says you're county."

"Right... you're. Y-O-U apostrophe R-E. The contraction for *you are*. The correct way to spell *your*, as in *belonging to you*, is Y-O-U-R. No apostrophe. No E."

"Well, thanks for the spelling lesson, Dorothy. Can we get back to minding our own business here? I got work to do."

"So do I, and that is my whole point. I have work to do and you are interrupting it by encouraging people to honk, and I will thank you to stop it right now."

"Well, don't bother thankin' me, 'cause I ain't stoppin' and you can't make me."

Dottie gritted her teeth and pursed her lips tight to avoid saying what came to mind. Instead, she took a deep breath, let it out and smiled. Then she ripped the cardboard from the pole to which it was stapled and tore the sign in half. Without saying another word, she dropped the pole at LouWanda's feet and marched back across the street to her own shop. Just before opening the door, she turned back to face her friend and ripped the sign into several more pieces, letting them float from her hands in the cool September breeze.

"I ain't pickin' that up!" LouWanda screeched from across the street. "Litterbug!"

Dottie just waved and went inside the store, kicking the door shut with a satisfying slam. When she looked out the window ten minutes later, LouWanda was nowhere to be seen.

"Thank you, sweet baby Jesus," Dottie muttered under her breath, then went back to setting up her new inventory.

30 - What Wicked Wind Blows?

The article in the *Tallahassee Times* appeared a week before the Founder's Day celebration and went viral on social media within twenty-four hours. Of course, it took a few more days for the folks in Mayhew Junction to catch wind of the uproar.

Randy Kerner was the first to bring it up at the Mayhew Café's round table. He didn't bother with diplomacy, nor even try to lower his voice when he accosted the source of his immense displeasure.

"LouWanda Crump, I swear…you have crossed the line for the last time. What the hell were you thinking, blabbing to a *reporter*, for God's sake?"

LouWanda was not surprised. She'd read the article on Monday when her neighbor dropped off his copy of the *Tallahassee Times* from the day before, as he'd done every single day for the past ten years.

"I don't know what you're talking about, Randall," LouWanda lied. "And don't take the Lord's name with me, either."

"I'm talking about the article in the Times, that's what. I know darn good and well you read it."

"I'm not having a conversation with you if you're gonna curse at me."

"LouWanda," Randy roared, "I'm telling you right now, if you have gotten this county national attention for all the wrong reasons, I swear…"

"You swear what? And what national attention? All's I did was get us some publicity for the Founders Day parade."

"Then what in God's name is she talking about? We don't have any Confederate monuments at our courthouse."

"Not yet we don't." LouWanda patted her wobbling beehive with both hands.

"You can't just put up a new monument on the courthouse lawn, for crying out loud. That requires a vote from the county commission, and we haven't seen hide nor hair of a plan."

"Well, if you don't like where we put the memorial, you can vote to have it moved. How's that?"

Randy took a deep breath and closed his eyes. He could feel his blood pressure rising—felt the swelling thrum of his arteries pulsing in his ears. "Not good," he growled. "Not good at all."

"I'm not talkin' about this no more, Randall. I'm sick of everyone tryin' to mess with my hard work. If you wanna see the new monument, you be at the courthouse after the parade."

"Oh, I'll be there all right. You can bet on that."

Town Celebrates Southern History
Marley Ann Maxwell, Intern

Mayhew Junction is a tiny town by any standards. Nestled in North Florida's rural farmland, its thousand or so residents make up ten percent of Fletcher County's entire population. It is a town where everyone knows everyone, and everyone recognizes a stranger, which I learned by stopping at the local diner. The welcome offered by townspeople is warm and generous, if a bit wary, and who can blame them when the stranger in town carries a camera and notebook?

After receiving an anonymous tip about a cache of old photographs found in the attic of the local B&B, an historical building that once served as the county courthouse, I made an appointment to visit what is now known as The Château. Current owner Will Thaxton is a transplant from Minnesota, a stranger in a strange land. He is warm, but seems mildly uncomfortable in his surroundings, though it is clear he loves the business he started with his partner – business partner he is quick to clarify - Beatrice Bradsher. Beanie, as she is called, is a self-taught pastry chef with a quirky charm that defies explanation. Both were gracious hosts despite my arriving in the midst of preparations for their newest venture, a bakery called La Pâtisserie.

We sat at the long kitchen table that serves as both a prep station for baked goods, and a gathering place for breakfast guests. Thaxton shared most of the photos, neatly cataloged black and white cabinet prints made in the late 1800s when the old courthouse was moved to make room for the structure that remains today. He was hesitant to produce the photos in question, but eventually agreed to show me one, with the stipulation that I not reproduce it. In the photo, a black man, his clothes bloody and torn, hangs from a noose tied in a tree on the courthouse lawn. Thaxton said these photos will be donated to the Meek Eaton Black Archives in Tallahassee for further identification of parties involved. There is good reason for their interest.

In a report by the Equal Justice Initiative, *Lynching in America, Confronting the Legacy of Racial Terror*, Florida ranks as first in the nation per capita for lynchings between 1877 and 1950. It is a legacy most want to forget, and few teach in history classes within the state. The Mayhew Junction Historical Society, led by local business owner LouWanda Crump, has struggled to resolve the issue surrounding what to include in their *Mayhew Junction: Then and Now* publication, available for purchase beginning on their Founders Day celebration next weekend.

In a conversation after the Thaxton interview, Ms. Crump indicated there had been some disagreements as to what should or should not be published in a book intended to "highlight our founding fathers." She has promised the town will be proud of the dedication of a new town memorial slated for the afternoon of the Founder's Day parade. When asked about the memorial itself, Crump declined to be specific, but offered this cryptic observation. "It bothers me, all this nonsense about Confederate monuments. Why shouldn't we be proud of our ancestors? It's our heritage. Some people just need to get over it, if you ask me."

This reporter will most certainly be in attendance at the Mayhew Junction Founders Day celebration and will publish a follow-up to this story in the coming weeks.

31 - *If I Knew You Were Coming,*
I'd Have Baked a Cake

The phone at The Château had been ringing off the hook since the article came out. At first Will and Beanie were pleasantly surprised. They booked every single room they had for the weekend of the parade and were now keeping a waiting list. It was hard to complain about business, but business itself was getting a little more hectic than they were used to.

Two days before the event, Will was putting the finishing touches on his parade cart while Beanie baked all the layers they would need for the log cabin cake they'd decided to make in honor of Founders Day. As soon as those cooled, they would add the filling, stack the layers and carve the top layers into a roof shape before icing with a crumb coat. Tomorrow, Will would finish the assembly and decorate with chocolate butter cream piped to look like logs.

But the calls, an unfortunate result of Marley Maxwell's article, were more disruption than Beanie could take. After one particularly obnoxious conversation, Beanie made her frustration known to Will when he came in to check on her progress.

"I don't know what's wrong with people, Will. When I tell 'em we ain't got any room for 'em, they act like I oughta know where else they could stay, and they get downright ugly when I cain't help 'em. There ain't but one motel, plus us, in the whole county, which none of 'em seem to believe in the first place." Beanie tucked a stray curl up under the rim of her hat and took another tray of cakes from the oven. "I don't know what's goin' on...we ain't never had this much business for Founder's Day."

"I've been wondering about that myself," Will slid a tray over on the cooling rack to make room for Beanie's tray.

"This last one was a doozy. Says he was looking for a set of rooms for eleven men. Eleven! I was glad to tell 'im we was full up. I get the heebie-jeebies just thinkin' about tryin' to clean up after all that mess. Wanted to know where else to look and I told him to try all the surrounding counties, 'cause he wadn't gonna find nothin' close by. Well, you'da thought I told him to jump in the lake. He got all indignant-like, so I said, 'Look, you ain't gotta take it out on me. I cain't snap my fingers and conjure up a room for ya, let alone five of 'em.' And he said, 'Lady, you don't know who you're messin' with.' And I said, 'You got that right, and I don't wanna know, neither,' and then I hung up on him."

"Something's not right here, Bean. Did he say who they were?"

"I don't know...the national something-or-other, I think."

"I have a bad feeling. All these people coming in from outside the county for a local event? I hope I'm wrong, but I think we are in for some trouble."

Beanie snorted. "Don't be silly. This town wouldn't know trouble if it rang the doorbell and announced itself. Stop bein' such a worry-wart and help me turn these cakes outta the pans."

The pair were well on their way to a solid crumb layer when the phone rang again.

"Just ignore it," Will said. "We don't have time to tell the world we're out of rooms."

But the voice that filled the room when the answering machine picked up was hard to ignore. Will thought it sounded an awful lot like Beanie, except more calculated—hypnotic in a way—like warm syrup laced with cyanide.

"Beanie? Beanie..." The caller's voice sang out. "I saw your picture in the news. Lord, child, I would recognize you anywhere. You are the spittin' image of your ol' mama. Your cousin Vernita gave me your number. Told me you'd won the lotto and opened a new business downtown. I gotta say, I'm surprised you're still there. I couldn't wait to get away from that hell-hole. Bolted the first chance I got. Anyway, I'm comin' down there to see you, soon as I can get somebody to take me down to the Greyhound Bus Station to buy a ticket. I don't have a place to stay yet, but I'm sure you'll have room for me there. You wouldn't turn your mama away, would you? No, of course not. See you soon, Punkin. You remember me calling you Punkin all the time? It was 'cause your head was too big for your little body. Like to've killed me when you were born. I swore I'd never have another baby, and I never did, either. Oh well, there'll be time for reminiscing when I get home, won't there, Punkin? See you soon..."

166

A dial tone droned for a few seconds before the answering machine clicked off and the room went dead silent.

Beanie stood frozen, both arms bent at the elbows, hands in mid-air. Frosting covered her fingertips on one hand and threatened to drip from the icing spatula she held in the other. Wide-eyed, she glanced back and forth from Will to the answering machine in the corner of the room without making a sound.

"Beanie? You okay? What the hell was that?"

Beanie did not respond. Or move. Will pulled the spatula from her hand, took the towel from her shoulder and wiped the frosting off her fingers. He watched her face quiver, lips first, then chin. He removed her hat and set it gently down on the table, then pulled her stiff body to his own and held her there a moment, her elbows pressing into his ribcage.

"It's okay, Beanie. I've got you. It's okay," He patted her awkwardly on the back and kept speaking soft and low until he felt her relax a little. The tears came in a flood then, and she buried her face in the hollow between his collarbone and shoulder and cried. When she seemed to finish, he moved her away for a moment and studied her face. She still did not speak, so he pulled a chair out from the table and sat her down in it.

"Can you talk to me about it, Bean?" Will asked.

She shook her head.

"What can I do? How can I help you?" he tried again.

She shrugged and wiped her face on her sleeve. He pressed the kitchen towel into her hands, and she murmured a thank you and blew her nose into it, which left a smear of frosting across her right cheek. Will wiped it away with his thumb, then simply cradled her face in his hand until she looked up at him and spoke.

"I don't know why I'm bein' such a baby. She left so long ago, I don't even remember what she looked like. All I know is…" Beanie's mouth turned down and her bottom lip poked out as she tried to control her emotions. "She's my mama and I ought to be happy she's comin', but I ain't happy at all. Is that bad?"

Will felt his chest tighten. He took both of her hands in his and leaned forward. Never in his life had he wanted to hold someone so much it physically pained him not to do it.

"Beanie, come here." Will scooted back his chair and pulled her toward him. He guided her onto his lap, crinolines and all, tucked her head onto his shoulder and sat there for a minute. "It's not bad at all. And whatever happens, I am right here. You don't have to do this alone. Okay?"

There was another moment of silence before Beanie settled into Will's arms.

"Okay," she said, and nestled her face into the curve of his neck.

32 - Royal Letdown

Fletcher County was notoriously laid back, which wasn't necessarily a bad thing, but when you had a family of five kids like Bubba John and Sweet Lee Atwater, you looked forward to the rare event like the Founders Day celebration because it offered a full day of activity for all ages. This year, Sweet had to admit that the older the kids got, the more difficult it became to manage the details. Bitty was slated to ride in the school literacy float, which Bubba John had volunteered to help build. He'd gone all out, too, and Sweet was looking forward to seeing the finished product, which Bitty declared "the coolest library ever." The two little ones would stay with Sweet Lee on the sidelines. Tate was gearing up to snag the most candy and trinkets thrown from the float. Inherently oblivious to public scrutiny, Tate snagged an old long-sleeve t-shirt from his daddy's rag pile, tied a knot in the bottom and wrapped the sleeves around his waist. This, he reasoned out loud as he showed his invention to his mama, would leave both hands free to grab candy and shove it through the neck-opening of the shirt. Sweet later remarked to Bubba John, "He's either going to be an engineer or a criminal. We'll have to wait and see."

T-Ray would walk with his baseball team, but as a contender for the Homecoming King, he would need to race back to the end of the lineup as soon as the team reached the Mayhew Café in order to ride at least most of the parade route on the Homecoming float. A golf cart stationed near the bank would handle the five athletes affected.

B-Kay's softball team was also marching, and she'd been invited to run for Homecoming Court, but she was not the slightest bit interested in anything that forced her to wear a tiara.

"Oh, right," T-Ray said when B-Kay made her pronouncement over breakfast one morning. "Like you haven't always been a princess around here."

B-Kay responded with an elbow to her brother's gut. "I got'cher princess right here, dude."

"Oof," T-Ray clutched his stomach, but grinned and yanked a sprig of B-Kay's hair before sidling up to Sweet Lee cooking bacon at the stove. "Hey, Mom, I'ma need a tux for homecoming."

Sweet gave him a side-eye glare. "I got news, son…it's not B who thinks she's royalty."

"Bam!" B-Kay said with a mouth full of cereal.

"Your suit is fine. It's still in the bag from the dry cleaners, hanging in your closet."

"They said it's a requirement this year. I need an actual tux."

"Who said?" Sweet swatted T-Ray's hand away from the pile of bacon he tried to raid.

"The director, Miz What's-her-face. You know."

"I don't know, but I'll call and find out. You have a nice suit that you've only worn once. That should be fine."

"Why are you being like that, Mom? We're rich."

"What do you mean, *we?*" Sweet leaned the business end of her spatula against the edge of a paper towel-covered plate and turned to face her son. "You don't own a thing in this house. Your daddy and I are…well…we have money, yes. Rich? Maybe not. Doesn't matter. If you want a tux, you can pay for it yourself. I'm not willing."

"That's harsh, Mom." T-Ray said, ignoring his sister's pantomimed *sizzle and burn* routine.

"That's reality, Son. Deal with it."

"Fine, I'll wear the suit, but don't expect me to come home with a crown in that thing." T-Ray stalked out of the kitchen and down the hall.

"Who's the princess now?" B-Kay called out to his retreating back.

"That's enough," Sweet Lee picked up her spatula and waved it toward the hallway. "Can you go hustle the little ones up for me? Tell 'em bacon's ready. I'll have the eggs cooked by the time they get to the table."

"Yes, Mama," B-Kay said, chastened but still smirking inside.

170

33 - What History Teaches

Corinne Barr reluctantly agreed to meet LouWanda at the library for some "last-minute research" before the Founders Day ceremony. Driving the few blocks across town, Corinne chastised herself for agreeing to help LouWanda when she knew for certain the event would be disastrous. There was something compelling— she had to admit—about having access to, and thus close scrutiny of, a mind like LouWanda Crump's. Corinne could not bring herself to believe her cousin was evil, despite seeing signs to the contrary, and she was willing to risk being wrong. She had decided to let things just play out so LouWanda could experience the consequences of her actions, no matter what they might be.

For LouWanda, ignorance was indeed bliss, if you didn't count the harassment she experienced from Randall Kerner and her best friend Dorothy Brentwood. She tried to call a truce after the sign incident. She didn't even go back out with the new sign she made, though she seriously considered it when Dottie rebuffed her attempt to make up with a large cup of half-and-half tea. Whatever. Dorothy would come around. She always did.

And if LouWanda were being honest, she owed her friend, though she didn't like to think of it for long. Let dead horses lie, she thought. Or was it dogs? Whichever it was, the dead should stay dead. And some of the living *ought* to be dead, but that was a whole nother story. Alton Crump could be dead or alive, she didn't care. Long as she didn't ever have to look at his face again. She'd like to see her son, though. See, this is why she hated thinking about the past. Sleeping dogs—that was it.

She thought about the last time she saw her boy, asleep in his crib. He was wearing the footie pajamas Dorothy bought him, and he was sucking his thumb. Every now and then he'd flinch a little. Then a shaky smile would spread across his tiny mouth and he'd start sucking again in earnest. Let sleeping babies lie. And never, ever, leave their side.

"LouWanda?"

Corinne had been standing beside her cousin for at least a minute and LouWanda had not noticed *her* any more than she'd noticed the stream of tears spilling down her own cheeks. At the sound of Corinne's voice, LouWanda snapped out of the sad reverie. She swiped at her face with both hands and scowled up at the voice.

"Lord, Coh-rinne, you liked to have scared me to death. You ought not sneak up on people like that."

Corinne stifled a smile. "I did not sneak up on you, Cousin. Why are you crying?"

"I ain't cryin'…"

"Right," Corinne drawled as she dug through her purse. "And I'm not your black cousin."

"You act like that's not in question at all." LouWanda wiped each cheek on her upper arms, then snatched the tissue from Corinne's outstretched hand.

"It's not and you know it. I showed you the DNA. Stop this and tell me what's wrong."

LouWanda sighed. "I don't wanna talk about it right now, okay? But thanks for askin'."

"Is it about Luke?"

LouWanda dropped her head like it was too heavy to stay upright. "Please don't say his name."

"I'm sorry."

"It's okay, it's just… How did you know?"

"About Lu… about your son? LouWanda, I've lived here all my life. Segregation didn't make us deaf, dumb and blind."

"No, I mean, how'd you know that's why I was cryin'?"

Corinne scoffed. "What else could possibly make you cry right here in front of God and everybody?"

"Fine, but I don't wanna…I can't, okay? I can't. That's all."

"Fair enough." Corinne placed her computer bag on the table and sat down. "So, what can I do for you today? Besides help you find your son."

LouWanda froze. She stared at her keyboard and tried to breathe but found that nearly impossible. "What makes you think you can do that?"

"I can try," she said. When the silence went longer than was comfortable, she repeated, "I'm willing to try. Are you?"

An almost imperceptible shake of the head preceded her answer. "I can't."

172

"Okay. I won't ask again, but the offer stands. So, what did you call me here for?"

"I need to know more about our ancestry, more about our great-granddaddy."

"Two greats, you mean?"

"Yeah, whatever."

Corinne flipped her laptop open and clicked it on. "What do you want to know? I may know it off the top of my head. I've done quite a bit of research already."

"Well, I was wonderin' what he was like, for one thing. I've heard all these stories and, you know, some of 'em was good and some was bad, and Randall Kerner seems to think they was all bad and won't shut up about it, and I don't know what to say to 'im."

"Hmmph," Corinne frowned. "You trying to learn the truth, or you just want to shut him up?"

LouWanda flipped her hands up and stretched her shoulders to her ears. "I don't know! I reckon I'm hopin' the truth will do the job. Whatever! But seems to me with all the hist'ry they got on this blasted thing, they ort to have somethin' about him on there. I mean, I gotta get a speech written by this weekend. I don't wanna embarrass myself and get it wrong."

Corinne nearly choked and said under her breath, "Well, there's a first time for everything."

"What was that?" LouWanda scowled.

"Nothing, Cousin. First things first. Something like that. Let's go to my Ancestry© page and I'll show you some documents I have."

"I don't want no fake news, I know that."

Corinne took a deep breath and held it for a moment. She closed her eyes and rubbed her palm over her forehead, stopping to squeeze her eyebrows toward the midline.

"You know, I feel you on that. Especially considering that black children have been subjected to the white version of history for years. All I can tell you is, you're probably fairly safe with what I have, given that most of it was written for whites by whites. You can decide for yourself if the spin suits the story you want to tell."

"Well, Lord, Corinne, I didn't mean to set you off. I was just sayin…"

"So am I, Cousin. So am I."

Corinne Barr knew all too well what happened to LouWanda Crump all those years ago. Perhaps it was why everyone gave her at least an ounce of grace no matter what the offense. No one should know the horror of a missing child, let alone the suspicion that followed. Imagine kissing your child goodnight and never seeing him again. She had every right to be bitter. The rest was how she was raised. Forgiving LouWanda was easy. Having a conversation with her was the hard part.

"So, do you want the good or the bad first?" Corinne asked once they were settled and looking at her Ancestry page.

"I don't reckon it matters. Just give me what'cha got."

"I'll start with the bad. You may need to end on a good note."

"Don't be smart-alecky with me. He's your grandpappy, too."

Corinne paused a moment and side-eyed LouWanda. "That's the first time you've owned it."

"Well..." LouWanda chuckled. "I don't reckon I have much choice in the matter, now do I? Stop foolin' around and tell me the story."

"I'm going to let you read it for yourself. It's too long and convoluted to tell. And I'm going to start with T.A. Kraft. He would be my biological grandfather, and *your* grandfather's cousin.'

"Wait, what?"

"My biological great-grandmother and your great-grandfather were siblings. Brother and sister. Their children—your grandfather, James Matthews, Jr. and my grandfather, T.A. Kraft— were cousins. That's where our cousin line started, but don't worry about all that. This right here," Corinne slid the cursor onto a bookmarked site and clicked the mouse, "is the most comprehensive and concise version of T.A. Kraft's story."

"Lord at the big words comin' outta your mouth," LouWanda groused.

"Oh, stop." Corinne slid the laptop to her right and stood. "I'm going to take a quick break and check out the new arrivals while you read this one."

"You just got here."

"I'll be right back. Read."

Corinne made her way to the non-fiction section, which was her favorite. She enjoyed a good novel every now and then, but she preferred to keep up with current events, especially the ones political in nature. When she'd made her selections, she dropped them off at the circulation desk for Miss Janice to check out and detoured to the ladies' room. By the time she made it back to her computer, LouWanda was fuming.

"He went to *jail*? That's what you wanted me to read?" LouWanda squinted at the screen. "Says here they convicted him of…what is that word there, Corinne? I ain't never heard of such."

"Peonage?" Corinne lowered herself carefully into the chair she had recently vacated.

"Yeah, that's it. What does that even mean?"

"The article explains it fairly well. Did you read the whole thing?"

"Well, no I didn't read the whole thing. Just the important parts."

"LouWanda, that *is* the important part. He was convicted of peonage—holding people against their will to pay off debts they probably didn't even owe. But if you'll read the whole thing, you'll see he was doing far worse than what he got convicted of doing. And even that was overturned."

"I don't get it. That's how they did business back then. Blacks didn't have work after they got set free. They had to do somethin' didn't they? They shoulda been happy to have a job, way I see it."

"Okay, I'm going to lose my temper in about two seconds. I am not going to sit here and hold your hand if you aren't even willing to read what I gave you."

Corinne started packing up her papers and was about to shut down her computer when LouWanda put her hand on her arm.

"Wait, don't leave. I… Could you read it to me? I have a hard time seein' all the words and I get turned around. I can read all the words, most of 'em anyway, but I lose my place and sometimes it feels like the letters all run together. It's better for me if I hear 'em."

Something inside Corinne Barr rose up then—the teacher in her if she had to guess—and suddenly it all made sense.

"I'll be happy to read it to you, LouWanda," she said.

And so, she did. And by the time they were finished, the library was ready to close and LouWanda had a history lesson she would never forget. She heard not just about L.B. Matthews, their common great-great-grandfather, but also about his grandson T.A. Kraft, the overseer at the turpentine plant where Corinne's grandmother was held captive and her grandfather murdered. She heard about the sawmill and turpentine industries which, in cahoots with law enforcement, the judicial system and even the government, found ways to force people of color into debt slavery and worse.

"I don't understand it," LouWanda said as they walked to their cars. "If all that's true, how come I didn't never hear a word about it? All I ever heard was how blacks was lazy and didn't wanna work. I never heard nothin' about all that mess a'goin' on."

Corinne paused at the back of her Cadillac. She almost had to admire the sudden candor. But only almost. She wasn't quite sure if this was LouWanda's attempt at being honest with her, or if she just didn't know any better than to say in public what she'd always said in her kitchen.

"Well, think about it, LouWanda. If you had conspired to enslave and kill people so you could make money, would you tell the truth about it? Seems pretty logical to me that anyone who could do those things are not the type of people to own up to it. What they did was vilify the victims, make them out to be the bad ones. And then they wrote the history books to pretty it up and make themselves heroes."

"I gotta go lay down. I feel like I been punched in the stomach."

"I feel your pain," Corinne said, rolling her eyes in case LouWanda didn't catch the sarcasm in her voice.

"What? What'd I say now?"

"Nothing. Nothing at all." Corinne popped the trunk of her car and placed her computer bag and purse inside. "I emailed you some stuff on Louis B. Matthews, too. That's our great-great-grandfather, the one on the horse in the picture of the last lynching in Fletcher County. The one you're so dead set on memorializing Saturday. I hope it helps you with your speech, but I have to say, Cousin, I don't think you realize what you're doing. There's already talk of trouble."

"Don't be dramatic. It ain't that big a deal. It's just a little plaque, and the statue ain't but four feet tall."

"But why on earth does it have to be a *Confederate* Memorial?"

LouWanda looked at Corinne like she'd lost her mind. "Well, what else do we have?"

"We, who?"

"Southerners. Who else?"

"White Southerners, you mean. 'Cause I'm just as Southern as you are, and I don't identify with the Confederacy. The Civil War is nothing to my people but a giant wound that reopens every time someone celebrates it. Does that not bother you at all?" Corinne felt the anger rise up in her chest and swallowed it hard, like she always, *always* did.

"But, see, that's what I'm sayin'. Why should I feel bad about something my ancestors did? I mean, I don't think it was right, I'm not sayin' that, but you're askin' me to make up for somethin' I didn't have nothin' to do with. Why can't y'all just get over it?"

"Because it's our history. You want *us* to get over *our* history while you celebrate the very same one. Why can't *you* get over it? The Confederacy lost, LouWanda, as well they should have. We wouldn't be the United States—we wouldn't be the *South*— if they hadn't. It's time *you* got over it. Move on. Start focusing on the things that actually make us special. 'Cause there's plenty to be proud of, if you think about it. And it would be really nice if we could—for *once*—celebrate together. But I'm telling you now, I'm not celebrating this. And you should know—I want you to be prepared—there *will* be a protest at the Founders Day program." Corinne tucked her bag under her arm and stared hard at LouWanda. "And I'll be taking part in *that*."

LouWanda, face red and heart beating hard and fast, watched Corinne get into her car and drive away.

"Well, good day," LouWanda muttered to herself as she climbed into her Bronco. "All's I did was ask."

34 - Founders Day Fiasco

With the parade scheduled to begin at 10:00 a.m. on Saturday, preparations began early. Downtown Mayhew Junction was buzzing with activity, most of which involved finding available parking spaces on side streets and vacant lots. Lineup for floats began at the Assembly of God church parking lot, two streets south of Main.

Sweet and Bubba John drove separate vehicles for practical purposes. Bubba John parked at the high school after dropping the twins off to meet up with their teams. Sweet delivered Bitty to the church at 9:00 a.m., where the Literacy Coordinator was waiting to corral students in the first-grade Sunday School room. Then she took the two youngest to her shop where Dottie had already set out five chairs along the edge of the sidewalk to secure their front row view of the parade. This also gave them good access to the festivities on the courthouse lawn afterwards, since they were on the block directly next to the courthouse square.

Beanie and Will had gotten up at the crack of dawn to prepare, and with a house full of guests, they'd kept breakfast simple and continental, offering an array of pastries and coffee from a buffet table. Nell would cover the bakery while Beanie and Will worked the parade route itself. The log cabin cake was huge, but sturdy, and sat atop the painted white cart Will had finally finished. They'd propped up the back to keep it level while they put the finishing touches on the scene, which included horses and people and trees fashioned from rice cereal treats and fondant. Beanie made period clothing out of fondant, with tiny fabric aprons tied on for dimension and texture. The scene was perfect, but both Beanie and Will were beginning to wish they'd opted for a more automated mode of transport. With the added weight of the cake and buckets of homemade caramels, the cart was teetering on the verge of unwieldy. Will was thankful he and Bean had built up some stamina on their daily walks. He was also thankful for the change in their relationship, however slight it might be. It seemed to Will a bridge had been crossed, a tension relieved. It wasn't exactly a romance yet, but they laughed a lot, made eye contact often, worked in closer proximity and touched more than ever before.

Like this morning, when Will was bent over the cake, tweaking the position of one of the trees and bolstering another, Beanie had leaned over beside him with one hand resting on his back.

"Looks good enough to eat," she said, then slid her hand back and forth across his shoulders and patted him twice before moving on to set up the buffet.

It's the little things, he thought. The little things mean the most.

Fortunately for Beanie and Will, they were halfway to the parade lineup when Reba Hill Bradsher Jessup Swindell showed up on the doorstep of the Château, luggage in hand. Nell had no choice but to let her in.

"Why, I'm her mama," Reba said, unwrapping the scarf she had tied around her mound of brassy red hair. "Can't you tell from lookin'?"

"Uh, of course... I just... Beanie never said you were coming, so I don't really know..." Nell stammered. Something didn't feel right, but she couldn't put a finger on why.

"She musta forgot. She always was a simple little thing. You got a mirror I can use? This hair's fallin' faster than the Niagara." Reba sighed and looked around. "Not as fancy as I imagined, but quaint. Homey, if you're into that. Be a doll and tell me where I can put these things? I been carrying them around ever since I got off the bus over in Lake City. I like to've never got over here."

The bell on the door to the bakery chimed and Nell had to make a quick decision even if it was the wrong one.

"Just put your luggage in the corner by the stairs. Bathroom's the last door on the left, through the sitting room. You can wait there if you want, but they won't be back 'til after the parade. You should probably walk on over to the courthouse and enjoy the festivities."

With that, Nell returned to the bakery.

In the meantime, Reba Swindell made herself right at home. Beanie found her in the kitchen when she ran back to the Château to grab something to keep the flies off the cake while they waited for the parade to start.

"Punkin!" Reba flung her arms wide to envelop her daughter in a vicious embrace that pinned Beanie's arms to her side and sent her Stetson flying.

Beanie grunted as all the air left her chest.

"Let me look at you!" Reba grasped Beanie's face in her hands and went in for a kiss.

Beanie's eyes went wide as she finally reacted, grasping Reba's hands and wrenching them from her face.

"Lord, Mama, your hands are freezing." Beanie spun to her right and eased around the far end of the kitchen table to create a barrier between herself and the woman invading her personal space. She bent down to retrieve her hat and, rather than place it on her head, held it to her chest like a plate of armor.

"Well, of course they are. Y'all keep this place like a tomb. Where's the thermostat? I'll turn it up a bit."

"Oh, gosh, no. We gotta keep things cool enough for all the frostin' to set. Speakin' a'which, I gotta grab some tinfoil and get back downtown. Will's waitin' for me and the parade starts in an hour."

"Who's this Will person? Is he a beau? Have you gone and gotten married and not told your ol' mama about it?"

"Lord, no." Beanie eyed the set of drawers in the cabinets behind Reba, calculating how she might get to them without being dragged back into an embrace. "We're friends is all. And business partners, of course. I really got to go, Mama. The flies is awful out there."

"Well, I never," Reba drawled. "Call me crazy, but I don't think you're all that excited to see me, and that cuts me to the quick."

Beanie, having no idea how to respond, said nothing. She took a deep breath, placed her hat squarely on her head, pushed past her mother and pulled open the drawer holding various boxes of kitchen wraps. Seizing the largest tube of aluminum foil she could find, she held it up and shook it in triumph, which Reba took as a threat and flinched.

Beanie noticed—and not without a tiny shred of satisfaction. "I'm goin' back down to the parade. If you wanna come with me, you better get your coat. It's a little nippy when the wind blows."

"I'm not tryin' to be a burden, Punkin. If I'm gonna be in your way, I'll stay here."

180

"Suit yourself," Beanie said, and immediately felt relieved. She didn't wait for a response. Brushing past her mother, Beanie exited the kitchen, calling over her shoulder on the way out, "See you when I get back, if not before. Get Nell to warm you up a sweet roll. It's Mommer's recipe."

"Oh, yeah? How's Mommer doin'?" Reba hollered at Beanie's retreating back.

"She's dead!" Beanie scooted out the front door without looking back. She skipped down the front steps muttering to herself. "That oughta good and shut her up."

Reba had to bite her tongue not to whoop for joy. She'd gotten her fill of Eulene Bradsher long before she took off for Tennessee leaving her husband and child far behind. Eulene was the reason she left and the reason she never came back. Until now, that is. And Reba could read the writing on the wall. She has poisoned my child against me, Reba thought. Well, we'll see about that.

When Beanie made it back to where the parade was in full lineup, she told Will about the brief encounter.

"She like to've squeezed all the air outta my lungs. And she smells like bread puddin' baked in a used ashtray. I can't take it, I just can't. I think she means to stay with us. I saw her suitcase in the sitting room."

"She can't stay with us. We're full for the next two days."

"Lord, Will, what am I gonna do?"

"We'll cross that bridge when we get to it. Right now, we have a cake to show off."

Will thrust one cake hat at Beanie and plopped the other onto his own head, wondering the whole time how he ever let himself be talked into something so ridiculous.

35 - Batter Up

T-Ray was looking forward to the parade this year. The team had decided to put on a little show for a change, rather than riding atop haybales on a trailer pulled behind the coach's dual-axel pickup truck. Dodson Coon came up with the idea. He'd been juggling for years. Peaches and lemons first because his daddy had a tree farm. He'd worked his way up to juggling with clubs and the occasional torch and had driven everyone crazy at practice tossing bats and balls into the air. After a while, though, the other players had joined in, often staying for an hour or more after practice perfecting their moves. They prepared an entire show for the parade, planning on stopping once in front of the local bank and once in front of the courthouse to wow the crowd with their skills. They all brought batting helmets, too, just in case.

The girls' team were lined up behind them. T-Ray wasn't sure if he was more excited about his sister having a front row seat, or his girlfriend Luciana watching from the courthouse steps. That is if she made it back in time. She was second in line and the parade didn't go much past the courthouse, so he remained hopeful. Either way, he prayed more times that morning than he had in a month of Sundays. Juggling baseball bats was tricky at best. Adding a routine and random baseballs made it a real crapshoot. But they'd worked hard. T-Ray was pretty sure they were ready.

They were tenth in the lineup, behind some kind of military color guard, T-Ray thought. It was a raggedy looking group dressed in Confederate gray suits that were either too large or too small for the men who wore them. Three men in the center held flags—the U.S. Stars and Stripes, flanked by the Florida state flag and the Confederate Battle flag. At one side was a man so tiny T-Ray first thought he was a woman, until he got close enough to see the mustache that framed his entire mouth. His musket, fit with a bayonet, was at least a few inches taller than the man himself, and the legs of his baggie wool pants were safety-pinned halfway up his calves and still the pants legs dragged the ground around his boots. As small as he was, he seemed to be in charge, shouting cadence and orders in nothing short of a high-pitched squeal. Two burly fellows marched behind the guard, pulling a small cannon with homemade yokes that fit like backpacks. On either side of the Confederate procession were several men who T-Ray thought didn't look like they belonged there. Not in the color guard, and not in Mayhew Junction for that matter. They were either too slick or too tattooed to fit in. A chill passed over him and he shook it off. By the time the parade started, he'd forgotten all about them and spent his time scanning the crowd for his ex-girlfriend Hannah and her friends, just as a precaution.

The parade coordinator had warned each group to be aware of their distance from the other participants. They should not get too close to the group in front, nor straggle too far behind. The exception was if they had a planned stop for a performance, after which they were to double-time it down the road until they caught up. They got these instructions every year to little avail. Dance teams and majorettes moved too quickly, and beauty queens perched in convertibles always slowed things down. That was just how it went.

This year, it was Will and Beanie causing backups from the start. Positioned in the number three pole, Will struggled to keep his heavy cart rolling while Beanie tossed caramels and coupons to the crowd. At first, they were greeted with ooohs and aahhhs as townspeople realized the log cabin was a cake. Rules about staying off the parade route went straight out the window as women had to see for themselves the details of the display.

Beanie kept saying, "It'll be at The Patsy after the parade, y'all. We're selling slices for a dollar a piece. You can see it then, I promise."

Once the mothers broke rank, the children followed suit and there were several swipes taken out of the bottom of the cake. Teens rushed out to take selfies, holding phones high in their outstretched arms to capture the cake in the background. Finally, two onlookers took pity on Will and Beanie and flanked the wagon on either side, effectively holding usurpers at bay.

The first time the parade stopped was for the singing of the National Anthem by Mayhew Junction high school senior, and T-Ray Atwater's new girlfriend, Luciana Munoz. The daughter of Columbian migrant workers, Luciana had been the darling of the community for years. She was hardworking and talented and was on track to be the Valedictorian of her graduating class, but it was her voice for which she was known. There was scarcely a church in the county that had not invited her to sing, nor a dry eye in the congregation when she finished. She and B-Kay had been friends since elementary school, though the beach was the first time T had noticed her as anything other than his sister's friend.

She rode perched on the back seat of a red Mustang convertible driven by local farmer Jimmy Thomas who'd employed her parents for the past ten years. They were second in line, behind the elderly couple chosen to represent the town's founders. As was the custom every year, the pair were dressed in period costumes and riding in a horse-drawn wagon.

The entire parade came to a halt when the convertible stopped in front of the courthouse. Eustace Falwell had set up his karaoke tent on the sidewalk, directly next to the statue and monument, which were covered tightly with an old tarp drawn tight at the bottom. Two men from Rooster's Civil War re-enactment group stood at attention next to the tarp, muskets resting on shoulders. Armed guards, such as it was.

The town had set up a sound system for Luciana to sing, but they'd forgotten to include a CD player for the accompaniment track, so Eustace volunteered to handle the sound for them. A couple of quick connections later and his karaoke machine was set to blast from four huge speakers set up around the courthouse lawn.

Beanie was first to notice something wasn't quite right. Beanie had always loved The National Anthem – loved how it gave her chills to hear it – loved how, no matter how noisy a place was, it became quiet when the first few bars began.

When Beanie saw the look of discomfort on Luciana's face, she thought it was because Eustace spent an unnatural amount of time gushing over the beauty of the teenager waiting to sing. She was pretty sure she wasn't the only one whose skin was crawling.

But as Luciana began the first bars of the song, "Oh, say can you see, by the dawn's early light…" a voice rang out from somewhere in the crowd.

"Go home!"

How rude, Beanie thought. She looked at Will and realized he'd heard it, too.

"What so proudly we hailed, at the twilight's last gleaming…"

184

"This is America!" another voice, this time behind them.

Luciana's voice quavered, but she pressed on. "Whose broad stripes and bright stars…"

"Go home!" This shouter used a bullhorn.

"…through the perilous fight…"

"You don't belong here."

"Dirty little Mexican…get out!"

More voices joined in and a murmur rose through the crowd. Beanie instinctively moved closer to Will.

"What's going on?" Beanie looped her arm through Will's at the elbow.

"I don't know," he answered. "It's not good though. This could get out of hand real fast."

"Are they talkin' to Luciana?"

Will nodded. "Yep."

"But this *is* her home."

"Unfortunately, not everyone agrees," Will said.

Luciana finished the song and was whisked off to the convertible under the protective arm of Mr. Jimmy, as she called her parents' boss. His face was red, and his lips set thin and tight. He was a long-time Conservative who'd voted for the man who'd promised to drain the swamp, but this was crossing a line, he thought, as he shepherded the trembling girl to his waiting car.

"Ignore them, honey," he said. "They're idiots. Don't worry, nobody's gonna bother you while I'm watching."

Sweet, standing less than twenty yards away, was livid. She plopped Daisy into Dottie's lap. "Can you hold her a minute?"

Sweet didn't wait for an answer, just made a beeline for Jim Thomas's car.

"Are you okay?" Sweet climbed into the back of the convertible and wrapped Luciana in her arms. "Where are your parents?"

Luciana sniffled and looked around. "They were by the courthouse when I started to sing, but I don't see them now. I'm sure they went home."

"Without you?" Sweet spoke without thinking.

Jimmy Thomas looked over his shoulder from the driver's seat. "She's with me."

"Oh, of course, yeah. I just mean…"

185

"It's fine, Miss Sweet. I'm fine. But they probably went on home just in case."

"What the heck was all that about, Jim?"

He stared through the windshield at the back of the wagon, horses moving nervously at the front. "Let's go!" he shouted, then turned again to Sweet. "We're about to start moving. Are you ridin' with us?"

"I feel like I should, I mean, with her parents gone and all."

"She's safe with me," he repeated.

"Okay, if you're sure." Sweet was anything but sure, but what could she do, short of leaving her own kids in an unsteady crowd? "Come straight back to us when you're finished, okay?"

Luciana nodded and mustered up a brave smile. Sweet waited for the car to slow to a crawl and hopped over the edge onto the pavement.

Sweet considered texting T-Ray to tell him what happened to Luciana, but she was afraid he might do something rash. She needn't have worried about being the one to break it to him. News in Mayhew Junction spread like trails of lightning across a cloudless sky. By the time Luciana reached the end of the parade route, the entire baseball team, girls and boys, were talking about it. B-Kay texted her friend first. *Wait for us by mama's store. Daddy's there, too. They won't dare mess with him.* She added a few heart emojis and a sad face.

T-Ray texted: *RU OK? Wait 4 me.* To which Luciana replied simply: *OK*

What she thought and didn't say was, *it's nothing new. I hear things like that every single day.* But this was different for sure. These were grown men, not pimply-faced boys or snotty girls who said things under their breath in the locker room, or the aisle of the grocery store where she worked part-time. Shake it off, she told herself, then smiled and waved to the crowd of people who loved her as much as they could.

36 - *It All Comes Down to This*

Luciana made it back to T-Ray's family as the raggedy color guard marched to a ceremonial halt for LouWanda's dedication ceremony. She settled onto the curb between Sweet and Bubba John's chair and angled herself to the left. She had no interest in watching the installation of the memorial, but T-Ray's juggling routine came directly afterwards, and she didn't want to miss that. She was still shaking from the incident before but felt better when Sweet put a calm hand on her shoulder and leaned down to whisper, "You were amazing. I still have chills."

Luciana was glad she didn't mention the name-calling. Some people were too ignorant to realize not every Spanish-speaking immigrant was from Mexico. Her own family had escaped from certain disaster in Guatemala. Her father, an agricultural scientist, had spoken out against corruption in government and they were forced to flee. Luciana barely remembered the country where she was born or the details of their arrival in the U.S. Her parents would not speak of it and forbid her to as well. They had moved frequently as migrant workers before settling in Mayhew Junction.

Jim Thomas knew a good thing when he saw one. Raphael Munoz was a genius with his crops. He set the Munoz family up in his best single-wide trailer, closest to his own house, and handed down his own truck to Raphael to use. Bought himself a brand new Ford F250 in its place. He didn't worry about whether or not they were legal immigrants. In these parts, law enforcement looked the other way unless there was a problem, which was rare. Half of the county officials grew up on farms; they knew what the migrant workforce meant to the local economy. Truth be known, Jimmy knew the answer to the question he never asked. It was better that way.

On the courthouse square, LouWanda Crump beamed broader than the Cheshire cat of a man she stood beside. Eustace Falwell was in his element, though he'd certainly be happier when he got the chance to sing later.

"This is go'n be good, Miss LouWanda. I'm tellin' you what. Makes ya proud to be American, don't it?"

LouWanda nodded her agreement, eyes fixed on the motley group of Confederate guards performing a series of choreographed moves before spreading themselves in a semi-circle around the tarped monuments. The small man at the left of the formation, drew a battered bugle from inside his coat and nodded at LouWanda.

"Go ahead, Rooster," she said and held her microphone up in front of him.

Rooster played a passing Reveille, with only a few wonky notes. Eustace's karaoke machine was still hooked up to the county speakers, so everyone within a half mile would be sure to hear.

LouWanda was so focused on the color guard and the speech she held in her hand that she failed to notice the movement of the crowd. To her right and behind her, Corinne Barr and a congregation of folks from her church and her neighborhood began to form three concentric circles. They held signs in their hands, upside-down and backwards so they could not be read, but obviously signs, nonetheless. Once their formation was complete, Reverend John Milton Milo began a soft, but fervent prayer and all heads bowed.

Halfway across the courtyard and directly behind LouWanda, a group of white men stood in two lines facing the prayer group. Across the street from the courthouse, two men stepped out of a truck parked beside the small convenience store. Each leaned into the bed of the pickup and retrieved an armload of tiki torches, the tags of which still hung from the base of each torch just as they were when the pair cleared out the stock on aisle five at the Dollar Mart.

LouWanda caught a glimpse of them out of the corner of her eye, but she dismissed any thought when the bugling stopped, and it was her turn to speak. She unfolded two pages of notebook paper and smoothed them as best she could before beginning to speak.

"Ladies and gentlemen," LouWanda croaked, then cleared her throat and continued. "On behalf of the Mayhew Junction Historical Society I am happy to welcome you to the dedication of a historical monument to our Southern heritage. We are gathered today to celebrate our county's *di*-verse history, which you can read all about in the books we have for sale today, right over there on the courthouse steps. *Mayhew Junction: Then and Now* is a complete history of how our county and our town were founded. Fletcher County was named in honor of William Bradley Fletcher, postmaster of Mayhew Junction 1859 through 1891...oh my," she blurted as a brisk wind tore the paper from her hands. "Oh, somebody get them things...get...oh shoot."

Remembering the microphone in her hands, LouWanda gathered what wits she could and forged onward, "Well, I had it all wrote out, but I'm not gonna bore you with all the details of the county courthouse. You can read all about it in *Mayhew: Then and Now*. Like I said, you can get 'em here today. And you can also get them at my shop across the street if you don't have no money today. Just stop in and see me. I'll have plenty. Anyways, we have a lot to be proud of, which is why the Historical Society was happy to commission these two pieces to be placed near the courthouse steps."

Stepping from behind the circle of soldiers, Randall Kerner approached LouWanda and took the microphone from her hands. "Now, look here, LouWanda, the County Commission never did any such thing and you know it. Do what you're gonna do but leave the commission and the Historical Society out of this."

LouWanda huffed and snatched the microphone back.

"As I was sayin' before I was rudely interrupted...we have done a lot of work to bring you this history and these monuments right here. And we did it for the WHOLE community, includin' black people, too. So there ain't nothin' for nobody to be upset about, as we was makin' sure everybody in the town was represented rightly."

"White Power!" The voice, amplified by a bullhorn, came from behind LouWanda. But when the group turned to look, there was no bullhorn to be seen, just a group of men holding lit torches in broad daylight.

"What the Sam Hill?" LouWanda scowled. "Who're those people back there?"

She was asking Randy Kerner, but her voice carried across the entire courtyard.

"Stop yappin', lady, and get to the good stuff," another voice rang out.

"I'm tryin'," LouWanda screeched into the microphone. "But y'all gotta get ahold of yourself and let me get this thing over with.

As I was sayin'… Oh, never mind. Rooster, pull up that tarp there, wouldja?"

After a bit of a struggle, two men from the Confederate guard released the covering over LouWanda's memorial. The concrete soldier, painted with Confederate gray uniform and an unnatural shade of taupe for skin color, stood less than five feet tall, about the same height as the owner of the monument shop. And the marble monument, more headstone than memorial, was blasted with the words that LouWanda read to the crowd:

Honoring our Confederate dead
You are gone but not forgotten
The South Shall Rise Again!
Fletcher County 2018

A murmur rose through the crowd and various groups of people moved toward the memorial to see for themselves.

Oh, my… said one woman.

Damn straight… from another.

Wow…

You got that right…

Can they say that?

Whoop!

You gotta be kiddin' me…

LouWanda and Eustace stepped back under the tent to make room for the throngs of people pushing in to see for themselves.

Meanwhile, T-Ray's baseball team moved into position for the juggling act and Eustace queued up the track he'd been given for the event, so half of the crowd turned their backs to the monument to watch the show.

But the throng of white men with torches faced off with a wall of protestors with signs reading "Black Lives Matter" and "Love Your Neighbor" and "God Created Us All" and "No Confederate Monuments."

With the noise of the show and the crowds of people gathered in the flat surface of the courthouse lawn, it was difficult to see how heated the confrontation had become. Will and Beanie came up in the middle of it, taking a shortcut through the courtyard to get the cake back to a place where they could cut it and sell slices.

The first thing Beanie noticed was her mama smiling up at a man with a crewcut. She recognized him as a guest who had been at her breakfast table. Reba's hands were wrapped around his bicep, under the tattoo of barbed wire circling the widest part of his flexed muscle. He's at least half her age, Beanie thought, then realized this was the least of her worries. The crowd was thicker than they'd bargained for and closing in fast. Voices were getting louder and louder, and Will could now make out the chants of the white nationalists he'd seen on the nightly news.

You will not replace us!
White Power!
Blood and Soil!

And from the protestors side:

We won't celebrate, a heritage of hate.
The Confederacy is dead. Put the flag to bed.

"Beanie," said Will, "I want you to stick close to me, okay? Here, hang onto my belt and don't let go." Beanie did as she was told, grasping Will's waistband over his back pocket.

"What does that mean, Will? Blood and soil, what does that mean?"

"It means they are white nationalists and they mean to start trouble. That's what it means. Have you seen any of the sheriff's deputies here?"

"They was one car at the end of the parade, and one parked over at the park. But that's all."

It was a real struggle to get through the crowd with the cart and the confrontation seemed to be reaching a boiling point.

"We have to leave the cart, Bean. We need to get out of this mess."

"We can't leave the cake…"

"Yes, we can. Come on. We're going."

And so, they abandoned the cart where it was, smack dab in the middle of the two groups now pushing toward each other.

When they'd finally squeezed through the crowd and made it to the front porch of the Château, Will pushed Beanie through the door and told her to call the sheriff's office and see if they had people coming.

"Lock these doors. Tell Nell to close up the shop and come into the kitchen with you."

191

"Where're you goin'?"

"I have to go back, Bean."

Beanie felt like something had sucked all the air from her chest. "Don't go, Will."

"I have to. I'll check on your mom and send her your way if I find her. You can watch the door and open it for anyone you know, but keep it locked unless you are sure you're safe."

And with that, Will sprinted from the porch and disappeared into the crowd.

***

Meanwhile, LouWanda finally noticed the commotion behind her, though she stood frozen, unable to speak for a few moments. Randall Kerner snapped her out of it.

"For God's sake, LouWanda, do something," he said.

"What's going on back there?"

"The mess *you* made, that's what. I told you. We all told you. Now look what you've done."

"Who are those men?"

"They're not from here, that's for sure. This is not good, not good, not good…" Randy pushed past LouWanda, heading for the conflict he saw brewing. One of the torch-holders had broken ranks and rushed a black protestor, knocking the sign from his hands with the unlit end of his torch.

"Whoa, whoa, whoa there…" Randy stepped in front of the man he recognized as having graduated with his son. Zeke something, he thought.

"Get out the way, Mr. Randy," Zeke said. "I ain't watchin' this go down."

Randy stood firm and addressed the white men in front of him. "I'm Randall Kerner, County Commissioner here. I don't believe we issued any permit for you boys to gather here, so I'm going to ask you to disperse now. Just go on home. We don't need this nonsense here."

"Don't need a permit, dude. We got a right to be here," said one man.

"You ever heard of free speech?" asked another.

192

"Look," Randall decided to appeal to their humanity, "we don't want trouble…"

And that's when the real trouble started.

LouWanda, feeling nervous and closed-in from the throngs of people pressing toward the courthouse to see what was happening, brought the microphone she still held up to her mouth and hollered, "Y'all back up now! Back up! Somebody call the law!"

It was as if someone had fired a starter gun. As the line of torchbearers pushed toward the protesters, Corinne Barr stepped forward with both arms spread wide.

"Stay calm. Stay still," she called out to her congregation. "Let them come to us. We shall NOT be moved."

LouWanda was never sure who threw the first blow. All she saw was a tattooed beast trying to grab the sign out of Corinne Barr's hands. Corinne fought back the best she knew how. She kicked the aggressor right in the shin, which only served to enrage him. As he drew back his fist a voice rang out so loud, he actually turned to look. There was an impossibly tall white woman barreling toward him, screaming at the top of her lungs, "YOU GET YOUR HANDS OFF MY COUSIN!"

T-Ray Atwater

I shoulda paid attention when Javon and Sergio were talking at practice the other day. I just thought they were bein' stupid. Javon was sayin' his church was protesting some new monument, and I'm like, protesting what? And Javon's like, "Dude, you okay with a Confederate monument?" And I'm like, what's the big deal? It's just a Southern thing. And Sergio was kinda in his face about it, too. Said his parents didn't wanna go to the parade now 'cause they were worried about a bunch of law bein' there because of the protestors. And Javon says, "Man, you don't even know what you 'bout to see. Them bitches ain't playin' comin' down here. Ain't no way we layin' down for this."

I mean, after a while, I could see both points, but I still thought they were making a big deal outta nothin'.

Then, on the day of the parade, I noticed these trucks we'd never seen before cruisin' around town. Javon elbows me and says, "Bunch of skinheads comin' down here just to start trouble, you watch."

So, then I get the text about them harassin' Lucy, and Javon's like, "What'd I tell you, bruh?" And when I get all pissed about it, Javon says, "Oh, yeah, you git your panties in a wad over your girl, but when it's us, we on our own."

When I saw my dad runnin' through the crowd, I knew it was as bad as Javon said it would be. Dad hollered at me that he was going to get Bitty and I should go straight to the store and look after Mama.

By the time we make it to where the trouble's started, I'm startin' to really get it. I mean, these are my teammates, right? This is my hometown. I hear racist stuff all the time, but I just usually blow it off. Stupid is as stupid does, as my mama likes to say. But I don't hate anybody, let alone over what color their skin is. Still, if I don't take a stand against it, I'm kinda lettin' it happen, right? That's what Javon was tryin' to tell me at the ball field that day, but I didn't want to hear it.

So, there we are in the middle of it, and we all decide right there together that if we're gonna be a team on the field, we better damn well be a team in the fight. Nobody had much time to think. Javon had the idea of forming a V, like we were gonna do in our juggling routine. And it worked great to move people out of the way. He wanted to get where his mama and daddy were with the church, but he said he'd be safer stayin' with the team anyway. Mama came up and tried to get me to come into the store with her, but I said no. My daddy didn't raise me to fight, but he didn't raise me to run from one either.

We had a good view of the guys with tiki torches when we were up on the float, so we knew where we needed to get down on the ground and we just grabbed our bats crossways, pointed ourselves in that direction and parted the crowd. You shoulda seen the looks on those assholes' faces when we got to them. They was all bowed up and bawlin' out the church folks who didn't have anything but homemade signs. They didn't expect an entire bat-wielding brigade from Fletcher High.

I'm not sure what set off the crowd—it may have been Miss LouWanda charging the dude who was pushing Mrs. Barr— but people started runnin' in all directions, mostly away but some of 'em actually sort of grouped up around us like backup. Miss LouWanda just full-on tackled the guy and he fell right beside the cake cart Miss Beanie'd been pushin' in the parade. When he tried to get up, Miss LouWanda grabbed two handfuls o' that cake and smashed it right in his face. Like to've smothered him, I think, and definitely blinded him. One of his buddies grabbed her then and flung her into the cake cart and I didn't see her move on her own again. I swear I thought she was dead, she was bleedin' so bad.

I remember feelin' a little bit scared, but I think all that kinda energized the team. We surrounded the group that was still mostly huddled up with their stupid dollar store tiki torches. As we circled 'em, they started shoving those torches at us and we just tee'd up on 'em and batted 'em outta their hands. Launched one of 'em right into this big dude's crotch. Set 'im on fire and watched him dance. That was the best shot of the day. He was fine, though. He got it out pretty quick.

I don't know how long the fight lasted. Coupla' minutes maybe? Anyways, we made it pretty clear we were willing and able to knock some heads off some blocks, just like the tiki torches. Some of 'em were outside the circle and I know there was kind of a free-

for-all behind us, but we stuck to our plan and kept most of 'em rounded up until the cops got there and hauled 'em over to the county jail, handcuffed to each other in a line.

By the time I made it back to the store, Dad was there with Bitty and B-Kay, and Mama had Daisy asleep on a pile of t-shirts on the floor and Lucy sittin' on her lap cryin' her eyes out. She said it was 'cause she was scared I was going to get hurt, but I think it was more than that. She's always been kinda quiet about her family, and when I try to talk to her about college, she says she can't go. There's more to it I don't know, and I think it's time for me to man up and pay attention.

37 - The Aftermath

Beanie likes to say her "come to Jesus meeting" commenced the second Will Thaxton left her in the safety of their home. She followed his instructions and closed down the bakery. Then she and Nell sat at the kitchen table with Sugar trembling at their feet, while the two women silently prayed for the next half hour.

Lord, if you let him come home, I'll…she thought, then stopped. After a minute, she said, "I don't know what I would do without him."

Nell's head snapped up. "Who, Will?"

Beanie looked confused for a minute. "Oh, gosh, I didn't realize I said that out loud."

Nell laughed. "Well, you didn't have to say it. I knew who you were praying for. You may be the last to know, Beanie. You're in love with the man."

"I am?"

"Pretty sure of it."

"How do you know? I mean…how do you know when you're in love? I thought I was in love with Suvi, but I don't reckon I was 'cause it wadn't that hard to let 'im go."

"You just know, that's all. I can tell he loves you from the way he looks at you. Cecil used to look at me that way." At that, Nell choked up for a moment, then went on. "I can tell you love him, because he always makes you laugh and I hate to break another truth to you, but Will's not all that funny."

That sent Beanie into a fit of nervous giggles, until she heard the key turn in the front door and then she was all business. She flew from her chair and nearly tackled Will when he entered. Her hat went flying when she wrapped her arms around his neck, and she burst into tears despite her elation.

"Whoa! What's this all about?" Will wrapped one arm around her waist and closed the door with his other one. He looked over at Nell, who grinned and shrugged her shoulders.

"Is the coast clear out there? I think I'll go open up the shop." Nell was nothing if not discrete.

"It was basically over as soon as it started. The cake's destroyed. Turns out our butter cream is quite effective at putting out tiki torches. You should have seen those dudes being marched over to the jailhouse. Looked like some of them had rolled in the cake. Probably did, now that I think about it."

Nell shook her head. "I never thought I'd see the day when we would have a protest at the courthouse. What happened to LouWanda's monuments?"

"They are no more, that's all I know." Will said.

"Was anybody hurt?"

"Yeah, LouWanda and the guy she tackled. She was bleeding pretty badly from her head. Suvi tossed what was left of the cake off the cart, loaded LouWanda onto it and wheeled her to where the ambulance was parked. Corinne rode with her to the hospital, I think, but they pulled out a little while ago, so I don't know how she is."

"Well, I doubt we'll have much business after all that, but I'm gonna leave you two alone. Beanie's got something to tell you."

Beanie looked wild-eyed at Nell. "I do?"

"Yes, Ma'am, you do. And I suggest you get to it," she said before making her exit.

Will, still shaken from what he'd witnessed, could only stare at Beanie with a look that could only be described as bewildered.

"What was that all about?" Will made a beeline for the coffee pot without waiting for an answer. "I need coffee."

"Oh, nothin'," Beanie said. "We was just talkin', that's all."

Will turned, the coffee pot in his hand. "About what?"

"I was awful worried about you. I wish you hadn't gone back out there."

Will's shoulders relaxed and he turned back to pour coffee into his cup.

"Is that all? I was fine. You should know by now I'm not likely to get into a fist-fight with anyone. But I do have to be able to live with myself."

"You could have been hurt. I was really worried," she repeated.

"Is that what you wanted to talk to me about?"

"Well, kind'ly... That and I reckon I love you is pretty much it."

Years later, whenever Will told this story, he would talk a lot about how everything felt like it was in hyper-slow motion. He set the carafe down on the countertop, then realized it was too hot and moved it back to the burner. He turned to face Beanie and no words would form in his brain, let alone his mouth. Finally, *finally*, he managed to say, "Really?" And Beanie just shrugged like, *what could she do?*

"Like *love* love?"

Beanie nodded.

"When did this come about?"

"Prolly a lot longer ago than I wanna admit, but for the main part, when I got scared you wouldn't come home, and Nell pointed out I was in love with you and I didn't argue."

"Oh, Beanie," Will crossed the floor in two steps and wrapped her in his arms. "That's the best news I've heard in a long, long time."

"Me, too," Beanie lifted her face to be kissed, and Will happily obliged.

Maybe it was a minute or two—they were never sure and argued about it for years on end—or maybe it was ten minutes, but whatever time they stood in the middle of that kitchen exploring their newfound joy, was interrupted first by Sugar whining to get in on the love action, and then by the grinding laughter of Reba Swindell.

"Well, ain't y'all the cutest thing? I thought you said he wasn't a beau, Punkin."

Will stepped back and gathered his wits. Reba stood in the doorway, clinging to the tattooed man Beanie had seen her with before."

"I was talkin' to ol' Travis here when that mess started in the square," Reba drawled. "He saved my life is what he did."

Beanie and Will stood dumbfounded for a moment before Will found his voice. "Were you with those men with the torches?"

Travis squirmed and looked down at the floor, so Reba answered for him. "Well, of course he was. And when those natives started gettin' restless, he swept me up and carried me to safety. Offered me a place to stay, too, since y'all apparently ain't got room even for kin."

"Well that's not going to happen, I can promise you that," Will said. "I'm sorry, Mr.—what was your name again?"

"Smith. Travis Smith." The man actually smirked at Will.

"Right. That should have been the tip-off right there. So, Mr. *Smith,* I'm going to have to ask you to pack up your things and leave."

"I paid in cash through tomorrow."

"Stop by the front desk on your way out," Will said. "I'll have a refund ready for you."

The man snorted and, without a glance at Reba, turned on his heel and headed up the stairs.

"Well, really, was that necessary?" Reba asked when the man was gone.

"Completely," Will said. "We don't want any trouble here, and that group is pure trouble."

"They wadn't the ones causin' the ruckus, it was all them—"

"*Stop!*" Will threw up one hand, palm facing Beanie's mother.

"What? What'd I say?"

"Whatever it is you were *about* to say, we do not want it said in our house," Will responded.

"Well, fine then. Lord, what is the matter with you two? First you throw a payin' guest out and then you… Hey, if he's leaving, can I have his room?"

Beanie found her voice then. "Absolutely not," she said. "You need to get your things and clear out. I'm sure Mr. Smith'll be happy to drive you to the bus station."

"Well, Punkin, what if I don't *want* to go to the bus station?" Reba snarled.

Beanie shrugged. "I don't care where ya' go, Mama. Ya just can't stay here."

38 - A Time to Heal

Corinne Barr did indeed ride to the hospital with her cousin, in part to make sure she was okay, and in part so she did not miss the opportunity to say, "I told you so." She waited until LouWanda's head was stitched up and she'd come back from having a CAT scan.

"All I can tell you, LouWanda, is that an awful lot of people warned you it was a bad idea and you barreled right on through like a bull in a china shop. And now look at you. You got stitches in your head, a split lip, and Lord at your hair. It's a mess, Cousin. Just a mess."

LouWanda had little to say. She groaned a few times, but mostly she lay there and felt sorry for herself. Not because she'd been physically hurt. She'd had stitches and busted lips before. They always healed. What she dreaded was facing the townspeople in the coming weeks.

"I really messed up, didn't I?" LouWanda's mouth quivered as she fought back tears.

"That's putting it lightly." Corinne snatched two squares of tissue out of the generic hospital box on the bedside table and dropped them into LouWanda's hands. "And you might as well dry it up, buttercup. Nobody feels sorry for you."

"Then why are you here?" LouWanda sniffled and blew her nose.

"Because that's what family does."

LouWanda stared at Corinne for a long moment. She couldn't for the life of herself figure this woman out. "We ain't *really* family. I mean, family is raised up together and celebrates birthdays and weddings and such. You don't hardly even know me. You ain't gotta be here."

Corinne nodded. "You're right about that. I don't have to be. But I'm here, aren't I?"

LouWanda paused for a moment and, for once in her life appeared to be weighing her words.

"Well, I thank you for it, Corinne. I may not be so good at showing it, but I thank you all the same."

The two women sat in silence for a bit. They tried turning on television, but several local stations had a breaking news banner about a "riot in Fletcher County."

"Why are they callin' it a riot, for cryin' out loud? It wadn't no such a thing." LouWanda groused.

"You got a lot to learn, Cousin. Riot's what they say any time my people are involved. Doesn't matter that we were peacefully protesting. It matters that a fight broke out and we were there."

"Well, that's dumb. Who were all them tattooed guys anyway? They's the one started it all."

"*You* brought them to town with all your nonsense. I hope you learned your lesson."

"I didn't bring 'em to town! It was that danged newspaper girl did that with her article that— Well, speak of the devil and the devil shows up."

Corinne turned toward the door to see a young woman with a mop of dark curls peeking her head into the room.

"Hey, Miss LouWanda. I hope you don't mind, I wanted to check on you. You remember me, don't you? I'm Marley Ann Maxwell? From the *Tallahassee Times*?"

"I know who ya' are," LouWanda finally responded.

"May I come in?"

"I reckon so. You're already here. Ya might as well."

Marley approached the bed tentatively. "I was awful worried about you, Miss LouWanda. I saw you hit your head. Are you okay?"

"Honey, it'll take a lot more'n what happened today to take me down, I'm just sayin'."

Corinne made a noise that sounded almost like clearing her throat, but more like stifling a laugh. "Truer words have not been spoken."

Marley turned as if she were just seeing Corinne. "Oh, hi," she said, stretching her right hand toward her. "I'm Marley."

"Good to meet you. I'm Corinne Barr."

"Are you a friend of Miss LouWanda's? I hope I didn't interrupt your visit."

Corinne's eyes twinkled as she considered spilling the familial beans. LouWanda caught the look and rolled her eyes. "Oh, go ahead. You know you wanna say it."

202

"I haven't said a word."

"Yeah, yeah, yeah..." LouWanda groused.

Marley looked back and forth between the women, trying to interpret the exchange.

"She's my cousin," LouWanda said to Marley, then turned back to Corinne. "There, are ya' happy now?"

What Marley noticed was, despite LouWanda's words seeming angry, LouWanda herself did not. She had a bemused look on her face, as if she were actually happy to deliver the news.

Marley took out her notebook and pen. This was going to be good, she thought. And it was.

39 - The Stars of the Show

Later that evening, when the exhausted younger children were put to bed, Sweet Lee and Bubba John sat at their kitchen table waiting for the twins to get back from a run to Walmart in Live Oak. Dylan and Luciana were with them, but the plan was to drop them off before returning home by ten o'clock. Normally, they'd be given a bit of grace, since the nearest stores were forty-five minutes away and the closest movie theatre at least an hour. The simple life wasn't all that simple. But, as nerves were running high and no one was sure if the interlopers had actually left town, Sweet insisted they come on home.

"Whatcha thinkin' about," Bubba John broke the silence. He sat across from Sweet, an empty Budweiser bottle resting between his cupped hands. Every now and then he would twirl it by the neck a few times, then rest again. He would have liked another, but somehow it just didn't seem important right that minute. Besides, he'd promised his wife he'd cut back.

"Oh, gosh, everything," Sweet said, fatigue pressing the words down on her tongue. She shook her head back and forth and paused between every sentence. "Everything. Today was so bad. And yet, in the weirdest way, so good."

Bubba said nothing. He didn't need to prompt her to speak. He just listened.

"Sometimes it takes something awful to remind you how amazing your kids are, you know?"

Bubba nodded and twirled his beer.

"I've been so worried about T-Ray. Seriously. I was beginning to think I had raised a little smartass." Sweet stood as she spoke. "I think I'm gonna have a glass of wine. You want another beer?"

"Sure," Bubba John instinctively swigged the last two drops from the bottle he still held. Don't mind if I do, he thought but kept to himself. Smartass, indeed.

Sweet plopped a bottle in front of him, grabbed the empty and tossed it into the recycle bin. When she sat back down, she had a glass of Kendall Jackson Chardonnay poured almost full.

"Cheers," Bubba John said.

"To what," Sweet said meeting Bubba's tilted bottle with her perfectly straight glass.

"To not spilling a drop. Impressive." Bubba grinned.

"To great kids," Sweet offered and they clinked again.

"To a beautiful wife." *Clink.*

"To a husband who thinks on his feet." *Clink.*

"To not raising a smartass." *Clink. Clink.*

"Double cheers to that," Sweet said. "I was proud of you both today. I was proud of our town. I don't know that I'd have bet on that kind of solidarity."

"Oh, I would have. Nobody likes outsiders stirring things up."

"Well, yeah, but I'm pretty sure we have a few people who agree with those men."

Bubba John gave a little shrug. "Probably so, but not to that extreme. And really, when you come face to face with evil like that, it'll make you think. I'm not happy it happened, but there'll be some good come out of it. Wait and see."

"Lord knows I hope you're right, hon."

"I'm still trying to get all that mess straight in my head. When did the boys get involved?"

"Well, I left Daisy and Tate with Dottie and ran out to try to get to the twins. I saw T-Ray and he said B went with you. He was surrounded by the whole boys' team— they had their helmets on and bats in their hands—and T-Ray was telling them to be quiet and listen. I tried to get him to come to the store and he just looked at me like I was crazy. He said 'Mom, go back to the store and stay there.' And I said, no, I wanted him to come with me. So, he just turned his back on me and kept talking to the kids, and about that time I heard this kind of roar go up. And T says, 'OK, let's go.' Honestly, maybe it's because they choreographed their routine, I don't know, but it was amazing how they moved together. T-Ray was in front and they formed a triangle. They held their bats in front of them, horizontal at the waist, and they started moving through the crowd and it was like Moses parting the water. They just pushed right through the center of the crowd and then between the two groups. And then the triangle just formed into a circle around the men, and the boys took batting stances. I have never been so terrified in all my life. A couple of the men pushed torches toward them and, one by one, they just smashed them, which may not have been the smartest move. There were little fires in spots where the oil spilled. Fortunately, they were the piddlin' littlest tiki torches you've ever seen, but anyway, it was enough distraction for a bit and by then there were deputies and a couple of locals with shotguns making themselves known and things sort of calmed down. It was a wonder no one lost their cool and started shooting, you know? But I think it was just because the boys were so calm and—what's the word?—*self-assured*. That's it. Self-assured. They were a team. They didn't freak out. They just did what needed to be done. It was terrifying, but I'm so proud of them."

There was a commotion at the door and the twins came in bickering about who carried what from the car.

"I just asked if you'd carry my backpack, T. It's not like you had your hands full."

"You can carry your own backpack. I'm not your servant."

"I had the cooler! Which I packed with *your* favorite sodas. You could have helped."

Sweet looked at Bubba John, who was stifling his laughter. "Well, that didn't last long, did it?"

"Nnnnope," Bubba John said before chugging the last of his beer. "Come on, Mama, let's go to bed before we have to kill one of these kids."

Sweet put her glass in the sink and followed her husband back to their bedroom, their sanctuary. She pulled a little cross-stitched flag from the back of the door and hung it over the front doorknob. *Shhhhh!* It read. *Do Not Disturb.*

And then she locked the door.

Historical Celebration in Mayhew Turns Violent
Marley Ann Maxwell, Intern

As news of Mayhew Junction's Founders Day celebration spread through social media, LouWanda Crump's Confederate Memorial dedication reached an arguably unintended audience in the form of white nationalists. Though the men involved in Saturday's event were loosely organized and not affiliated with any one particular organization, a quick check of the social media accounts of those arrested revealed a wide range of alliances and interest in ideologies ranging from white supremacy and white separatists to neo-Nazi terrorist groups.

Facing off with the outsiders were members of Mayhew Junction's black community, who had gathered to protest the installation of Confederate memorials at the county courthouse downtown. The protest started out peacefully enough, though townspeople were distressed by the heckling of a Fletcher County High School student who performed a moving rendition of the National Anthem despite the harassment.

I personally witnessed the fights that broke out shortly after the memorials were revealed and, from my perspective and from video footage of the event, physical contact appeared to have been made first by men wielding torches and sticks. Protestors held signs and sang quietly, directed by their local leaders who urged non-violence even as the men advanced on their group. The skirmish lasted only a few minutes before being broken up almost exclusively by boys from the high school baseball team, who circled the men and held them at bay until the sheriff's deputies could arrest the entire group.

As deputies marched the interlopers across to the county jail, one bystander was heard to say, "I don't know how it is in them liberal towns, but aye God, you don't come in here and mess with our folks."

I sat down with LouWanda Crump Saturday evening at the hospital where she was admitted after incurring a head injury. Ms. Crump wanted to clarify that the memorial statues were not commissioned by the Mayhew Junction Historical Society as previously reported. "It was all my fault," she said from her hospital bed.

"Everybody told me it was a bad idea and I didn't listen, so I ain't got nobody to blame but myself." She went on to say she would be dropping out of the upcoming race for the County Commission seat in her district. "Suvi Jones will make a good commissioner. I ain't going anywhere. I'll help him however I can." When I asked if there were anything specific she had learned from her experience, she had this to say, "Mostly I learned what love looks like. That's about as good a lesson as a body can want."

Several arrests were made at the scene and charges are pending.

40 - A Bump on the Head

Randy Kerner was the first to say on Monday morning what everyone at the round table was thinking, "If I'd known all it would take is a bump on the head to bring LouWanda to her senses, I'd have knocked her out a long time ago."

Eustace cackled, Mac choked on his coffee, and Dottie stifled a laugh saying, "Be nice, Randy. She was really hurt."

"Lotta people were hurt, some more than others, but she got one thing right in that interview. She's got nobody to blame but herself."

"Aw, she didn't mean no harm, y'all," Eustace piped up. "I was kinda bummed my karaoke got shut down before I even had a chance to sing somethin'. I worked up a whole show and everything." Eustace had already said this four times that morning, but no one minded. They were all shell-shocked from the confrontation and mostly happy things were back to normal.

Half the town thought Marley Maxwell made up the quote she attributed to LouWanda. Never in a million years, or at least the past fifty, had anyone known LouWanda to apologize for anything. It was always someone else's fault.

"You think she actually said it?" Randy directed his question toward Dottie.

"I know she did. She said it to me, too. But really, we *all* told her. She can't deny that with a straight face. I think she's doing damage control right now, and it's likely more for her own benefit than for the town, so I'm not a whole lot of impressed. Truth be told, I'll believe it when I see it."

"Bingo," said Randy, pointing his finger for emphasis. Then he turned his attention toward the door, where Suvi was entering with Gabe on his heels. "Congratulations, ol' son!" Randy stood and intercepted Suvi with a hearty handshake. "All's well that ends well, eh?"

Suvi smiled. "I'm not sure it's a done deal yet, Randy. I need to hear it from the elections supervisor before I celebrate. How's that work, anyway?"

"You'll run uncontested. You had it in the bag anyway. You've always been a hometown hero. Even more now that you saved LouWanda's life. Pretty generous, considering she's your opponent."

"I'm not sure how anyone could look at someone hurting and think of them as the enemy." Suvi said.

"Trust me," Randy grunted, "not everybody thinks the way you do."

Suvi waved Randy away and took a table a little farther away than usual. Gabe punched Suvi in the arm as he sat down.

"So now you're a hero, huh?" Gabe said, sliding into the chair across from him.

"Oh, stop. It's just a phrase."

"Maybe so, but you did save her."

Suvi closed his eyes and took a deep breath. "Don't remind me. I don't know what it is with me and cake, but seems like every time I get near one, I get publicly humiliated."

"I don't know who posted the video, but you do realize you're already a meme, right?"

"What the hell's a meme?"

"Oh-em-gee, Suvi. I-D-K what I'm gonna do with you." Gabe goaded.

"You could always unfriend me." Suvi waved at Sissy and unfolded his newspaper.

"Touché! I didn't know you had it in you."

"There's a lot you don't know," Suvi groused, "and I'd like to keep it that way."

"Pfff, you like it. Don't lie."

They went on this way until Sissy brought coffee, and they settled into a comfortable silence. Suvi pretended to read his paper, but what he was really doing was thinking.

If that one newspaper article had gone viral and brought skinheads from as far away as Mississippi, what attention would come to videos of him heaving his unconscious political opponent onto a cake cart and wheeling her to the safety of an ambulance? It wasn't heroic. It was humiliating. But he'd done what any decent human being would do, no matter how much LouWanda Crump had brought it on herself. And the outcome wasn't bad, except he was no longer sure he really *wanted* to be on the county commission. What good would it do? What real, actual good would it do? That was the question.

"Come on, old man. Snap out of it," Gabe said. She'd been sitting there watching him worry. It was almost as if she could see his hair turn gray. "It's going to be fine."

He looked up at his friend's face. It was calm, serene. It was compassionate and kind, concerned, but not bothered. Maybe she was right. He said nothing. Just nodded a few times, folded his paper back into a rectangle and tucked it under his plate.

"We playing a round this afternoon?" he asked.

"Absolutely. Want me to get us a tee-time?"

"Nah, I'll call the club if you'll drive."

"Deal. Dinner afterwards?"

"Yep. Dinner as usual."

As usual. There is something infinitely comforting in that phrase.

41 - All's Well That Ends Well

Sweet wouldn't say that things returned to normal. What's normal anyway? She would say the town was in a period of reflection. Most were stunned at what happened, some were secretly thrilled, and others were horrified at the national attention the event attracted. The churches were the first to take action, scheduling special joint services to come together as a community and discuss what could have been done better, what should be done in the future to better understand what was happening. It would take a lot more than that, but it was a start.

The town had decided not to cancel the afternoon events that day but rescheduled the parade for one month later. At that time a new plaque, paid for by an online fundraising account set up by the boys and girls baseball team, was ordered from the Suwannee Monument company and installed at the foot of the flagpole in front of the courthouse. It reads simply:

In respectful memory of Dellwood Connolly
and other victims of racial violence and injustice.
May we all be a part of bringing reconciliation,
atonement and peace among neighbors and friends.

LouWanda recovered and kept her word. She pulled out of the race and vowed to be helpful to Suvi when he took his place on the county commission. Of course, she also insisted the Historical Society revise their memory book to include a picture of the new monument. She said it would increase sales of the book, and she acted like the monument was her idea all along. Some things never change.

***

Beanie and Will settled into a new normal, for them anyway. Beanie didn't want to rush things. After all, she'd not even met Will's daughter yet.

"I was thinking of inviting Natalie down for Thanksgiving," Will said one evening over a rousing game of Phase Ten. "She could bring her new fiancé and we could make a big meal here, or we could go out if you'd rather."

"Oh, I wouldn't want to go out, though I wouldn't mind ordering a batch of that dressing from the café. I ain't never been able to make it that good. Do you think she'd come? Is she ready for…you know…for us?" Beanie wagged a finger back and forth between Will's chest and her own.

"I think so. We've talked about it a little. Might be a little weird, us sleeping in the same room."

"Oh, right…well, I can move back to my room for a while. All my clothes is still in there anyways."

"Well, I guess that's an option, but…um…I was thinking maybe we'd…I don't know…get married or something?"

Beanie squinted her eyes and stared hard at her partner. "That's the worst proposal I ever heard. You should be ashamed." Then she started to laugh.

Oh, what Will Thaxton would do for that lovely sound. His face turned bright red, but he laughed along with her.

"Well, it wasn't an actual proposal. I just didn't know where we stood on the whole thing, so I guess I was just bringing it up as a point of discussion."

"You and your points of discussion are gonna be the death of me. I'm just sayin…"

"So, is that a yes?"

To which Beanie laughed even louder.

"I reckon it is a yes, since you put it that way. I'll marry ya', even if you don't have the good sense to ask me right."

"I can fix this," he whispered, and led her by the hand into the sitting room where logs were crackling in the fireplace for the first time that fall. He sat her down in her favorite chair, reached into his pocket and pulled out a tiny box, which he had no intentions of telling her he'd carried in his pocket for two weeks now.

He knelt before her and opened the box to reveal a ring it had taken him over an hour to choose. But Beanie didn't even look at the ring as Will asked her to be his wife. She looked at his face— his kind, handsome face holding eyes so blue they would disappear against a summer sky—and she answered this time with a kiss.

Author's Note

First a note to those of you who waited patiently for the second in this series: Thank you for caring enough about my characters to ask me when you could read more. It is your persistence and interest that motivated me to finish this work, and I am deeply grateful.

As most of you now realize, I am not a prolific writer. I'm a busy writer. I am cramming everything I possibly can into this late-in-life career as an author. As I type this note in preparation for publication, I am sitting in an apartment in Johnson City, Tennessee where I moved last year to go to grad school. I am currently enrolled in ETSU's Masters in Communication and Storytelling program. It's a long story. Hit me up to FaceTime with your book club (reading any of my novels) and I will tell it to you. You can email me at CassieSelleck@aol.com.

At the front of the book, I tell you that all the characters here are fictitious, but that is not strictly the truth. There is one character who is absolutely real and is napping beside me as I type these words. Sugar is a little chihuahua my husband likes to claim in jest that I stole, but I have proof otherwise. The story of her arrival on my doorstep is a little sketchy, but the very day she arrived I posted pictures on Facebook looking for her owners. By the time we found them, I had gotten her shots done and accidently named her, just like in the story. Except it was my mother on the phone with me and not the veterinarian's office. I did offer to give her back when we found the owners, but they took pity on me and let me keep her. Perry just likes his "she stole her" story better. He's not the only one who can stretch the truth in this family.

By the way, a little shout out to Dr. Lindsey Jackson at Mayo Town and Country Animal Hospital and his staff, including Caroline, Tiffany, and Dylan. I am so grateful to have these wonderful folks who have cared for our pets for many years now. They are amazing.

The Chateau is a real establishment in Mayo, my hometown for the past twenty years, and it was indeed the former courthouse of Lafayette County, but that's where the truth about the building ends. The story of Dellwood Connelly is a figment of my imagination. I have used some historical details, such as the information from the report referenced by the Equal Justice Initiative on the number of lynching's in the United States. Those statistics are all too real, but the details of the story I tell are fictitious. Please go to www.eji.org for more information on racial justice and criminal justice reform in America. Other details, such as the naval stores, or turpentine camps, are a real part of Florida's past as well, but the characters and details in my story are also fictitious.

The reason I include these unpleasant reminders of our history are not to stir up trouble, but to remind us where we have been so we will not repeat the past. I want to be a voice for justice in this country, and I hope you will join me in that endeavor. We are not free unless and until we are all free. There is no justice unless and until there is justice for all. We can all do better if we step outside of our own limited perspective and walk around in the shoes of another.

As I write these words, we are self-quarantining due to the Covid-19 pandemic. I know it has been a struggle for a lot of folks, and there is much tension over how to move forward. During this time, I have realized exactly how little control I have over any given situation. For a control freak, this was a hard lesson. But what I also realized is that sometimes the most important thing you can do is to pause and reflect on what you can change going forward to be your best self, and to make the best of the circumstances. I have taken this time to consider how I want to live in this world going forward. It has been almost like a "reset" for me. I hope we come out of this more resolved to live alongside each other in harmony. I hope we stop trying to homogenize each other and recognize that our differences make us no less human, no less loveable, no less deserving of a peaceful existence, and no less entitled to pursuing happiness, however different that may look. I hope we are kinder to each other from this day forward.

Lastly, I want to tell you a little bit about my husband. He has been my biggest cheerleader, staunchest supporter, and humblest recipient of what little time I have left over to spend with him. No one should be this lucky. He works harder than any man I have ever met, and he does it because he loves his family. My goal is to help him retire in the next few years while he still has some time to enjoy a little travel with me. You can help me and other independent authors by telling your friends about the books you love. Share on social media, choose independently published books for your book clubs, and buy new books directly from Amazon, rather than from secondary sources. Better yet, buy digital books to save the environment and help cut printing costs for the author. Whatever you do, however you read, I thank you for reading my stories. You have helped make my dreams come true.

Made in the USA
Coppell, TX
09 June 2021

57146070R00125